KU-060-598

The COLOUR OF HOPE

ROSS MACKENZIE

ANDERSEN PRESS

First published in Great Britain in 2022 by
Andersen Press Limited
20 Vauxhall Bridge Road, London SW1V 2SA, UK
Vijverlaan 48, 3062 HL Rotterdam, Nederland
www.andersenpress.co.uk

2 4 6 8 10 9 7 5 3 1

British Library Cataloguing in Publication Data available.

ISBN 978 1 83913 202 5

Printed and bound in Great Britain by Clays Ltd, Elcograf S.p.A.

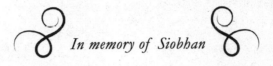 *In memory of Siobhan*

PART ONE

THE WISH

CHAPTER ONE
IN WHICH A WISH IS MADE

'Tell me again about colour, Grandma.' The boy sits on the floor at the old woman's feet, staring up at her with large, shining eyes.

The old woman's hands are resting on her substantial belly. She drums her fingers. 'Tsk. You should be in bed, child.'

'Please, Grandma! Please!'

She purses her lips like she's sucked on a lemon, but he can tell that her displeasure is an act. She reaches for her glass, swirls the liquid around, takes a sip. 'Fine,' she says with a sigh. 'What do you want to know?'

The boy sits in silence for a moment, questions hurtling around in his little head. The only sound is the delicious pop of the fire as the white flames lick the air. The room is cosy, bursting with moreish smells of rabbit stew and carrot soup from the stove.

At last, the boy smiles and says, 'Tell me about orange.'

The old woman's skin is mid-grey, her cheeks dotted with freckles. Her dark eyes are deeply set within bundles of wrinkles, but now, as she casts her mind back to another time, not so long ago, those old eyes twinkle. She smiles and looks at once much younger. 'Orange? Let me see now. Yes. Well, you know the walks we take in the forest when harvest season is all sewn up, my love? Those days when the air is crisp, and you can taste the winter on the edges of everything?'

The boy nods.

'And you remember when we return from our walks to warm our fingers by the fire and sip mulled cider? When we are warm and cold both at once, and so very glad to be alive as the cider heats us from the inside?'

Again, he nods.

'That feeling of heat and cold and life and spice all tied up in a pretty bundle,' she says. 'If we could see it, that is what orange would look like.'

The boy is smiling now. Imagining. His eyes are filled with a faraway look. Such pretty eyes. Like his mother's eyes.

As the old lady watches him, she wonders, as she has done so often since he was born, if her grandson's eyes are the same shade of blue his poor late mother's were. How she remembers those eyes. Blue as the ocean – when the ocean was still blue.

Before.

Before the colour disappeared from the world.

No. Not disappeared.

Before it was stolen.

4

'Can you tell me one more, Grandma?'

She tuts. 'Are you determined to get me arrested, boy? The Emperor's snitches are everywhere, and his Black Coats would string me up in the City square if they found me talking like this.'

The boy edges closer. 'No one can hear us way out here in the farmhouse, Grandma. Besides, I don't think anyone would ever try to arrest you. Not even the Black Coats.'

The old lady takes another sip from her glass. The hint of a smile plays on her lips. 'Oh, they would *try*.'

'Just one more colour, Grandma. Tell me about green.'

'You, boy, are as stubborn as a mountain. I'll tell you for one minute. But then it's bedtime.'

'OK, OK. C'mon!'

She drains the final sip from her glass. 'Close your eyes. No, shut them properly. Good. Now think of how the world feels after a rainstorm. Are you doing that?'

He screws up his eyes and nods.

'Well?' she says. 'How does it feel?'

He thinks for a long moment. 'Clean. And new. And more alive. A little bit like when I'm swimming in the river and I dive down deep. When I come back up and take a big breath. It feels like that.'

She nods. 'Aye. Now imagine you could see *that* feeling. That's what green looks like, child.'

The boy has heard all of this before, a hundred, hundred times, but it never ceases to make his heart soar. 'So that's how grass looks? And frogs? And trees in the springtime?'

'Yes.' The old woman narrows her wrinkled eyes. 'Now I want you to imagine something else. I want you to imagine climbing up the stairs and going to sleep, Darroch, because that is exactly what is about to happen.'

A few minutes later the old woman is tucking the boy in for the night. He insists she check under his bed and in his cupboard to make sure there are no Black Coats or Ripper Dogs lying in wait.

'Safe and sound,' she says, planting a kiss on his forehead.

Moments later Darroch is alone in the silent dark. He listens as the old lady makes the house secure, puts out the lamps and goes to her own room. Only when her snores rumble does he climb out of bed and creep to the window. He pulls the heavy curtains open, slides the sash window upwards and breathes the sweet warmth of the late summer night.

The sky is clear and black and patterned with a great scattering of twinkling stars. He looks to the west, over his grandmother's farm towards the rolling hills and the forest, and then to the east, to the City and the sea. The moon is dazzling as a new coin, and its soft light brushes the high walls and spires of the city.

He tries to imagine what all this might look like should colour suddenly come rushing back into the world. But no matter how beautifully Grandma describes the wonder of colour, all Darroch has ever known is a world in black and white and shades of grey, and his imagination cannot truly comprehend anything else. How he longs to see the green of the sheep meadows, the blue of the clear sky, the glimmer of golden sunlight on the City rooftops.

He sighs and is about to come in and close the window when something catches his eye. High over the sea, a streak of iridescent light flashes beneath the curve of the moon and is gone again in moments.

A shooting star.

Darroch's eyes widen and then close tightly as an idea burns in his head.

He whispers, 'I wish for somebody to bring colour back.' Then he opens his eyes, shuts the window and climbs back into bed.

He falls asleep without giving his wish another thought.

He has no clue that he has just changed the world, and the fate of one person in particular, forever.

Chapter Two
In Which a Remarkable Child is Born

At exactly the moment the boy is making his wish, a fisherman named Tom Laurie is pacing around the kitchen of his cottage on Harbour Street in the City.

He walks around the table, wringing his trembling hands, and then to the foot of the stairs, where he stops and listens. He hears his wife cry out, puts one foot on the bottom step, but stops himself from climbing any further; he knows that the midwife is looking after his beloved Sarah the best she can, and his presence will not help the situation at all.

Back to the kitchen it is, then, for more helpless pacing.

Then, finally, after many hours of labour, Tom hears the sound that he has longed for: his child's first cry.

He rushes for the stairs and bounds up them two at a time, but when he is almost at the summit, a new sound makes him freeze.

A scream.

The bedroom door flies open and out rushes the midwife, hurriedly closing her leather bag. He blocks her way at the top of the stairs, and when he looks at her face, he sees something that turns his heart to ice.

She is terrified.

'Mistress MacLean?' he says in a tremulous voice. 'What is wrong?'

She does not speak, only continues to stare wild-eyed at him.

'Mistress MacLean,' he says again. 'Please. Tell me, what has happened? Is it the baby? Is something wrong with the child? Or is it my wife? Speak, please!'

She opens her mouth, and for a moment it seems that she is going to say something. Her eyes fill with frightened tears. Then she pushes past him. Stunned, he watches her go, down the stairs and out of the door to the night. Then his senses return and he rushes into the bedroom.

His mind has conjured terrible images of what he might find there, but thankfully none of these are true. And yet he stops, still as a stone, and can do nothing but gawp, amazement and wonder and, yes, fear coursing through his every fibre.

His wife is sitting up in bed. There is a bundle of blankets in her arms, and within the bundle is a tiny, perfect baby. Tom is looking at the very scene he has always dreamed of. He is a father. He has a family.

But this scene has one difference to his beloved fantasy.

One very important difference.

The baby's skin is not light grey like her mother's skin, or the dark grey of Tom himself. No. Tom remembers colour from when he himself was a child, before the Emperor and his Necromancer took it away.

He recognises that his baby's skin is light brown.

'It's impossible,' he says.

'She's a miracle,' Sarah says in a hoarse whisper.

'She?'

'Yes, Tom. You have a daughter.'

The baby makes a fussy little sound, wriggles, and the blankets swaddling her turn from whitish grey to pale blue. Then the colour continues to spread, turning the smooth skin of Sarah's arms pinkish white. The colour blossoms, filling the stripes of her nightgown with blue, reaching her neck and pretty face, reddening her cheeks.

This all happens in a blink, and Tom, who has never seen his wife in colour before, almost falls to the floor in shock.

'It's all right, Tom.' She holds out a hand, beckons him. He has always thought that she is beautiful, but now that he can see the colour in her face, the emerald green of her eyes, the shining red of her hair, he feels that he is looking at an angel.

He edges towards her as she holds his daughter out. Trembling, frightened that he might drop her, or break her, he takes the tiny bundle in his arms. She is warm and asleep and completely perfect. When next he looks at his wife, all trace of colour is gone from her.

'Look,' she says.

He looks.

It begins with his hands and arms, the skin turning from dark grey to a brown deeper than the colour of his daughter's skin. The colour reaches the sleeve of his heavy jumper, suddenly burned orange, and continues to billow outwards until every bit of him is alive with vibrant hues.

'It must happen to whatever she touches,' says Sarah. Her face becomes grim. 'Tom, we're going to have to get her out of the City. Tonight. Now.'

A lump of panic rises in Tom's throat. 'But how? You've just had a baby! You can't go on any long journeys.'

'I'll just have to,' she says. 'I'm not staying in this City a moment longer than need be. You know how it works. The Ripper Dogs will probably have already picked up her scent. It'll only be a matter of time before they lead the Black Coats here. We might have an hour – and that's if Mistress MacLean doesn't go telling them first.'

'The midwife?' Tom's heart stutters. 'She wouldn't do that, would she?'

Sarah is climbing from bed, teeth clenched in effort.

'You can't!' says Tom. 'It's too dangerous!'

'I think I know better than you what I can and can't do, Tom Laurie. Now put the baby in her crib and help me get changed.'

Chapter Three
In Which Tragedy Strikes
and Fate Intervenes

'Did the stable man ask any questions?' Sarah says. She is walking around the kitchen, the baby warm and asleep in a sling close to her heart. Sarah made the sling when she first discovered she was going to have a baby, though back then she did not know what colour of silk she was using. It turns out that the diamond pattern is shining gold and royal blue.

'No,' says Tom. 'Not a word. People hire horses at all times of the day and night, my love.'

A skinny black horse stands hitched to a post outside the door. The horse is secured to a small cart, the type of which is usually used to deliver vegetables or sacks of coal. Tom is busy loading some essential supplies. 'There,' he says with a final tug of the leather straps on a heavy pack. 'Time to go.'

He helps her onto the cart with great care, trying to hide the tears welling in his eyes. She makes herself as comfortable as possible on the blankets he has placed on the flat bed and sits stroking the soft wispy hair on her newborn daughter's head.

Tom unhitches the horse, climbs to the driver's bench, takes the reins and urges the horse on. As they turn the corner out of Harbour Street, Sarah watches the grey front door of the little cottage she loves until it is out of sight. Then she holds her baby and begins to cry.

It takes half an hour to clear the city boundaries, and soon after that the road becomes rocky and uneven. The cart judders and jumps, but still the child sleeps peacefully. The horse pulls them past a small sheep farm atop a meadow, and then the road takes them into the woods.

The trees soon become so tall and dense on either side of the road that the only sign of the sky is a long strip of star-dusted grey overhead. The air is thick with the scents of sap and pine, and the sounds are distant and wild.

'Where shall we go?' Sarah asks.

'Wherever we must to be free,' Tom says. 'There is a village half a day's ride away. I'll find a safe spot in the woods for you and fetch some supplies there. After that, we'll keep riding.'

'But where, Tom?'

Tom does not answer at first, because he does not know. 'We'll ride until we find the end of the Necromancer's spell.'

She hugs her daughter. 'But most folk say there isn't an end to it. Nobody's ever found it.'

Tom's shoulders are slumped. 'Well, we'll be the first, my love, won't we?'

No sooner has he spoken those words than something catches her eye. She sits up and squints back the way they have come. Her heart begins to thud faster and faster. A series of points of light bob up and down on the road a long way behind them. She knows instantly what they are, because she has seen them before. Each dot is one of a pair. Each dot is the eye of a Ripper Dog.

'They're coming!' she cries out. 'Tom, they're coming after us!'

He glances back and his eyes widen in the light of the oil lamp upon the cart. With a whip-crack of the reins he drives the horse on, and the cart jumps and jolts as they pick up speed. The baby wakens and begins to cry.

'They're gaining!' Sarah watches the points of light grow larger, until she can see the shapes of the dogs appear on the edges of the cart's lamplight, bear-sized and shaggy and dark, the guttural sounds of their slobbering growls echoing all around. Upon the dogs' backs are their riders, tall, thin creatures that might once have been human, hidden beneath long coats and hoods. Black Coats.

One of the Ripper Dogs lunges forward, knocking the edge of the cart with a long muzzle filled with teeth the size of daggers. The cart veers wildly, tips onto two wheels, and crashes back down. The baby is screaming now, Sarah clinging to her as she rolls uncontrollably around the flat bed of the cart. The dog has another lunge, and this time its huge front paws land on the flat bed, tipping it, making Sarah slide forward towards its waiting jaws. The dog snarls and snorts, sending globs of thick drool spraying. Sarah screams, kicks out, and one of the dog's fangs punctures her leg. The pain is searing, blinding, but still she clings to her child, kicks and fights, knocking one of those deadly teeth out, making the Ripper Dog fall back and the cart right itself with a crash.

Two of the Ripper Dogs go sprinting past the limping cart, overtaking it, blocking the road, causing Tom to bring the horse to a skidding stop. Instinct kicks in. He leaps from the bench, draws his fish-gutting knife and tosses it. It plunges handle-deep into the nearest Ripper, and the creature growls and lunges at him, grabbing him around the waist in its jaws, sinking its teeth in, shaking him around like a wet rag and then throwing him twenty feet down the road.

Upon the cart, Sarah's world is growing fuzzy, far away. The pain in her injured leg is burning worse with each passing moment. She can feel the Ripper's poison invading her every cell. One of the great black dogs climbs onto the back of the cart, making the wooden beams groan and buckle. Sarah tries to back up, but all of her strength is gone. The dog's hot, stinking breath blows her hair back as it comes closer, its enormous wet nose twitching, brushing against the child she holds to her chest.

'No!' she cries. With one final effort, she rolls over so that her back is to the dog, her body shielding her crying little girl. She waits for the fangs to bear down upon her.

From far away there comes the fizzing sound of something travelling fast through the air, and then the *THWACK* of contact, and an echoing howl of pain.

More growls, more howls, more *THWACK, THWACK, THWACKS*.

Sarah does not know what is happening around her. She no longer has the strength to lift her head. As she closes her eyes for the last time, she prays that her baby will be saved.

All is still and quiet. Nothing moves. Nothing makes a sound. Then a shadow detaches from the solid black of the woods and steps onto the road.

The man's face is weathered and leathery. He wears a long tweed coat and a wide-brimmed hat. His nose is long and bears the crooked angles of several breaks. His top lip is hidden under a long, untidy black moustache.

He moves under cover of dark, first to make sure that his special arrows have done their job. The Ripper Dog carcasses are bubbling and melting, and the Black Coats have already turned to dust. He retrieves the arrows, wiping the poisoned blood from the silver arrow tips upon the mossy woodland floor.

When he is sure all is safe, he checks on the man lying crumpled on the road. By the soft light of the oil lamp on the cart, he can see the man is young. He feels for a pulse.

'Deid,' says the man in the tweed coat with a shake of his head. He stands, walks to the cart and frees the horse. 'Go on, ma beauty,' he says, patting the horse, watching it run back towards the City. Next, he moves to the cart, climbs onto the flat bed and finds a young woman face down.

He stops. His sharp, shining eyes narrow. He reaches for the cart's lamp, brings it down, holds it nearer her so that he can properly see. His breath catches in his chest.

'Colour?' he whispers, reaching out a trembling hand, lifting a lock of the young woman's shining red hair. 'Colour! But how can it be . . .'

A soft sound makes him draw back. It is a muffled, cooing noise, and when he realises where it is coming from, he gently rolls the dead woman over and finds a surprise.

'A wee babby!' he cries. 'And crivens! You have colour too!'

And so she does. Her skin is light brown, her hair brown. She has stopped crying now, and she looks up at him with large, dark eyes that melt him. He reaches out a finger and her little hand wraps around it.

And that is when it happens.

First his finger and then his hand turn from grey to sunbeaten gold. Soon the sleeve of his tweed jacket is flooded with shades of tan and cream. His mouth drops open.

'Goodness me!' He holds his free hand out, watching the colour come alive in his fingers. 'A wee miracle! I see now why these devil dugs and their riders came after you.' As gently as he can, he unwraps the sling from the baby's mother and lifts the tiny child free. She coos and gurgles as he cradles her in his arms.

'Yehr mammy and daddy are away now, my wee lamb. But don't you worry about a thing. Sandy Burns will see you right.'

He wraps the sling around himself, makes sure the baby is safe and warm and then, with one final look around the scene, he sadly shakes his head and disappears once more into the shadows of the woods.

PART TWO

A Thing Called Colour

(Six Years After the Wish)

Chapter Four
In Which a Journey Begins

The Emperor's dominion is large and rambling, stretching as far as the eye can see and beyond in every direction. There are snow-capped mountains and winding rivers, patchwork crop fields, towns and villages both pretty and ramshackle. There are shadows, and things that live in them.

But mostly there is the forest, grey and sprawling and colourless.

Look.

See there, far below? Where the road cuts through the trees like the gouge from a giant's blade? Something is moving along that road. A travelling caravan pulled by a handsome shire horse. Upon the wagon, clutching the reins, sits Sandy Burns. Beside him is a small girl with a serious face.

Her name is Hope.

'Are yeh still sulking, lassie?' Sandy says with a sideways glance.

She doesn't answer, folding her little arms across her body and jutting out a shining bottom lip.

Sandy shakes his head. 'Well, yeh sulk all yeh want and see how that works out for yeh.'

'You shouted at me,' she says at last, still not looking at him.

'Shouted?' Sandy almost falls off the seat. 'Crivens, you can hardly blame me! We'll never be able to go back to that toon.'

'It's town,' she tells him. 'We'll never be able to go back to that *town*. Oliver is teaching me to speak more proper like him. He says I should . . . *enunciate*.'

This time it's Sandy's lip that juts out. 'Oh, aye? And who is Oliver to decide what way of speaking is proper? Anyway, don't change the subject. What yeh did back there was not acceptable. We're drifter mages. Our job is to help folk. We're no supposed to get involved in the politics of any place – and that means yeh don't go turnin' people intae pigs. Especially mayors!'

'He was *very* rude to you,' Hope says.

Sandy tries to keep his expression serious, but he feels it soften. 'Well . . . aye. He was. Some people tend to turn nasty when they realise that we can't solve all their problems wi' magic. But I would have handled it. Yeh cannae go turning everyone who is rude to you into an animal. If you did that, there'd be no people left.'

She looks at him and blows a raspberry.

'In my opinion,' comes a smooth voice from the caravan,

'it wouldn't be so bad if all the people in the world became animals. In fact, I think it would be somewhat of an improvement.' A small, scruffy black dog appears in the open doorway, sits, yawns.

Sandy casts a sharp look over his shoulder. 'Don't yeh go encouraging her. I thought you were supposed to be man's best friend?'

The dog makes a movement that might be a shrug. 'That depends on the man.'

'And how did Hope manage to get her wee handies on one of my spells back in that village anyway?' says Sandy. 'I thought yeh were keeping an eye on her?'

'I had to answer a call of nature, if you must know,' says the dog.

Sandy shakes his head despairingly. He tugs on the reins and his horse, Gloria, turns off the dirt road and trundles over uneven ground between two mighty redwood trees, the fingers of reaching branches scratching along the top of the caravan, until they come out in to a clearing of long grass. The caravan comes to a stop, and Sandy hops down and stretches his creaking bones.

'Why've we stopped?' says Hope, looking around.

Sandy has begun to walk away towards the grey trees. 'Because now *I* have to answer a call of nature.' He disappears behind one of the thick tree trunks, then his voice calls, 'Oliver, take Hope to stretch her legs a wee bit, will yeh? But don't go far, mind!'

Oliver, the dog, looks at Hope with shining eyes. He

twitches one of his sticky-up ears. 'Would you care to join me for a stroll?'

Hope nips down from the wooden bench of the caravan. She is small for her age, with dark grey skin, a mop of tangled hair and large, fierce eyes with whites so pure and bright they almost glow. 'C'mon then,' she says.

They walk to the opposite end of the clearing, away from Sandy, following the winding path of a narrow brook into the trees. It is midsummer, and the day is fine and warm.

'Sandy is right, you know,' says Oliver, sniffing around the base of a tree. 'You really shouldn't mess around with his spells. You might hurt yourself.'

Hope picks up a twig and tosses it into the brook, watching as the colourless water carries it away. 'He never lets me do any proper magic.'

'You help him gather spell ingredients, don't you?'

'But that's *boring.*' She sits down on the soft mossy grey carpet of the woodland floor. Oliver stretches, lies beside her and rolls over. Hope starts to rub his belly.

'It might seem boring,' he says, 'but it's important. He is teaching you, you see? Imparting wisdom. Making sure you understand the basics of magic before you use it.'

Hope wrinkles her nose.

Oliver sits up. 'The point is, Sandy is protecting you, as he has always done.'

Hope ruffles the untidy fur atop his head, and he reaches up and licks her chin with a wet tongue, making her giggle.

'You want to play fetch?' she asks.

He sighs. 'Must I?'

'It's what dogs do! And I know you like it.' She stands, hops onto a fallen tree trunk, and tiptoes the length of it, her arms outstretched either side for balance. Then she jumps down, picks up a suitable stick and tosses it.

Oliver watches it spin between the trees and land on the forest floor among some knotted tree roots. Hope watches him, smiling. She knows that he is trying with everything he has to stay rooted to the spot. She also knows that no matter how many books he might read or fancy words he may use, Oliver is a dog, and every bit of him is screaming out to chase after that stick.

At last, he can fight the urge no more. He darts away between the trees and returns a few seconds later with the stick clenched in his jaws. He drops it at her feet and looks up at her, his tongue lolling out and his tail wagging madly.

She acts surprised. 'Oh, you want me to throw it again?'

'I despise myself for it,' he says, 'but yes. Please.'

Hope snatches the stick from the ground, rears back and throws. Once again Oliver goes careering after it. On his way back this time, though, he skids to a stop. The stick falls from his mouth and lies forgotten on the ground as he stares at her.

'Your hand,' he says softly.

Hope holds both hands up. Soon her left hand drops back to her side. But the right . . . the right she continues to hold up, even as her breath catches in her chest and her heart thumps and bangs. Something is happening to that hand. The grey tips of her fingers are slowly filling up with a strange, warm, brightness, so different from the rest of the world that at first it hurts her eyes. This thing, this creeping, beautiful strangeness, fills the entirety of her fingers, and moves to the palm of her hand, and then her wrist. And there it stops.

'Stay exactly where you are,' says Oliver, and the fear in his voice is palpable. 'I'll fetch Sandy.'

Off he runs, back towards the clearing, leaving Hope alone with her alien hand. Should she be frightened? Perhaps. But, as she examines the warm change in her skin, she does not feel scared at all. It doesn't hurt, or tickle or anything like that. It simply is. She brings her left hand back up, holds it next to the right, which is exactly as it has always been, smooth and dark grey.

The rustle of approaching feet, and Sandy bursts between the trees, skids, and stands gawping at Hope's hand. He comes forward, takes it and turns it gently over in his, eyes shining beneath the brim of his hat. 'Did you take your medicine this morning?' he says a little breathlessly.

Hope's nose wrinkles. '*What?*'

'Did yeh take your medicine, lassie?' His grip on her hand tightens, and for the first time a needle of unease pricks at her spine.

'Aye. Every morning, just like you always tell me.'

Sandy leads her by the hand, out to the grey brightness of the clearing, up the step and into the dark grey caravan. It is bigger inside than it ought to be. This is because, as

Sandy has told her a hundred times, it is made from enchanted wood. There on the left is Sandy's desk, littered with papers and ornaments, and on the right the pantry cupboard and the little wood-burner with its chimney reaching up through the ceiling. At the far end is Sandy's neatly made bed. Hope's bed sits on a mezzanine above, accessed by a wooden spiral staircase. The entirety of the rounded interior wall and ceiling is one gigantic bookcase, curving up and around, and where the books should fall out directly overhead, they cling on, their spines facing down towards the shining grey floorboards.

'Fetch yehr medicine,' Sandy tells her. Hope gives him a puzzled look and then does as he asks, climbing the steps to the small mezzanine area where she sleeps. Dropping to her knees, she reaches under her bed, brings out a wooden box and opens the hinged lid to reveal a scattering of trinkets. There are a few colourless marbles, a handful of coins, some black-and-white fishing lures and a dull grey metal toy soldier. And there is a tiny bottle upon which Sandy has affixed a label and scrawled, in his messy hand:

Hope's Medicine

She takes the bottle, and as she reaches for it, the thing that has changed her hand spreads up her arm to her elbow, filling the skin with that silky glow. As her fingers brush the box, the wooden edges flash for a moment and she takes a sharp breath and draws her hand away.

'Hope? Whit is it? Has something else happened?'

'No,' she replies. 'Just coming.' She touches the box again and watches in astonishment as it too fills up with the strange substance from her hand, much darker than her skin. It spreads around each side of the box, and to the lid and floor, and then to the items within the box too. The marbles look cold. For some reason they make her think of ice. The toy soldier's jacket is bright and loud and causes her to imagine heat. When she breaks contact with the box, all this returns to lifeless shades of grey.

And now the bottle changes as it nestles in her palm. The glass remains clear but the liquid inside is flooded with summer warmth.

She takes the bottle down to Sandy, pops it into his waiting hand and watches it change back to the shades of grey she has always known it to be.

Sandy holds the bottle up, shakes it, uncorks it and gives it a sniff.

'Well?' says Oliver, sitting at Sandy's feet.

'There's nothing wrong with it,' Sandy says, holding the bottle up to the light and examining it through one eye. 'It's fine.'

Hope has been watching him carefully. Although she is only six, Sandy has already instilled in her the knack of people-reading. People, he has told her, are much easier to read than books. Hope agrees. Words are tricky things. People are simple compared to words. A person's story is written in their face and body and hands. It's in the way they move. A flick of the eyes. A twitch of the head. And it always tells the truth – even when a person's mouth is trying to do the opposite.

She is reading Sandy now. She can tell that he is scared, and this frightens her, because she has never known Sandy to fear anything.

'Have I done something wrong?' she asks.

'Whit?' Sandy tears his gaze from the medicine bottle, looks down at her and his shoulders slump a little. 'No, lassie, yeh haven't done anything wrong.' He slips past her, sits on the edge of his bed. 'Come here.'

She sits beside him. He holds the little medicine bottle out in his open palm.

'Why do yeh take this each morning?' he asks.

Hope thinks for a moment. 'Because I have a . . . condishun.'

'A condition.' Sandy nods. 'Aye. And what does that mean?'

Again, Hope's nose wrinkles as she thinks. 'It means something is wrong with me?'

Sandy offers her the bottle. 'Take it.'

She does, and as soon as it touches her newly changed hand, the liquid inside flushes with warm light once more. She does not yet know why, but it makes her think of bees, of honey and summer mornings.

Sandy watches this happen, the fear written on his face again.

'Is *this* what's wrong with me?' she asks, holding up her hand.

Oliver jumps up on the bed beside her and pushes his muzzle into her side gently. 'I think it's time to tell her, Sandy.'

Sandy sighs. 'I was hoping she'd be a bit older before I put such a weight on her wee shoulders. But yeh're right.'

Hope looks from one to the other. 'Are you sure I'm not in trouble?'

'Aye, lassie, I'm sure.' Sandy gathers his words. 'Yeh were right when you said that having a condition means that something is wrong. At least, that's what it means in usual circumstances. Yehr circumstances are not usual. They are very unusual. Yeh see, Hope, there is nothing wrong wi' you. In fact, there is something very right – and that same something is what's wrong wi' the rest of the world.'

Hope frowns. 'I don't get it.'

'This,' says Sandy, taking her hand. As her skin touches his, his own hand changes too, flooding with brightness. 'This is how the world is supposed to be, Hope.'

She tries to understand, but his words don't fit properly in her head. Still clutching her hand, he leads her back outside to the long grass. He sweeps his free arm around the clearing. 'This is the way yeh've always known things to be. But it's a lie. See yehr hand there? That strange thing that's filled it up with warmth? That's called colour, lassie. Colour!'

He lets go of Hope, and the warmth – the *colour* – fades from his own hand. 'It used to paint the whole world. So many shades and hues you wouldnae believe.' He dashes away across the clearing to the trees, plucks a wide leaf from a hanging branch and brings it back. He offers it to her. When she takes it, Hope watches bright, dazzling colour fill every part of it.

'That,' says Sandy, 'is the colour green. Green is nature, Hope. This whole forest used to be a sea of green – until autumn o' course, when the leaves would turn the colour of fire each year. And look here, lassie.' He's quite animated now, moving away again, this time picking a delicate flower from the floor of the clearing among the long grass. Hope takes it from his open hand. The flower has a long stem that curves at the top and hanging from that curve are a dozen or so tiny, bell-shaped flowers. The colour creeps from her hand, into the stem, turning it green like the leaf before it, but when it reaches the flowers, it fills them with a different colour, so beautiful it makes Hope's breath catch.

'And that colour is blue,' Sandy tells her.

Hope cannot tear her gaze away from the flowers, from the beauty of them. Deep within her there is a shift. Somehow, in some hidden-away part of her, she knows that this is right. This is the way things should be.

'Blue,' says Sandy, 'is the colour of the summer sky. The sea, the lochs, the Crystal Pools to the west. Blue. All of them. At least, that's how it used to be.' He crouches beside her, and Hope is shocked to see that his eyes are pooling with tears.

She has never seen him cry before. She drops the flower, reaches up and gently touches Sandy's weathered face. He closes his eyes, tears spilling from them, and she watches the colour wash across his face, lighting up his skin, his lips, his dark hair and moustache. He opens his eyes, and she takes a sharp, astonished breath when she sees that they are green.

'Why is all the colour gone?' she asks.

He clasps her little hands in his. 'The Emperor took it,' he says.

Hope's nose wrinkles again as her little brain tries to puzzle things out. She has heard of the Emperor of course, mostly in the whispers of the people in the many places that she and Sandy have visited. The Emperor takes something called taxes from them, and in return he lets them live on and farm his land – though she cannot understand who decided the land belongs to him in the first place. 'Why'd he do that?' she says. 'Did he want all the colour for himself?'

Sandy shakes his head. Hope can see that this subject troubles him greatly. 'He did it because of jealousy. Yeh see, Hope, the Emperor was born into a family of powerful mages. But when he came into the world, he came in black and white and grey. No colour lived in him, and nobody could sort him, not even his all-powerful mammy and daddy. The old Emperor and Empress hid him away. They tried to protect him, y'see, because they knew he'd never be accepted, that people would be frightened of him – and fear and ignorance can make people do terrible things. But he was lonely, and his heart grew cold and bitter. When his parents died . . .' Sandy pauses, and Hope sees that he is trembling. It is a sad story, she thinks, but she cannot understand why it should affect him so. 'When they died, the boy took the throne, and he made his aunt his only advisor. She is powerful in the dark art of Necromancy.'

'What's *that*?' Hope asks.

'Someone who messes with things they shouldn't,' says Sandy.

'What things?'

Sandy pauses, and Hope can tell that he is considering whether to tell her. At last, he says, 'A Necromancer uses magic in ways they shouldn't. Necromancers talk to the dead. They summon spirits and demons and such. And there's never been one as powerful as the Emperor's auntie. Together, they've used necromancy to steal all the colour from existence, and to summon an army of Black Coats and Ripper Dugs to destroy anybody who tries to bring colour back. Yeh can get thrown in jail for just talking about colour, Hope.'

She holds up her little hand, and her eyes widen. Her belly swirls with fright.

'I don't want to go to jail.'

'And I'll never let that happen,' Sandy says. 'That's why you've been taking your medicine since you were a baby. It hides your colour, Hope. It hides that you're different.'

She thinks about this. 'Why *am* I different?'

Sandy stands with his hands in his pockets. 'I don't know, lassie. I wish I did. And I wish yeh didn't have tae hide it. But yeh do.'

Hope thinks some more. There is a new, burning

question in her head. 'Do you think my mummy and daddy were the same as me?'

She is sitting on the edge of the bed, and Sandy has been pacing while he talks. Now he crouches and takes her hands again, and the colour from her hand spreads into his. His eyes are large and sad.

'The night I found yeh,' he says, 'yehr mam and dad were trying to get you out of the City. They must have been frightened the Emperor would kill yeh as soon as he found out about you – and they were right. His Ripper Dugs and Black Coats came after yehr parents, caught up wi' them in the forest no far from the City walls.'

'Did they hurt them?' Hope's little eyes are wide.

Sandy squeezes her hand. 'Aye, lassie. They did. I don't like tae go near the City, but I was picking some potion herbs that grow only in that part of the forest the night it happened. By the time I stumbled across your parents it was too late. Yehr mammy and daddy died trying to protect yeh. I picked yeh up and took yeh away, and I've protected yeh ever since.'

Hope dabs at her eyes with her knuckles.

'It's my fault.'

'What?' says Sandy with a frown.

'Well, my mummy and daddy would have been OK if it wasn't for me, wouldn't they?'

Sandy gently tilts her chin up so that her eyes are looking into his. 'Don't you ever think that way,' he says, 'you hear me? Nobody can control how they come into the world.

But you can control what you become, and the mark you leave while yeh're here. The Emperor and his Necromancer are the ones to blame, lassie. Not you. Never you. They're the ones who took colour. They're the ones who were frightened of you and set oot to kill you. And they'll still be frightened of yeh today if they ever find out you're alive.'

'Frightened of me?' The idea is almost too silly to imagine. 'Why would they be frightened of a wee girl?'

'Because,' says Sandy, 'there are a whole load of folk who would see your gift as a miracle, who would remember the way things used to be. That makes yeh powerful. But you must hide your colour while you are young. You must protect it until the time comes when you choose to use it. And it must be your choice.'

She nods, but she does not understand a lot of what he has said. He talks a lot. She yawns. 'I'm tired.'

'Aye,' he says. 'Take your medicine, there's a good girl.'

He hands her the tiny medicine bottle, and she uncorks it and lets a few drops of the liquid drop onto her tongue. The taste is honey-sweet and it warms her as it goes down. Almost at once, the colour in her hand and arm begins to recede, leaving her wrist, her palm, her knuckles. Leaving her fingers, her fingertips.

Hope examines every part of her hand, seeing only shades of grey. The colour is gone.

'From now on,' says Sandy, 'yeh must keep your medicine with yeh always. Understand? And I think yeh should take a few drops morning, noon and night.' Still crouching beside her, he pats her shoulder. 'I know it's a lot to take in, lassie. And I don't expect yeh to understand all of it. But know this: as long as I'm breathing, yeh have a place tae belong.'

Hope nods. She tucks the bottle in her pocket as Sandy stands and goes back to his driver's bench at the front of the caravan. Soon the wheels are rumbling over the uneven ground once more as the horse pulls them back onto the road.

Hope curls up on the bed while Oliver the dog jumps up and cuddles in.

'Are you all right?' he asks.

'No. I don't want to be different from everyone else.'

'I know. Are you frightened?'

'No. Maybe. A wee bit.'

'I'll protect you too,' says Oliver.

She scratches him behind the ears, and he leans into her hand. 'I know you will.'

Oliver leans his head on her legs, closes his eyes and, in the way only a dog seems capable, falls asleep in three seconds. Hope looks around the caravan, wondering how, just half an hour ago, her life seemed so safe and grey and every day.

Now she knows a great and terrible truth: that the world is wearing a mask. That what she is seeing is not real. That behind the mask is colour, and it is a wonderful, shining thing. She has only seen it for minutes, but already her heart feels a little empty without it. *It's not fair,* she thinks, *that everyone in the Dominion should have to live without it just because one person says so.*

And her heart feels emptier still because that same person, the Emperor, also stole away Hope's might-have-been life. A shadow life with a mummy and daddy dances in her head. Maybe a life with school and friends her own age and a real, stone house.

Not that this life is so terrible though, she thinks, scratching the snoozing Oliver behind the ears. But still . . .

One day she'd like to meet the Emperor. She's not sure exactly what she'll do when that day comes, but she knows deep in her little soul that, for the Emperor, it will not be a good day.

Chapter Five

In Which Darroch Begins
a New Project

Far away from Sandy's caravan, on the outskirts of the shining grey City, Darroch Gwendle sweeps the cobbled yard of his grandmother's rolling grey farm. It is a hot day, and as he sweeps back and forth, back and forth, Darroch watches beads of sweat run down the gentle slope of his nose and drip to the stone.

He sweeps out to the corner of the yard, adding to the bundle of loose hay and grime, and then he stops, leans on the broom, and looks up. The sky is a vast, never-ending expanse of diamond grey. But, as Darroch enjoys the warmth of the sun's rays on his face, a pang of sadness gnaws at him.

It shouldn't be grey, he thinks. It should be *blue* – whatever blue looks like.

'You're a million miles away.' Gran's voice startles him. She is coming across the farmyard holding a glass of water for him. He drinks it down thirstily.

'You've done a grand job of the yard,' she says, looking

around. 'Spick and span.' She taps her foot on the cobbles. 'Aye. Very grand. I suppose that'll be you done for the day, then.'

Darroch looks from the empty glass to his grandmother. 'Done for the day? As early as this?'

Mrs Gwendle nods. 'Well, I can hardly expect you to work all day, can I? Not on your birthday.'

Darroch blinks. 'You mean . . . But I thought . . .'

'You thought I had forgotten my only grandson's eleventh birthday? Jings, son, I'm not as old and dithery as that. Not yet.' She gives him a smile. 'Come on.'

Darroch follows the old woman into the house, through to the kitchen, where the smell of spiced carrot soup greets him like a hug.

'My favourite,' he says, peering into the bubbling pot, inhaling deeply.

'Close your eyes.'

He turns to face Gran. '*What?*'

'Close your eyes, boy.'

As always, he does as she says. He hears a cupboard door opening, hears a rustle of something, but does not dare sneak a peek.

At last, just as he thinks he might explode with curiosity, she says, 'Right. Open.'

He looks. She stands in front of him, holding something out towards him. It is a long leather pouch. Slowly, he reaches out and takes it, feeling the soft leather in his hands, smelling it. And inside . . . something else. His heart begins to race as his fingers trace the shape of the thin, hard objects nestling inside.

'Open it, then!' Mrs Gwendle chuckles.

Darroch's trembling hands find the opening and peel it back. He stares inside and finds five brand new paint brushes. Not the sort for painting walls or fences around the farm. The other kind. The sort of brushes used for painting pictures.

He brings each brush out, examining its smooth wooden length, running his fingers across the varying sizes of soft sable bristles.

'I know your grandfather's old brushes are getting a bit past it now,' she tells him. 'And though you've looked after them, everything has its season. I thought it was time you had something of your own. Some brushes that are just yours.'

Darroch does not know what to say. Tears leave streaks across his vision. 'Thank you, Gran.' He hugs her. 'I'll always keep Grandad's brushes. I'd never get rid of them.'

'Oh, I know that,' she says with a sniff. 'Now, on you go. Try them out!'

She shoos him away, and off he goes, hurtling upstairs to his room. He gently places the leather pouch on his bed, opens it, and arranges his new brushes in size order, smiling down at them. Then he turns his attention to the far side of his bedroom, where a lopsided easel stands, surrounded by bits of old canvas and wood. Beside the easel, Darroch's little desk is almost totally hidden beneath a jumble of more wooden scraps, pots of grey paint, a palette, and a scattering of his grandad's battered old brushes. It is here, in this little space, that Darroch has, for the past few years, been learning to paint.

His grandfather loved to paint, or so Gran has told him. Grandad's paintings are hung around the house. They are pretty things, mostly of the farm and the sea and the rolling hills. There is even one of Gran, although it was painted when she was much younger.

He moves to the cluttered desk, his fingers brushing tubs of paint with names that make his heart light. Yellow Ochre. Raw Umber. Burnt Sienna. To Darroch's eyes, these paints are nothing but varying shades of grey. He wonders now, as he has wondered countless times, what these paints must have looked like when his grandfather gazed upon them. When there was still colour in the world.

The hunger to know is almost painful.

Darroch moves beyond the desk, picks up some of his attempted paintings. There is one of the farm at sunrise from the highest point of Gran's land. He likes that one. Another shows crab fishing boats heading out from the City towards the open sea. Though he would never say so, Darroch believes that he is getting quite good. His latest painting, still on the easel, is a self-portrait. When Gran saw it, there were tears in her eyes. Tears of pride.

Darroch steps back again, his arms folded. This time he is not looking at a particular painting, or a brush, or speculating on a colour of paint. No. This time he is staring at the blank grey wall and imagining.

For a while now, he has known that he wants to do this. But it's a big job, and he has been waiting until he thinks he's good enough. Now he thinks maybe he is. And Gran has just given him new brushes, hasn't she? Surely that's a sign?

He nods, still staring at the blank wall, picturing what it might look like when he is finished. A smile creeps across his face as he goes to the desk, picks up his palette and pours several splodges of grey paint onto the wood. Next, he selects one of his new paint brushes, and there he stands, facing the wall, tickling his chin with his brush.

Then, after a while, he takes a deep, deep breath, dips the brush into the paint, reaches out and, with a long exhalation, touches the tip to the wall.

A few hours later, Mrs Gwendle passes Darroch's room. She has not planned on stopping there, but a sound makes her do so. She hovers at the door for a long moment, listening. The sound from within brings a smile to her face. Darroch is humming to himself as he works.

Mrs Gwendle nods. This is good. Darroch is happy. She has known, since he has been a tiny little thing, that he is more curious about the world than is good for him. He is just like she was when she was young. Always asking questions. Never accepting the sorts of silly answers that other little children fall for. No. Darroch has always been able to see that the world is wearing a mask.

One day, she is sure he will want to join the Rainbow League, to help bring colour back. She has seen glimpses of what is to come. Snippets in the tea leaves her own grandmother taught her to read. Whispers in her dreams. And will she stop him? Of course not. If she were younger, if she didn't have responsibilities, why, she'd be out there herself, wouldn't she?

But still, the thought of her only grandson putting himself in danger makes her shiver.

One day he will go. But not yet.

Chapter Six

In Which Moonlight
is Collected

A lunar cycle after Hope's first experience with colour, she stands with Sandy at the open door of a humble cottage, the light from inside spilling out onto the night. In the doorway there is a dishevelled, skinny man in his twenties. He is shaking Sandy's hand madly.

'Thank you,' he is repeating over and over. 'Thank you, thank you! And thank you a million more times! Oh, how can our family ever repay you for what you've done? I wish we could spare a few coins!'

Sandy manages to pull his hand free. He flexes a little life back into his fingers. 'Coins? I wouldnae hear of such a thing.'

'But you saved our wee girl,' says the man in the doorway, staring at Sandy with wide-eyed reverence. 'When she fell out of that tree . . .' He swallows. 'Her injuries were so bad, we thought we'd lose her. If you hadn't been passing through . . .'

'We're always passing through somewhere,' says Sandy. 'I'm happy we could help.'

'But surely there must be some way we can repay you?' the man says.

Sandy smiles, pats the man's shoulder and looks down at the cracked dirt path. 'It is a drifter mage's duty to help those in need. The only repayment I ask of yeh is that yeh will show us kindness if we are ever in need.'

'Of course,' the man says.

Sandy nods, tips his hat. 'Aye. Very good, then. We'll be away. Remember to give your wee girl the rest of the potion when she wakes.'

'I will.'

Sandy turns away, and then pauses. 'And keep her away from trees for a while.'

'Where are we going so late?' Hope rubs her eyes and stares up at the clear night sky. Midnight has come and gone already, and the moon is fat and dazzling. They have left the caravan back in the tiny village where Sandy treated the little girl's injuries.

'Yeh'll see in a minute.' Sandy holds a metal lantern in one hand, though the bare light of the moon is enough to show the way tonight.

Hope frowns down at Oliver, who trots beside her as they climb the steep, rocky hillside. Far below is the forest, which looks in this light like a vast black sea. Here and there Hope can make out white village lights twinkling like the lamps of far-off ships. 'Why can't he just tell me things?'

45

'He's being mysterious,' Oliver says. He is walking at her feet, stopping every now and then to sniff and leave his scent. 'You know how he likes to be mysterious.'

'My legs hurt,' says Hope.

Sandy does not slow down. In fact, Hope is quite sure that he has quickened his pace. 'Nearly there. Come on, lassie.'

'Do *you* know where we're going?' Hope asks Oliver.

The raggedy black dog twitches an ear. 'I'm not at liberty to say.'

'That's just a fancy way of saying you're not going to tell me, right?'

'In a word, yes.'

Hope huffs, stuffs her hands in the pockets of her grey coat and speeds up.

'Don't pout,' says Oliver. 'It doesn't suit you.'

They walk on in silence, until Hope darts down and plucks a little grey flower from the rocky ground. 'What colour do you think this is?'

'Oh, Hope,' says Oliver. 'Not this again. Sandy told you it's not safe to speak about that. You must forget about colour.'

'But I can't,' she says, her cheeks flushing. 'How can I forget something as wonderful as that?'

'Because if you don't, the Emperor's Black Coats will come riding through the forest on their great Ripper Dogs and find you.'

'Sandy wouldn't let them,' she says.

46

'Oh, and you'd be willing to put him in danger? And me?'

'Well, no . . . but . . .'

'Because that is exactly what you'd be doing, Hope, if you ever broke the rules. Do you want that?'

'No!'

'What are yeh two yapping aboot?'

Sandy has stopped and is looking back at them with an expression of suspicion.

'Oh, nothing,' says Oliver. 'Hope was just saying that she thinks you're lost. I was sticking up for you, of course.'

A frown creases Sandy's deep brow. 'Oh, aye? Lost, yeh say? Ha! Follow me and yeh'll soon see.'

He turns away and Hope clambers after him, up the increasingly steep hillside until they reach the crest of the hill, where they meet a rolling heather moor. The land is soft and spongy, quite difficult to walk on.

'You should try growing another pair of legs,' Oliver says smugly.

After another ten minutes of almost falling over, the moorland reveals a very large pond surrounded by grey reeds and scrawny, twisted trees. The water is black as coal and gently rippling. Hope can see the light of the moon scattering over the pond.

'What are we doing here?' she asks. Then she adds, 'And . . . where *is* here?'

Sandy is already striding down towards the pond. 'C'mere, Hope.'

She joins him at the edge of the pond while Oliver sniffs

around the heather, picking up the scent of rabbits and stuffing his nose into anything that might be a rabbit hole.

'Yeh've seen me makin' spells loads of times, haven't yeh?' says Sandy.

'Aye.'

'And what's the special ingredient that makes every spell work?' Sandy asks.

'Moonlight,' says Hope. 'Everybody knows that.'

Sandy smiles. 'Aye, moonlight. And I'm fresh out of it. Used what I had left mending that poor wee lassie's bones.'

'So we're here to get more?' Hope asks.

'Indeed we are,' says Sandy. 'And how do yeh think we might get it, Hope?'

Hope opens her mouth to speak. She pauses. 'Do you not just pick it out the sky?'

Sandy chuckles. 'Pick it oot the sky, she says! As if it's as easy as picking a ripe apple oot a tree!'

Hope feels her cheeks flush. She crosses her arms. She sticks out her tongue. 'Don't make fun of me.'

'I'm no makin' fun,' says Sandy. 'Yeh cannae get moonlight from the sky. It's too spread oot, and too wild. Yeh need to find somewhere where it gathers, see? A place where it gets trapped.'

Hope looks up into his craggy face, and then out across the water, where the light of the moon falls in rippling pools across the surface. Her large, dark eyes grow larger. 'You mean, like a pond?'

Sandy gives her a proud smile. 'Aye. Like a pond. But

no' just any pond, mind. A *moonpond.*' He indicates the glistening water. 'There's many of them, scattered about the land. Moonponds are ancient places. Some say they were once bewitched by faeries. Whatever the reason may be, a moonpond traps the light from the moon. And there it lies until the sun comes up.'

Hope gazes out over the still blackness of the water, her eyes flicking around the places where the moonlight has collected in silvery pools and swirls.

'Yeh want to know how to tell a moonpond from the rest?' Sandy asks her.

Hope nods. 'I really, really do.'

'There,' says Sandy, pointing to one of the trees surrounding the pond. It is a great, knotted oak, much larger than the other trees.

'Every moonpond has an oak,' says Sandy. 'That's the first sign, and anybody can spot it. But only a mage can detect the other two. The second is . . .' he sniffs at the air. 'You smell that?'

Hope takes a deep breath through her nose. 'I do smell something. It's like . . . like strawberries!'

'Oh, there's magic in yeh and no mistake,' says Sandy with a clap. 'Aye, a moonpond always smells sweet to a mage.'

'What's the last one?' asks Hope, bobbing up and down in anticipation.

Sandy crouches at the water's edge, reaches out a hand, dips a finger in the water. Then he pops the finger in his mouth for a moment. 'Try it,' he says. 'It's safe.'

Hope crouches beside him, reaches out and dips her little hand into the water. As her fingers break the surface, the silvery moonlight dances around on the tops of the ripples she creates. She takes a finger and tastes the droplets of water hanging from her fingertip. Immediately, her mouth fills with a sweet, tingling warmth.

'I can tell from yehr face that yeh taste it,' says Sandy with a chuckle.

'It's lovely!' She goes to dip her finger back in, but Sandy stops her.

'A drop is enough,' he says. 'It might taste like honey and cream but if yeh drink enough it'll make yeh unstable. Magic might come burstin' out yeh when yeh least expect.'

Hope stares at her finger, then dries her hand off on her coat.

Sandy stands up, reaches into his coat pockets and brings out two glass jars. He hands one of the jars to Hope, then goes back into his pockets and brings out a tiny leather pouch. 'Yeh want to have a go at moon-collecting?'

She nods so vigorously that her brain hurts.

'Do as I do,' Sandy tells her. 'Look.' He takes a careful step to the very edge of the pond, leans, and dips the jar into the water. To Hope's astonishment, the moonlight on the surface swirls away from the opening as it moves through the water. 'No as easy as yeh might think,' he says. Then he winks. 'Unless yeh have a few of these wee beauties.' He brings the dripping jar out, tucks it under his arm and then opens the leather pouch and empties a few tiny stones into his palm. After a long moment, the stones begin to glow, brighter and brighter, until they are so dazzling that Hope shields her eyes. 'Sunstones,' Sandy tells her. 'When I throw these into the pond, the moonlight will think the sun has come up and run away from the glow, see?'

He tosses the stones, *plonk*, into the pond then quickly crouches and dips the open jar into the water just as the moonlight pours across the surface towards him, away from the light of the stones. In moments he brings the jar out of the water.

It is filled to the brim with swirling moonlight.

Hope edges closer to the jar, reaches up and taps the glass.

'Hold out yehr hand,' says Sandy. She does, and he pours five glowing sunstones into her palm. Their warmth is comforting, like holding happiness in your hand. 'On yeh go then,' Sandy tells her. 'Find a spot and catch me some moonbeams.'

Her blood tingling with excitement, Hope looks around the edge of the large pond, spots a shimmering pool of moonlight near the old oak tree and decides that's the place to start. She makes her way around the pond, Oliver following closely behind. At the base of the enormous tree Hope readies her empty jar, creeps to the water's edge and opens her tightly closed hand, revealing the dazzling stones.

As she winds her arm to throw, Oliver says, 'Do try not to fall in. It might be deep.' Hope shoots him a withering look before chucking the stones. They land with a *plip plip plip*, immediately scattering the moonlight. Startled by the speed at which this happens, Hope makes a quick move, dipping the mouth of her jar into the water, letting the retreating moonlight cascade in. Then she scoops the jar up, pops the lid in place, and holds it up, smiling proudly at the magical light that is shifting inside.

'I did it, Sandy!' she calls across the pond, holding her jar up in triumph. 'Look!'

Sandy, who has already filled another three jars, stands up, illuminated by his catch, and waves. 'Good lass! Come on back round.'

Hope is so happy she feels like she might lift off the ground and float over the pond. 'Did you see, Oliver? Did you see me?'

The little dog wags his tail and walks in a circle around her. 'You,' he says, 'are a marvel. A natural.'

Hope begins to walk proudly back around the pond. She is a few paces away from the old oak when she stops, turns back, and becomes very still. 'You hear that?' she asks Oliver.

The dog, who has had his nose stuck in a pile of something Hope would rather not think about, stands straight. His ears twitch. 'Something's coming.' He looks up to the star-dappled darkness. 'There.'

Hope spins around, stares up and spots an irregular shadow blocking out a patch of countless stars. The shadow is spinning and tumbling, growing bigger as it comes closer.

Hope thinks for a moment that she sees the shape of huge wings, folding and unfolding and thrashing around.

'Look out!' comes Sandy's call across the pond. 'Take cover!'

CHAPTER SEVEN
IN WHICH A WYVERN FALLS
FROM THE SKY

Hope is frozen in place, gawping up as the falling shadow looms large overhead. Just as it seems to block out the entire sky, Oliver clutches Hope's coat between his teeth and drags her to the ground.

A whistle of rushing air splits the night, and a crashing boom shakes the ground and sends ripples spreading out across the water.

Hope lies on her back for a moment, her eyes squeezed tightly shut. Oliver's weight is on her chest, and his warm breath in her face. 'Are you all right?' he asks.

'I think so.'

Oliver hops nimbly off her, and she gets to her feet just as Sandy reaches them.

'Are yeh both safe?' he pants.

Hope hugs him and immediately feels safe, though her entire body is still trembling. 'What *was* that?'

'I dinnae know, but whatever it was, it came crashing doon somewhere behind the auld oak.'

'It was big,' says Oliver, hackles standing up all along his back. 'And I think it was alive.'

'We have tae investigate,' says Sandy. 'It's our responsibility as mages.'

'I was afraid you'd say that,' says Oliver with a sigh.

'What's responybilty?' Hope asks.

Oliver lovingly nudges his muzzle into her leg. '*Responsibility* means it's up to us.'

'That's right,' says Sandy. 'Part of a mage's job, if we do it right, is tae keep an eye on the unknown. There are worlds other than this one, and sometimes things come through where the borders are thin. If that happens, we have to put them back. Tidy up, if yeh like.'

Hope stares up at him, then at the darkness behind the ancient oak. She swallows hard.

'Stay close,' says Sandy.

Hope does not have to be told twice. She sticks at Sandy's heels. He has begun to teach her how to move unseen and unheard – to shadow-walk – but she does not have the hang of it yet. Sandy's feet do not make a sound, and Hope must concentrate deeply to keep him from becoming a shadow and sliding from her vision.

They are moving away from the pond now, and the pale, bright light of the dazzling full moon reveals a pile of hulking darkness a hundred paces away.

Sandy holds up a hand, turns to Hope and Oliver and says in a raspy whisper, 'Stay here for now – don't even think aboot arguing with me, lassie! Oliver, make sure she disnae move a muscle.'

Hope flashes a fiery stare at him, but Sandy has already turned away and is moving towards the thing that fell from the sky. Again, he shadow-walks, and Hope uses every bit of her concentration to keep him slipping from her eyes. When Sandy is maybe twenty paces from the thing, he suddenly freezes. Hope sees his arms drop to his sides, and then he rushes forward towards it.

'Yeh can come over!' he shouts across, and there is great urgency in his voice.

Hope scrambles over the spongy moorland, watching the hulking dark thing grow bigger with every step, until she is within ten paces and stops with such a jolt that Oliver bundles into her.

'It's . . . it's a . . .' She cannot form the words until she takes a calming breath. 'It's a dragon!'

The creature is enormous, with a body as big as Sandy's caravan, a long, muscular neck and a head as big as a pony. It is black as a lump of coal, covered in shining black scales that reflect the light of the moon. One of its great leathery wings lies crumpled beneath the body, and the other stretched out to the side, twenty paces across.

'No,' says Sandy. 'No a dragon. A wyvern. Just two legs, see? And a moon wyvern at that. But what's happened to you, pal, eh? What's made yeh fall oot the sky?'

He takes a step closer, and a deep, unhappy rumble escapes the wyvern's throat, making Hope jump back.

'No, ma beauty,' Sandy says in a gentle, musical voice. 'I'll no hurt yeh. Don't you fret about that . . .' Another step takes him within touching distance, and Hope holds her breath as Sandy reaches out slowly, very slowly, and places his hand on its side. The wyvern rumbles again, but it is a different sound this time, sad and tired. Its head is wide and horned, with a long muzzle and a mouth filled with teeth the size of elephant tusks. The eyes are glowing orbs, like miniature moons, though they are almost completely shut.

'Is it sick?' Hope asks.

'I'm no sure yet,' Sandy says, his hands gently searching the wyvern's body. It lies twisted, mostly on its front. He crouches, begins to examine what he can see of the belly. 'Aw no. But who would do such a thing?'

'What? You find something?' Hope edges closer, but Oliver steps between her and the wyvern. His hackles are up.

Sandy waves her over. 'Come and see for yehrself. It's all right, Oliver, let her come.'

Oliver steps aside and Hope dashes around to Sandy, causing the great animal to shuffle and rumble.

'Slowly, lass!' Sandy hisses. 'He's hurtin'.'

'Sorry. Can I . . . touch him?'

Sandy nods, and Hope reaches out a shaking hand and places it upon the heaving body. It is cold to the touch, hard like stone and smells like the burning embers of a campfire. Its sides expand and contract with each laboured breath, and Hope can sense the awesome power in it. She feels awfully small.

'Look there,' Sandy says, crouching, indicating a place on the belly. Hope crouches too. Illuminated by the moonlight from one of Sandy's jars, she can see that the wyvern's belly is not plated with armour like the rest of it. Its skin is exposed here, thick and cracked like old leather, and there, something long and metal is sticking out.

'Looks like some kind of spear,' says Sandy.

Hope can see dark blood pouring from the place the spear has punctured. The sight of it makes her mouth dry up and sends waves of hot anger through her body. 'Will it die?'

Sandy shakes his head. 'No if I have anything to do with it.' He moves around to the moon wyvern's head, takes the lid from one of his jars and carefully empties the moonlight onto the ground, where it gathers in a pool of viscous, silky glowing liquid. The wyvern's eyes open a little more, and from its mouth comes an enormous, rough tongue that laps up the moonlight. Another low rumble begins in its chest and escapes its mouth.

'Right,' says Sandy. 'You two stand back. On yeh go. That's it. A wee bit further.'

Hope and Oliver move back until Sandy is satisfied that they're a safe distance away.

'What's he going to do?' Hope asks.

Oliver is pressing against her leg, his entire body rigid and his ears alert. 'I don't know,' he says. 'You know what he's like. Whatever he's up to, I bet it's dangerous. I hope he doesn't get swallowed up.'

'Don't say that! Look, he's doing something!'

Sandy has walked in a circle around the moon wyvern, coming back to the place where the spear is stuck in its belly. He takes a big breath and cracks his knuckles, then turns his attention to the moon wyvern, leaning over, reaching out.

Hope gulps. 'He's grabbed the spear!'

The moon is bright, and the light from the remaining jars of moonlight illuminate Sandy's face. Hope sees him close his eyes, take another big breath, then . . .

With a mighty heave, Sandy pulls the spear out of the wyvern's belly.

The great beast's eyes widen. It lets out a deafening, rumbling roar that shakes the ground. It kicks out its legs and then, as it tries to get up, it throws out a wing, catching Sandy, lifting him, throwing him high through the air. He soars overhead as Hope and Oliver watch open-mouthed. There he goes, arching over the old oak tree towards the moonpond, his arms and legs flailing, until he is out of sight.

SPLASH!

The wyvern crashes back down onto its belly and lies still. Hope and Oliver stare at each other, then they dash over the spongy moor to the pond.

Sandy is already wading out of the water, soaked to the bone. As he walks towards them, pondwater runs out of his sleeves, his trouser legs, from beneath his hat, which has, magically, somehow stayed in place.

'Don't say a word,' he tells them as he walks past, tall and straight-backed.

Hope does not say a word. She and Oliver follow Sandy back towards the wyvern, which has not moved after its efforts. Sandy raises a hand to tell Hope and Oliver to hang back, and on he goes, back towards the beast as if he has not a care in the world.

'There there, ma beauty,' he says in soothing tones. 'Old Sandy's only tryin' tae help.'

As he edges closer, the wyvern rumbles again, and snorts. Hope's thinks her heart might leap into her mouth.

'He's mad,' says Oliver in a voice filled with admiration.

Sandy reaches out, puts a hand on the wyvern's head, strokes down the side of its face. 'That's it. The worst bit's over with now.' He picks up one of the two remaining jars of moonlight, removes the lid. Then he moves around and crouches to the wyvern's belly, pouring the moonlight into the puncture wound. The wyvern moans a little, but this time it doesn't make a move, and soon Sandy seems satisfied.

'Will it recover?' Oliver asks as Sandy comes back to them.

'Too early tae tell,' says Sandy. 'He'll need watchin' through the night. Oliver, do me a favour. Go back tae the caravan and keep an eye on the horse. Hope and me will stay here and watch our big pal.'

Oliver wags his tail, stands on his hind legs and puts his

paws on Hope's chest. He licks her face with his rough little tongue. 'See you soon.' Then he turns and, with a bark, darts away into the night.

'He's a good dug,' says Sandy, watching after him. For the first time, Hope notices that he is holding the spear he wrenched from the wyvern's belly.

Sandy walks to the oak, slips off his soaking tweed coat and hangs it on a branch. Then he sits on the soft ground and leans his back on the tree. Hope sits beside him as he examines the tip of the spear in the bright moonlight.

'Why did someone hurt him?' she asks.

'I don't know,' says Sandy, shaking his head.

Hope frowns. 'Do people eat wyverns?'

'No. But I've had run-ins with people who kill animals and keep them as trophies.'

'What's a trophy?'

'It's kind of a souvenir,' says Sandy.

'What?' Hope screws up her face. 'People keep dead things as souvenirs?'

'Well, with something as big as a wyvern, they'd probably just keep the heid.'

'The *head*?' Hope is so disgusted by the thought that she doesn't know what to say. She can't imagine how anyone could think killing a creature like a wyvern and taking its head could possibly be better than watching it fly free through the sky. Then another thought comes into her mind, and she shivers. 'Do you think the people who hurt him are near?'

Sandy's eyes have not left the spear all this time. 'He can't have flown very far with an injury like that,' he says, 'so I guess the hunters must still be in the neighbourhood. Don't you worry, lassie, if they come across me, I'll make sure they never hunt again.'

'You're really interested in that thing.' Hope points to the spear.

Sandy's eyes flick away from the spearhead for a moment, then back to it. 'Something's no right about it,' he says. 'I cannae tell quite what, but it feels wrong. I don't like it.'

Hope is more interested in the wyvern than the spear. She peers across the lumpy moorland at the hulking black shape of it. The light from the moon is glistening on its scales, and deep, rhythmic rumbles are drifting out of it. 'I think he's asleep.'

'Aye,' says Sandy.

'Can I go see him again?'

'No, lassie, yeh can't.'

'I won't go too close. Please?'

'Crivens, lassie! Has there ever been a minute of the day when yeh've been happy tae sit still? Yeh cannae go near him. If he wakes up, he might throw out a wing and skelp you into the air like he did me. I've no wish to see yeh flyin' across the sky like a wee robin.'

Hope folds her little arms, turns away from Sandy and puffs some air out from her cheeks.

'Yeh did a good job collecting that moonlight though,' says Sandy after a moment of silence.

Hope tries not to smile. 'I did?'

'Aye. Yeh're a natural.'

She turns back to face him. 'Will you let me make a spell soon? Please?' She thinks of the secret room beneath the floor of the caravan, filled with spell candles, all different sizes and shapes. And the tall glass jars of wands, their ends dipped in magic, looking like oversized matches. She has watched Sandy make spells to trade in the witch markets since she was tiny, smelled the magic in the cauldron, seen the sparks and fizzing wisps of light. She wants more than anything to learn to make those spells and potions.

Sandy gives her a rueful smile. 'Yeh never give up, do yeh? I've told yeh before, I'll start teaching yeh magic when yeh turn ten.'

'But that's so long away!'

'It seems that way to a child,' Sandy says. 'But I promise yeh, it'll be here before yeh know it. In any case, there's nae point in arguing. It's the way mages have always done things.'

Hope huffs again, and they sit in silence for a time, looking up at the stars. Then Hope feels a familiar warmth tingling in her fingertips and looks down to see that colour is creeping into her skin again. Her eyes widen and her heart quickens as the warm light brown colour reaches her hands and then touches the sleeve of her coat, turning a ragged patch of it yellow.

Sandy sits forward. 'When did yeh last take yehr medicine?'

'After dinner like always.' Hope holds her hands up, and

a breath catches in her throat. The colour is in both hands, which has never happened before.

Sandy nods. 'It's getting stronger. Take some more medicine. I'll need tae mix up a more potent spell.'

Hope brings the potion bottle out from her coat pocket, watches the liquid turn yellow. She opens it, raises it to her lips. Before she takes it, though, she pauses and imagines what it might be like to let the colour spread. She imagines the yellow filling up her coat, imagines the light brown colour in her skin bringing a glow to her face and her skinny legs. And what then? Would the grass she's sitting on turn green? That's the colour of grass, isn't it? But she shakes these thoughts away like a midge and takes a sip from the bottle. In moments the colour recedes once more and is gone, leaving that familiar ache in her chest.

Chapter Eight
In Which Hope Visits the Stars

Hope wakes with a start, unsure for a moment where she is. Then she hears Sandy snoring and remembers that they are beneath the oak tree near the moonpond.

And that there is an enormous moon wyvern sleeping a stone's throw away.

The grey-black sky is still cloudless, the moon huge and full and bright enough to see by. Hope peers over the shadowy moor, blinks, sits straight up.

She rubs her eyes.

She blinks again.

The wyvern is gone.

Her eyes widen as they turn to the sky, wondering if she will see the shape of its huge wings against the stars. She does not.

'Sandy,' she whispers.

Sandy has placed his hat over his face, and deep snores spill out from under the brim. Then, unsettled a little by

Hope's voice, he begins to talk in his sleep. He does this sometimes and, when it happens, he uses a strange voice that doesn't sound like Sandy at all. It seems that he becomes another person in his dreams.

'Back,' he moans. 'Get back. Get away from them.'

'Sandy.' Hope shakes him gently, but he does not open his eyes.

'It wasn't my fault,' he says in a half sob. 'You must believe me. Not my fault . . . I tried. Mother . . . Father . . . I tried.'

Hope reaches out to shake him again, but she stops when a sound from behind the tree catches her attention. It is the sound of something very large moving slowly.

Holding her breath, Hope inches up and leaves Sandy to his dreams. She peeks around the trunk towards the moonpond, her entire body jangling with curiosity and excitement, and takes a sharp breath.

The wyvern is standing in the middle of the pond. Most of its great body is submerged, and its long neck and the top of its enormous head form a strange, glistening island in the middle of the water. Its eyes are closed as it bathes in the moonlit pool. Swirling moonlight currents dance across the water as the wyvern's wings move beneath the surface.

Hope instantly forgets about the rest of the world. At this moment, all that exists is this beautiful creature, and the pond, and her hammering heart beneath the night sky.

Then she steps on a twig.

The wyvern's glowing eyes shoot open. Its head swings around, sending a wave of water out across the moonpond. Its gaze locks on Hope, whose feet seem to have sprouted deep roots into the earth. She is frozen, completely unable to move even a single muscle as the wyvern rumbles, as its leathery wings, big as ship's sails, rise out of the water, as it comes across the pond towards her in four huge steps.

It towers over her, peering down like she is an insect. She hopes that she does not look tasty.

When the wyvern makes another low, vibrating rumble and lowers its head towards her, Hope thinks about shouting out for Sandy, but quickly changes her mind. She might only be six years old, but Sandy has taught her well. She knows that making such a noise might frighten an animal and cause it to lash out.

She doesn't want that.

She stays perfectly still as the beast's muzzle comes close enough to touch, blinking as its hot breath blasts her face. The smell of it, of burning wood and glowing embers, fills her head, makes her dizzy.

'Please don't eat me,' she manages to squeak.

The moon wyvern blinks.

'I don't think you will eat me,' she says. 'You only eat moonlight, don't you?' Her eyes go to its belly, but though the light of the moon is bright, she cannot make out the wound. 'Wait there,' she says, and it is only when she has walked back around the tree and lifted one of Sandy's moonlight jars that she realises she is hurrying back towards a creature big enough to gobble her up as easily as she might swallow a munchberry.

She slowly approaches the wyvern and shines the light from the jar upon its underside. The wound has all but closed up.

'That must feel better,' she says. Then, after a pause, 'Would you like me to put some more moonlight on it?'

The wyvern lifts its wing so that she can get a better view of the wound, and she stares up at it. 'All right. Hold on.' Her little hands have a bit of trouble unscrewing the lid, but she frees it eventually. Then she pours some of the thick moonlight onto the wound and gently rubs it in. The wyvern's eyes close as the wound is soothed.

'I can't believe someone would do this to you. You know what I think? I think they'll be in deep trouble if Sandy ever finds them. Nobody messes with Sandy. Nobody with half a brain anyway . . .' She stops short, because she feels that familiar warm tingle in her hands again, and when she holds them out, she can see the colour flushing into her skin, turning it light brown and her coat sleeve bright yellow. 'Oh my,' Hope says with a sigh. 'You see that? Sandy says there's folk would hurt me if they ever found out about it, just like they hurt you.'

At the sight of the colour, the moon wyvern's glowing eyes widen. It makes a short series of rumbles and sniffs, and it shifts from side to side. Then it does something that Hope does not expect at all. It brings its great muzzle towards her hands and rubs against them. She stands very still for a moment, amazed. The wyvern is cool to the touch, and its shining scales are not black as she thought. They are a dark red and they shine like pearls when the moonlight catches them. The colour from Hope's hands paints the wyvern's muzzle. There are patches of lighter red scales, and above its eyes are arches of fiery yellow. The eyes themselves are a glowing, silvery blue.

'What a beauty,' says Hope, her heart swelling. Feeling bolder now, she takes her hands and runs them back and forth across the small part of the muzzle she can reach. A low, gentle rumble comes from the wyvern's chest. Then it shifts, lowering one of its wings to the ground and nudging Hope towards it, sending her toppling to the mud.

'Watch it, will you?' she says, getting up, dusting herself off. She should have taken her medicine by now. The colour has spread all the way up her arm to her shoulder, further than she has ever seen, but part of her knows that this is a special moment, and that it will fade if she lets the colour go. The wyvern is colourless again without her touch. It nudges her once more towards its lowered wing.

'What do you want? Oh!'

A final nudge sends Hope onto the leathery wing, and then with a great, effortless rush the wyvern stands tall and tilts its wing so that Hope rolls into a huge dent between its shoulder blades.

'What are you doing?' she demands, watching as colour paints the scales of the wyvern's back pearlescent, blackish-red. 'Put me dow—'

She does not finish the sentence, because there is a great, heaving movement. Hope rolls backwards, feels her stomach lurch into her guts and scrambles up to feel the wind coursing through her hair. Her hands cling to the scales of the wyvern's back, her eyes wider than the moon high above.

High above, but getting closer.

Because she is *flying*.

Hope is flying on the back of the moon wyvern.

At either side, its enormous wings take them higher every time they cut through the still night with a thunderous whoosh. Up and up and up they go, the air growing colder, until, at last, the wyvern ceases its climb, levels off, and begins a smooth glide. Only now that the beating of the wings has calmed does Hope dare lean over and chance a look down.

She takes a sharp breath, and her mouth hangs loosely open at the sight that awaits her.

She had thought that the view from the hilly path to the moor was something. But this ... this is everything. It's forever.

Under the dazzling light of the huge moon, Hope can see all the way to the edge of the darkness of the forest. She can see beyond the faraway shadow of the Dragon Tooth mountains to the beginnings of the great frozen tundra of the north. And there, far, far below, is the moonpond, so small that she can easily block it out with her thumb.

'Hey! Where are we going? I can't go too far!' she yells over the whistle of the approaching night air.

The wyvern turns its enormous head to glance at her. Hope could swear that it is smiling. Then its head swings away, and with effortless grace the beast throws them into a steep dive.

Hope grabs on tight and shuts her eyes as the roaring wind steals her breath, cutting off her scream. She opens one eye a fraction, sees the darkness of the moorland rushing towards her, closer and closer . . .

The wyvern pulls up just in time; she hears its belly brush the moorland heather, then there is an exhilarating whoosh as the wyvern climbs high into the night sky again. Hope cannot help herself now. Such a rush of happiness, of adventure and wonder and freedom, courses through her that she punches the air with one hand and lets out a whoop of delight.

The wyvern answers her with a call of his own, a two-tone, roaring bellow that carries off over the sky like musical thunder.

Again they dive, faster and faster, and again they pull up in the nick of time, soaring so quickly and so incredibly high that there is a moment, as the wyvern reaches the crest of its climb, that time seems to stand still and Hope feels that she could reach out and pluck one of the stars from the sky.

Thwack!

The sound rips Hope from the moment. The wyvern lurches and a terrible scream escapes it. Hope is thrown to one side, almost rolls off, but manages to grab a thorny scale and climb back up as the wyvern thrashes around in the night and begins to fall.

Hope can do nothing. Nothing but hang on as they drop out of the sky, spinning, tumbling. She sees the stars then the ground, the stars then the ground, again and again as the world flashes past with every spin.

Sky.

Ground.

Sky.

Ground.

Sky.

Then the Wyvern's great wings wrap around her, enveloping her, cutting her off from the world and encasing her in a leathery shell.

She hears muffled cracks and snaps and is thrown this way and that, and then . . .

Boom.

It's all over.

CHAPTER NINE
IN WHICH HOPE FIRST ENCOUNTERS BABA

Hope's eyes crack open a fraction. Her head is spinning, pulsing with pain, and her ears are filled with ringing. She is still wrapped in the wyvern's wings, and as the ringing fades she can hear the course sound of the great beast's ragged breathing

Using all her strength, she pushes and wriggles out from her protective shell and into the dark. A glance up tells her that they have crash landed in the forest, but there is no way of telling how far from the moonpond and Sandy they have come.

Through the thick trees she catches glimpses of the night sky, where she was soaring only moments ago. But what happened?

Beside her is the hulking blackness of the wyvern, lying on its side. Perhaps, she thinks, it is simply exhausted. Maybe it flew too soon after its injury. But . . .

She reaches her hand out to touch its snout. Its eyes

open, and the glow from them is bright enough to illuminate the immediate area. Hope gasps when she realises that the colour has spread to every part of her. She stares down at the light brown of her legs, and then her eyes flick to the side, and she understands at once why the wyvern fell from the sky.

Another large spear has pierced it, this time just beneath the shoulder joint of its right wing.

Dread and fear and helplessness begin to tear through her like poison. Sandy might be miles away, and Hope does not know what to do. Tears well in her eyes.

'Don't worry,' she tells the wyvern. 'I'm here. You're not alone.'

It blinks sadly, rubs its muzzle against her hands as she strokes it. She presses her forehead against it, closes her eyes and lets her tears drop onto its scales.

A snapping from nearby breaks the silence. Hope's head whips around. 'What was—' But before she can finish, the wyvern uses its muzzle to lift her off the ground and toss her through the air. She lands with a muted thump on the soft black carpet of moss and fallen leaves some distance away. She gets her breath back, then begins to get up. 'Why would you do that?' she begins, then stops and stays still.

She listens.

What is *that*?

Something is moving among the blackness of the trees, something that sounds large. It's difficult to tell in the dark, but she thinks it is coming from the direction of the wyvern.

She spots the shaky, bobbing white light of a hand lantern stalking between the trunks and branches.

Hope edges closer and hears what she can only think of as the rasping breath of a dying thing. It rattles and gurgles and makes her think of stink and death.

'A lovely thing,' it says. The last part of the sentence is dragged out: 'thinggggggggg,' in a breathy wheeze. 'Not damaged too badlyyyyy.'

Something about the voice sends a chill through Hope's bones. In the dark between the trees, she creeps forward towards the colourless light, praying she doesn't step on a dry branch. She comes closer, closer still, until she is maybe thirty adult paces away from the place where the wyvern fell. Close enough.

She ducks down behind the hollow trunk of a long-fallen tree and stares out towards the figure standing beside the wyvern.

It appears to be a woman, though it is taller than any woman Hope has ever seen. She can smell the thing even from here, a stench of rot and decay. It sticks in her nose and her throat.

The tall woman has her back turned to Hope. She is wearing a long, ragged dress that trails on the ground and over her head she wears a light grey shawl stained with smears of dark liquid.

She must be half again as tall as Sandy, thinks Hope. And Sandy is not a small man. But her proportions are strange and unnatural. Her legs look too short, her body too big, her head well oversized. And her arms . . . her arms are so long that the lamp almost touches the ground as she lets it hang in her hand by her side.

'You thought you'd got away from old Baba, ehhhhh?' she breathes. 'Thought I wouldn't find you?' The tall woman coughs, raspy and dry. Her movements are jerky and unpredictable, and the way her head is constantly on the move makes Hope shiver. The tall woman makes a noise like she's smacking her lips. 'Let me tell you somethinggggg,' she tells the wyvern, patting it with a grey hand that is too long and ghostly pale. 'When I decide to collect something, I always get it in the ennnnnnd. Now let me see.' She moves around the wyvern, and it shifts and grumbles.

'Now don't you beeee like that,' says the tall woman, pointing a long, long finger in the wyvern's face. 'There's no point in fightiiiiiing it. Let me see . . .' She moves in a jerky half dance around to the spot where the spear has impaled the wyvern. Then, in a movement so quick it shocks Hope, the tall woman reaches out and yanks the spear from the wyvern's shoulder.

Hope covers her mouth to stop from crying out as the wyvern roars in agony. It flaps a shaking wing, tries to get up, and then collapses back on its belly. Hope wishes more than anything that Sandy was here.

'That's right,' says the tall woman. 'No more fighting. You belongggg to Baba now. I'll fix you up, and how lovely you'll look in my collectionnnnn.'

There is a moment of deep silence, when the air seems

to grow heavy and press against Hope's skin as she crouches behind the fallen tree. Then the tall woman starts to hum a tone-deaf, eerie tune that makes strange shapes in Hope's mind as it drifts between the trees.

Hope blinks.

She peers over the fallen log, her disbelieving eyes searching.

The wyvern has disappeared.

No. Wait.

The tall lady has leaned over, crouched down. Hope can only see her from the back, her wide, bony shoulders jerking busily. What is she doing?

When she straightens up and turns around, Hope sees that the tall woman is now holding two objects. In one hand is the lantern. And in the other she is clutching a small cage, the sort in which a person might keep a pet bird.

But there is no bird inside this cage.

A dark shape quivers behind the thin bars, something with a long neck and two eyes that glow with a silvery light.

It's the wyvern, now tiny and trapped. It lets out a small, helpless whimpering call, and Hope's heart aches. She wants to do something, wants to jump out and snatch the cage from the tall lady's hand, but fear keeps her rooted to the forest floor.

The tall woman smacks her lips again, lifts the cage with her freakishly long arm and chuckles. For the first time Hope can see the tall lady's face. Her head is huge, several sizes too big for the strange body. Her brow juts out like a ledge above her large, watery, bloodshot eyes and her mouth slopes to one side. She examines the shrunken wyvern in the cage, humming. It seems she is delighted with her catch.

'Time to get you hommmmmme,' she breathes. 'Back to Baba's house—'

She stops, becomes as still as the surrounding trees. A lump of fear rises in Hope's throat as Baba begins to sniff about.

'What's that?' she says, letting the cage drop to her side and raising the lamp in her other bony hand. 'Somethinggggg's here.' She holds the lamp out, swings it jerkily about, peers between the trees, all the while sniffing.

It's me, Hope thinks. *She knows I'm here.*

She considers running, but where would she run to? She is lost. And anyway, Baba might be fast, might catch her as easily as Hope could catch a snail.

'Who's there?' comes Baba's voice. 'I can smelllll you.' She swings around and in Hope's direction. Hope gasps, ducks down behind the fallen tree. Her heart is thumping out of control.

Baba begins to move. As the sound of shuffling steps comes closer, Hope drops down on her belly on the forest floor, pushes herself as far under the fallen grey tree as she can manage and lies still as death.

Baba comes closer.

Closer.

To listen to her breathing is painful. Each breath is a

tearing, ragged wheeze. The smell of her is eye-watering, like a dead thing in the summer heat.

Closer.

Baba stops on the other side of the fallen tree, and Hope can sense her towering above, can see the grey light from Baba's lamp shining on the nearby branches and trunks and roots.

'What is that?' Baba says. 'It's something I haven't smelled in a long time.' A pause, and another sniff. 'Colourrrrr.' She wheezes. 'I smell colour!'

Lying on her belly, Hope's eyes bug wide. Colour. Colour is giving her away. The only thing separating her from this monster is a rotting tree trunk. She curses herself for not taking her medicine.

Her medicine!

Slowly, holding her breath, Hope moves her hand down towards the pocket of her coat. Baba is beginning to crouch, to lean over the tree trunk. Hope can smell the rot just inches above her head. Her hand finds her pocket, touches upon the cold glass of the bottle. Silently she brings the medicine out, carefully uses her teeth to take off the lid and swigs the potion.

The effect is instant. She feels the warm colour draining from her body, replaced by the coldness of grey shades.

On the other side of the log, Baba grunts, straightens up. Hope closes her eyes as Baba sniffs wildly about.

'Gonnnnne. Where have you gone, lovely colour?' She smacks her lips, steps over the log, one of her hideous grey feet landing on the forest floor just a couple of inches from Hope's shoulder. Hope squeezes her eyes shut tight, her body rigid with terror, expecting to feel Baba's long, bony fingers on her any second . . .

A familiar sound in the distance.

The barking of a dog.

Could it be?

Oliver?

'Hope!' A distant call echoes through the trees. 'Hope?'

Sandy! Hot tears well in Hope's eyes.

I'm here, Sandy, she thinks. *Please come and get me. Please.*

Baba sniffs the air again.

'Magics,' she spits. 'Strongggg magics coming this way. A mage.' She holds the wyvern up in its little bird cage. 'Time to go, my beauty.' And her footsteps recede into the forest.

'Hope? Hope, are you here, lassie?'

She wants to shout out, but she is still so scared.

More sniffing nearby, and for a terrible moment she fears Baba has come back, but then Oliver's wet nose is nudging her, his tongue lapping at her face.

'Sandy, over here! Found her!'

And now Sandy is there too, breathless, scooping Hope up in his arms, holding her tight as she sobs.

'It's all right, lassie. You're all right.'

When she is calm enough, Hope tells Sandy the story of the wyvern, of how she flew on its back until someone shot it out of the sky. She tells him about Baba. How close she came to joining the wyvern in a cage. Or worse. But although Sandy searches the surrounding area, he can find nothing. Baba is gone, and the wyvern with her.

CHAPTER TEN
IN WHICH A DARING
PLOT UNFOLDS

✦

At exactly the moment Hope is riding on the wyvern's back, far across the Dominion, the spark of adventure is about to light a fire in another soul. Over six years from the night he made a wish upon a falling star, in his little bedroom in the farmhouse outside the City, Darroch Gwendle wakes in the night to the sound of muffled voices.

At first, he thinks that maybe he is dreaming. But the voices persist, and he sits up and listens intently. As far as he can discern, there are three people directly below him in the kitchen. He recognises his grandmother's voice, of course, but not the two others. He frowns. He cannot remember the last time Gran had visitors — and it is an especially strange occurrence at this hour.

Darroch sits on the edge of the bed, straining his ears, curiosity burning hotter in him with every passing moment until he can hold himself back no longer. He creeps out of bed, wincing as one of the floorboards moans, out of the door and halfway down the stairs, where he stops and peers over the old wooden bannister. The kitchen door is a little open, the lamplight falling on the floor in a bright, colourless bar.

He can hear the voices quite clearly now.

'We can't tell you how much we appreciate your help, Mrs Gwendle,' says the voice of a woman.

'Aye, that's fine,' comes Gran's reply. 'This was the best place to hide it until tonight. Don't expect me to make a habit of it, mind. I have a grandson I have to think of. Keeping him safe is my priority.'

Back on the stairs, Darroch frowns. Keeping him safe? What are these people up to that she must keep him safe from?

'Of course,' says a man. 'Like we say, we appreciate you keeping it for us, and your hospitality.' There is a slurping sound, like someone draining the last of a drink, then the man says, 'Well, I suppose we can't put it off any longer, eh?'

The sound of chair legs scraping on the kitchen floor sends Darroch scurrying back to the top of the stairs. He ducks behind the bannister as footsteps echo down in the hall. Gran comes into view, fully dressed despite the hour. She unlocks and opens the door, and two people walk out, a short, stocky man and very thin young woman with tightly-cropped dark hair. Both are dressed completely in black. They stop just beyond the door, turn back.

'Thank you again,' the woman says.

Gran nods, folds her arms across her chest. 'Good luck.'

As Gran closes the door, Darroch catches a glimpse of the man and woman pulling black masks down over their faces, and his heart skips a beat.

When the strangers are gone, Gran stands at the front door in silence for a moment, before she says, 'I know you're up there, Darroch.'

A jolt of shock steals his breath.

'Come on out, boy.'

She doesn't sound angry. Darroch does as she asks, leaving the shadows of the upstairs landing and coming down to the hall. He is eleven years old, and already taller than Gran, but it feels like she towers over him as he stands across the hall from her.

'Sorry,' he says. 'I didn't mean to spy.'

She nods. 'So you were spying accidentally?'

'Who were those people?' he asks.

Gran sighs. 'Nobody you need to know about, boy. Trust me.'

'But they put on masks when they left. Are they robbers or something?'

Gran takes a step closer, puts a hand on his arm. 'Do you really think I'd tolerate robbers? Here?'

He shakes his head. 'No. Course not. But then who were—'

'Back to bed,' Gran cuts him off. 'They were just friends of a friend passing through. It's nothing you need worry about and that's my final word.' She points up the stairs, and Darroch's chin drops onto his chest. He turns around and stomps up the stairs, his head spinning with a hundred questions as he climbs back beneath his sheets.

He hears Gran going up to her room shortly after, and then all is quiet.

Darroch tosses and turns for a while, but there is no way he's going to sleep now that his mind is alight with curiosity. Life on the farm is quiet. There are the sheep to tend to, and the crops to plant and harvest. Everything works on an endless cycle, regular as clockwork. Darroch has never complained. In fact, he finds the work rewarding, and he loves spending time with Gran. But there is a part of him that longs for more.

Quiet as he can, he slips out of bed and goes to the window, opening the curtains and pushing up the sash to the cool late summer night. He can smell the sweetness of the ripening corn. Soon the fields will be alive with seasonal workers picking the grey harvest, but for now all is quiet and still.

The sky is clear, the moon full. To the east of the farm, the City is asleep, save for the glow of a lamp here and there. Darroch's mind travels back a number of years, to a night very much like this one, when he made a wish on a falling star.

A wish for colour to return to the world.

He gave up on that wish a long time ago.

After one more deep breath of sweet harvest air, Darroch reaches up to close the window.

He stops, his hand frozen on the frame.

Out over the City, a zipping fizz of light is tearing up towards the sky. As it climbs, the light emits a high, screeching scream.

Darroch has seen fireworks before, of course, white in the dark sky – but only ever during special occasions, like the Emperor's birthday or the end of the harvest season. Never in the middle of the night like this.

The firework screams up and up, leaving a blazing, searing white tail behind it. Higher and higher it goes until, finally . . .

BOOM!

It explodes in a blossoming plume of fiery light.

Darroch's legs weaken. His fingers grip the windowsill and his mouth hangs slack like an open trapdoor.

The firework is different to anything he has ever seen. The shower of light in the sky is alive with a vibrance and beauty that makes his heart sing.

His eyes blur with tears as he realises that he is seeing colour for the first time.

Another firework blazes into the sky over the City, and another, and a dozen more after that, each a different colour to the last, a symphony of life and joy.

For reasons that he cannot explain, Darroch begins to laugh. Delight fills him as he watches the plumes of colour erupt in the night sky.

His bedroom door bursts open, and in rushes Gran, over to the window to join him. Her face is full of worry.

'Look, Gran! Look!'

'Aye, boy. I see it.' She does not seem to share his happiness.

'That's colour, isn't it?' he asks, pointing.

She nods.

Another boom rips the night as the largest explosion yet lights up the heavens, sending a hundred falling stars out over the far-off rooftops.

'What colour are those, Gran?' Darroch asks, then he holds up a hand. 'No, wait. I'll try to remember what you told me. That colour feels like . . . feels like the meadow out the back of the house where the sheep graze. It feels like spring. Like life. It's green, isn't it? Am I right, Gran? Is it green?' He tears his gaze from the sky to look at her. She nods.

'Aye, Darroch. That's green.'

BOOM! BOOM! CRACK! BANG!

'Oh, look at that one, Gran! What colour is that?'

'Red, Darroch.'

The show continues for another few minutes, and lamplight blinks on in windows all over the city as people wake up with the sounds and bright flares. When at last the fireworks stop, Darroch finds that he is breathless with excitement, that his chest is rising and falling and his mind is buzzing. When he closes his eyes, he can still see the after images of the burning patterns. But Gran doesn't look so happy. In fact, she looks troubled.

'Didn't you enjoy that, Gran?'

She closes her eyes for a moment. 'It's not that, Darroch.'

Darroch puts a hand on the old lady's shoulder. 'Do you feel all right?'

'Aye. Fine.'

A terrible sound from the City makes them freeze then, the high, bone-chilling howl of one of the Emperor's Ripper Dogs.

'Someone's in trouble,' says Darroch. 'Must be because of the fireworks.' For the first time since the excitement began, he finds himself wondering exactly how someone managed to bring those flashes of colour back to the world. Then his memory shows him the two mysterious visitors who stopped by the house earlier. He sees them slipping the black masks over their faces as they leave . . .

'Gran,' he says, a sick feeling swirling in his belly. 'Those people who came to see you. Did they do this?'

Gran sighs. 'I knew I should have kept out of it. But I let her talk me round, despite my better judgement.'

'What are you talking about?'

She pats his hand. 'C'mon. We'll go downstairs and get some tea.'

Five minutes later they are sitting at the kitchen table nursing cups of steaming tea.

'I was hoping,' says Gran between sips, 'that you'd be asleep when it all kicked off tonight. That you'd sleep right through, none the wiser.'

Darroch sits forward, his elbows on the table. 'So you *did* know about it?'

She nods. Darroch stares at her as if she is a stranger. How could his gran, the woman who raised him to follow the rules and never even speak of colour in public, be involved in something so incredibly dangerous?

'I know what you're thinking,' she says. 'And you're right, Darroch. I haven't followed my own rules. I'm sorry.'

'Who were those people?' he asks. 'The ones who were here tonight?'

Gran seems to gather her words for a moment. 'Listen to me, Darroch. There are people out there who would like to fight the Emperor and his Necromancer. Folks who wish to remind the people of the world that colour is their right, that it has been stolen from them – and with it a huge part of the imagination and vibrancy of life. And these people are not afraid to take a chance, to face down a Ripper Dog or a Black Coat, to face even death, if it means they can get their message out. If it means they can make people remember. Make them want change. There are pockets of these people all over the Emperor's domain. They call themselves the Rainbow League. Their numbers have been growing for the past few years, but this is the first time they've been able to organise such a . . . powerful message.'

Darroch stares into his teacup. 'Are you in the Rainbow League, Gran?'

She shakes her head. 'I've never been to one of their meetings, and until now I'd only ever met one of their members. I have an old friend who asked for a favour, and that is why I agreed to what happened tonight. I hid their fireworks on our land until the time was right to use them. But I would never become more involved than that. I wouldn't want to put you at risk.'

Darroch stares across the table at Gran, his heart swelling with pride. He has always known that she is a strong woman, both in body and mind, but he never imagined she'd do something like this. 'What if I don't mind?' he says.

She frowns. 'What?'

'You don't want to put me at risk, but what if I don't mind?'

She shifts uncomfortably. 'Darroch . . .'

'What the Emperor and the Necromancer have done is wrong,' he says. 'Everyone knows it, but folk are too scared to do anything about it. At least that's what I thought until tonight. You weren't scared.'

'But I was, Darroch,' says Gran. 'I still am.'

'Well, that's even better,' says Darroch, reaching across the table and taking one of his grandmother's calloused hands. 'You've always told me that bravery is being scared and doing something anyway.'

Gran smiles, her grip tightening on his hand. 'Gran, I'm eleven years old now, and tonight was the first time I've ever seen colour. It's . . . something has awakened in my heart. I just have this feeling that we need to help.'

Gran's eyes are fierce and sparkling. She makes a slight movement with her head. A nod? But then . . .

'What was that?' she says.

They both sit very still, listening.

Somewhere out in the fields, someone is shouting.

Gran pushes her chair back and jumps up. 'Stay!' she tells Darroch, making him freeze halfway to his feet. He sits back down. 'Don't leave the house. Not one foot out the door.'

Then she is down the hall and gone.

Darroch's chest thumps and he does not know what to do. He paces around the kitchen, then out to the hall, to the front door. With trembling fingers he opens the door and listens. Is that . . . is Gran shouting something? He thinks so. And then another noise makes his feet root to the floor.

The ear-shattering howl of a Ripper Dog makes him wince. It sounds so close.

'Gran!' he whispers, and, ignoring her warning to stay put, he dashes out to the cobbled yard, not knowing which way to run. 'Gran?'

A shape comes out of the darkness towards him. Gran! And someone else, someone leaning on her.

'Back in the house!' says Gran. Darroch spins around and runs to the kitchen. A moment later Gran helps the woman through the door and lays her on the floor. 'Get a pillow, Darroch.'

Again, he does as she asks without hesitation, fetching a cushion and slipping it under the woman's head. She moans and grits her teeth, and Darroch sees that she is clutching her side. Beneath her, a puddle of dark grey blood is growing.

'Gran!'

'I know, Darroch. Stand back.' Gran has a pair of scissors in her hand. She kneels beside the woman and cuts away the clothes from her midsection, revealing a row of puncture marks and a large, bubbling grey-black wound beneath the ribs of her right side. 'Crivens, what a mess.'

'Tony,' the woman manages to say. Her words are breathless and weak. 'Tony's gone. The Ripper Dog had me but he took it on so I could get away.' Her eyes are streaming and Darroch feels a stab of fear.

'Gran, what if they come here to the house? What if the Black Coats bring the Ripper Dogs here?'

Gran is still kneeling, examining the wound. 'No Ripper Dog is setting a rotten paw on my farm,' she says without looking up.

'But how do you know? I heard one just before you came back. It sounded close.'

'They will not come here!' Gran's voice is powerful enough that Darroch takes a step back. 'Our family have farmed this land for generations. Our blood and sweat lies deep in the soil. My great great granda is buried here. There was magic in his blood, and in some of the others.' She looks to the ground, shakes her head, and when she speaks her voice has become low. 'My daughter is buried here. We have a connection to this land, and there is power in that magic. Those creatures can feel it. They won't cross the border. Look at me, Darroch!'

This snaps him out of his fearful daze.

She says, 'I have a little moonlight in a bottle in my

dresser drawer. Bring it to me. Then get me some clean towels and fetch my sewing kit. After that, go up to your room and stay there until I call for you.'

'But I can help.'

'Do as I say! You are not going to want to see what I'm about to do. Go!'

Shaking badly, he follows Gran's instructions, only pausing for a moment on the stairs before he goes into his room. His window is still open from the fireworks, and the acrid, smoky scent of them has drifted over from the City, filling his room. He looks to the edge of the farm, and he can see no sign of the Ripper Dogs' glowing eyes. Have they gone? Do they think the woman is away into the forest? He prays that they do.

When the woman's screams begin to drift up from the kitchen, Darroch buries his head beneath his pillow and cries into the warm dark.

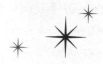

Chapter Eleven
In Which a Gift is Given

In the castle in the City, the Necromancer sits in a private courtyard, warming herself by the flames of a fire.

This is a secret garden, hidden by high walls, lined on four sides with thick grey ever-blossoming trees.

The fire sits in the centre of the garden, built upon a circle of stone. Its flames are high and fierce.

And the fire is in colour.

The Necromancer sits on the grey grass around the orange flames, her shimmering silvery dress catching the light. Her eyes are closed, and her hands are folded in her lap.

'Did you see?' the voice jolts her from her meditation. The Emperor bustles into the garden from the secret door, a young man with pale, freckled skin and dark wavy hair. His grey, oval face is flushed at the cheeks. 'Did you see, Aunt? Fireworks over the City. In colour!'

The Necromancer gazes up at him coolly. 'Yes. I saw.'

'And?' says the Emperor. 'What are you going to do about it?'

'The Black Coats are already hunting down those responsible,' she says.

The Emperor nods. 'Good.' But she can tell from the way he is fidgeting that he is worried.

'You're troubled?'

'It's nothing,' he says. Then, still fidgeting with his hands, he adds, 'I had the dream again.'

The Necromancer indicates that he should sit with her by the fire, which he does. 'It's only a dream, nephew.'

'It was a little different this time,' says the Emperor.

'How so?'

'Well . . . he came from the forest, like he always does when I dream about him. But this time there was someone else with him. A girl.'

'And?'

'She was in colour,' says the Emperor. 'Dazzling colour. And when the people saw her, they cheered and gathered around her and forgot all about me. And colour came back to the world, lit everything up, except me. They laughed and pointed and locked me away in my tower, just like before . . .'

'Listen to me, nephew. It. Was. A. Dream. He is not coming back here, not ever. Not after what he did. And if he ever does have the nerve to show up, I'll take care of him. As far as colour coming back . . .' She nods to the fire. 'Look at those flames. They burn stronger than ever. All the power and magic and beauty of all the colour in the world is trapped in this fire. It keeps us frozen in time, you and I, young and strong, and from it comes the power to summon armies of Ripper Dogs and Black Coats. The only way colour will ever come back is if those flames die out – and the only way the flames will die out is if my heart stops beating. I have no equal in this world, nephew, so you have nothing to worry about.'

The young Emperor stares into the flames. 'Our people hate us.'

'Yes,' says the Necromancer, 'but they also fear us, and that is more important. Fear is the string that moves the puppets, do you see?'

'The Rainbow League aren't scared enough of us to stop them letting off those fireworks tonight.'

'The Rainbow League will wither and die. Time is on our side, and against them. We will outlive and outlast them, and eventually people will forget all about colour. Now, it's late, nephew, and you need your rest. Go back to bed.'

The Emperor gets up, walks across the garden, and then stops. 'I'm in charge, you know,' he says, though he sounds unsure of himself. 'I'm the Emperor.'

The Necromancer smiles. 'Of course you are.' Then she turns back to the warmth of the coloured flames and closes her eyes.

Two weeks after the night of the fireworks, the woman from the Rainbow League has finally recovered enough to leave the Gwendle farmhouse. Her name is Beth and, as she has grown stronger, Darroch has taken the opportunity to speak with her while bringing her meals upstairs to the spare room. Their chats have been brief, but her stories of the Rainbow League, of risk and bravery and adventure, have lit his imagination on fire. Her life could not be further removed from his tranquil existence. One day that will change, though. One day he knows he will join the fight.

It seems that Gran was right about the farm being safe. The Black Coats have not come, and nobody has been to the house to question Gran. He will ask her more about that in time.

On the morning Beth is to leave the farm, Darroch is upstairs in his room. He has a rare day off from milking and sweeping and handiwork, and he is using this time, as he always does, to paint. He has been working on the mural on his bedroom wall for a couple of lunar cycles, and yet still only the bare bones of it are sketched out in rough, free brush strokes. He has drawn the view from the farm, towards the City and the sea, and the beginning of the great forest to the west. Parts of it he thinks are quite good, but others . . .

His hand snatches the paintbrush away from the wall, and he curses under his breath, scowling at the mark he has just made. It is supposed to be a boat, far out in the water, but it looks . . . well, it doesn't look like a boat, and that's for sure.

A gentle knocking on his bedroom door brings him out of his artistic trance.

'Come in.'

The door opens, and there is Beth, short-haired and large-eyed.

'Hello,' she says.

'Hi.' He feels a little awkward. No one apart from Gran has ever seen his room before.

'I'm sorry to disturb you,' she says.

Darroch puts his brush and palette down. 'That's OK. Is something the matter?'

'No. I just wanted to come and say thank you for everything you've done to help me.'

Darroch nods. 'Oh, I didn't do anything really. Just brought you food and stuff.'

'You talked to me, Darroch,' says Beth with a sincere smile. 'You asked questions about the world, about colour and the Rainbow League, and telling you about all of that made me more excited than ever to get back out there and kick the Emperor's backside.'

'Oh,' says Darroch, not quite understanding. 'That's good.'

Beth laughs. 'Yes. It is.' She shakes her head, leans against the doorframe. 'There aren't many children in the world, Darroch, with the bravery to ask the questions that you do. Jings, there aren't many grown-ups with that bravery.'

'What d'you mean?'

'I mean you don't just accept that the world must be this way. You wonder, Darroch. You ask "why?" and "what if?".

If there were more people like you in the Dominion, the Rainbow League would be much stronger.'

Darroch stares at her. 'You really think that?'

'I know it.' She glances out into the hall, then takes a step into his room. 'Your grandmother is a good woman. A strong woman. But I get the feeling she wants to keep a lid on your questions and your dreams.'

Darroch frowns again, this time feeling protective of Gran. 'She doesn't do it out of badness,' he says.

'Of course not,' says Beth, holding her hands up. 'I didn't mean that at all. She's trying to protect you. But you can't be protected forever. And that spark in you can't be contained for very much longer, I think.' She stops, listens, and the sounds of Gran making bread drift up from the kitchen. Then she reaches into her coat and brings something out. A short, thin candle, made of grey-black wax. She offers it to Darroch, and he takes it.

'What's this for?'

'For the time when you decide you want to join the fight.'

Darroch stares down at it. 'I don't understand.'

'If I'm right about you,' says Beth, 'the day will come when you can't hold back your dreams any longer. It happened to me too. One day I woke up and I looked around and realised that something had been stolen from me. From all of us. And I could not look myself in the mirror knowing that I wasn't doing anything to put things right.' She points to the candle. 'When you feel like that, and you will, light the candle and talk to me. I can start you on the journey.'

Before Darroch can say anything else, she has turned and left the room.

He stands rooted to the spot for a while, his mural forgotten, staring at the candle. The sight of it makes his heartbeat quicken, makes him imagine adventures far beyond the farm.

But what would Gran say?

The question brings him round, and he goes to his desk and stows the candle inside the leather pouch with his paintbrushes.

Later, Beth leaves the house with a final gesture, placing the tips of her fingers together and making an arch with her hands. A rainbow.

Darroch and Gran watch her walk over the meadow before she disappears between the tall stalks of grey corn and is gone.

In the coming days, the harvest will begin. There will be much work to do. And although the endless cycle continues, Darroch feels that the path of his life has just changed forever.

PART THREE

DEATH AND HER FRIEND
(Eight Years After the Wish)

Chapter Twelve

In Which a Message Comes

The raven arrives on a cold, still morning under a grey curtain of drizzle.

'Ha! Got another one!'

Hope jumps to her feet and grabs her fishing rod from its stand. When she pulls the rod, its tip bends sharply towards the water as the fish on the end of the line tries to flee downriver.

'You have not!' says Sandy. He sits on an upturned bucket, his chin resting on his hand, looking quite miserable.

'I believe she has, actually,' says Oliver. The scruffy black dog trots over to Hope's fishing spot and lifts the landing net, taking the long handle in his mouth and manoeuvring the net into the grey, swirling water.

Hope wrestles with the fishing rod, winding, being careful not to lose the fish or break the line, until a silvery bar catches the light just beneath the grey surface and, at last, the fish is in the net.

'Oh, good show, Hope!' says Oliver, his tail wagging as the fish flops around in the net. 'It's a beauty! Maybe the biggest catch of the day. How many fish have you caught now?'

'That's number five,' says Hope, putting the rod down and admiring her catch. Her arm is aching after landing the fish, but she doesn't care.

'And pray tell, Sandy,' says Oliver, 'how many fish have *you* managed to catch?'

Sandy gives his dog a look like thunder from beneath the wide brim of his ever-present hat. He mumbles something in a very low voice.

'I'm sorry, Sandy,' says Hope, loving every moment of his misery. 'Didn't quite hear that. How many did you say?'

'Both of yeh know perfectly well I've caught nothing!' says Sandy, kicking the handle of his rod. 'Nae fish. No even a wee nibble. I swear you two have been messing about with my bait.'

'You're just in a huff because the loser has to gut the fish and cook dinner,' says Hope. 'Fried fresh fish and boiled potatoes with butter sounds just the job to me, eh, Oliver?'

'Aye, aye,' Sandy says with a wave. And although he is clearly annoyed, there is also a hint of a smile playing on his lips. He loves a bit of competition and banter, and now that Hope is a little older, she is proving quite capable of providing both. She's already better at fishing, and though Sandy will never admit it, she's a better shot with a catapult too – last time they went hunting for wild rabbits, it was

Hope who caught dinner. He is still much better with a bow though.

'Right,' says Sandy with a wave. 'That'll do for the day, I think. I've no wish tae be humiliated any further by an eight-year-old.'

Hope laughs, and in that moment, looking out over the river towards the foot of the Dragon Tooth mountains, she feels happy. Two years have passed since the day her colour first appeared. She is now eight years old, tall and lanky, and her dark hair is long and unruly. She has taken her medicine every day, and though she sometimes daydreams about colour, imagines it in the wings of a bird or the sunset sky, she has been too busy learning the skills of tracking and hunting and survival to devote much of her brain to it. It has never gone away, though. Some nights she dreams in colour, and when she awakens to a black-and-white world there is a cold, empty ache in her heart. This always passes, though.

They walk along the river a short distance, Sandy carrying the box of freshly caught fish, until they come to the spot on the riverbank where Sandy's caravan and horse are stationed. On top of the caravan sits a huge black raven, and when Sandy sees it, Hope can tell that he is troubled.

'What's wrong?'

'I don't know yet,' Sandy says. 'See that raven? There's a message tied around its leg.'

'A message? You've never had a message before.'

'I've had plenty,' Sandy corrects her. 'But you've always been asleep when they've arrived. Ravens are the way mages send messages to each other. Regular folk use doves, but I suppose mages like to be dramatic.'

'How do you know it's bad news?' Hope asks. 'Could be something nice.'

Sandy sighs. 'I know it's bad because it's here during daylight. Mages always send messages after dark, unless it's an emergency.'

Hope suddenly finds herself itching with curiosity, her eyes stuck on the small roll of paper tied around the raven's leg. 'Are you going to open it?'

'Course I am,' says Sandy. 'C'mere, my beauty.' He holds out a hand, and the raven swoops down and lands on his forearm, allowing him to gently untie the note from its leg.

As he reads the message, his eyebrows knit as his eyes move across the paper, and when he is finished, he scrunches the note up and exhales.

'Well?' Hope asks.

Sandy continues to stare at the little ball of rolled up paper in his hand. At last, he blinks and says in a faraway voice, 'Pack up yehr things, lassie. We're leaving.'

'I still don't really understand,' says Hope. She is sitting on her bed in the caravan beneath the impossible bookcase ceiling. Oliver lies spread out across her knees as she scratches behind his pointy ears. Sandy sits outside on the driver's seat, guiding his horse along a dusty road between vast tracts of farmland, way out beyond the western edge of the great forest.

'It's not exactly an easy thing to get your head around,' says Oliver.

Hope keeps scratching the little dog's ears absent-mindedly. 'So, an old friend of Sandy's, a mage called Rab McCabe, has died. I understand that bit. And now Sandy has been summoned by his widow, Effie, to . . . to do what?'

'Well,' says Oliver, 'I've only ever read about it, but it seems that when a mage passes away, he or she is permitted by Death to appoint a companion to walk with them to the other side.'

'The other side of what?'

'I'm not sure. The books talk about a great desert made of ground-up bones,' says Oliver, and Hope wrinkles her nose at this.

'And if Sandy goes, how will he get back?'

'I haven't the faintest clue,' says Oliver. 'Only mages know that.'

Hope looks out to the driver's seat, where Sandy sits hunched over the reins. 'Do you think he's all right? It's been two days since that message arrived and he's barely said a word.'

'You know what he's like,' says Oliver. 'He's not very good at talking about things at the best of times, never mind when he's had a shock like this.'

Later, they stop beside a field of tall, swaying grey corn so that Sandy can stretch his legs. They eat the last of the fish Hope caught, with bread and butter, though Sandy leaves most of his for Oliver.

'Not much longer to go now,' he says, breaking the silence. 'We'll be there by evening.'

Hope finishes her fish and puts the plate down so that Oliver can lick the juices. She looks at Sandy from the corner of her eye, as he is staring far off into the gathering dark clouds. 'Sandy?'

'Aye?'

'What happens to us when we die?'

His grey eyes leave the clouds. 'Well, I've never done it myself, of course, but they say Death takes yeh by the hand and leads yeh to the edge of a great river. And there the Ferryman is waiting to take yeh across the water.'

'To where?' Hope asks.

One side of Sandy's mouth twitches into a sad smile. 'Nobody knows that, lassie. And we never will – not until it's our turn to make the journey.'

'Do you think it hurts?' Hope asks. 'Dying, I mean.' She is thinking of her parents, what they might have felt when the Ripper Dogs came for them.

Sandy must be able to tell what's going through her mind, because a look of kindness fills his colourless eyes. 'Some people get sick and die, Hope. Some people die in battle, or in other sudden ways. The pain they feel is in life. But dying? The actual moment we leave this world and move on tae the next? Naw, lassie, I don't think there's any pain in that. I think there's peace.'

'Your pal,' says Hope, 'Rab. Was he sick?'

'I don't know. Effie didn't say in the note.'

'Rab was very old, lassie. Jings, he was old when he and Effie took me in when I was a young man!'

A pause.

'Sandy?'

'Aye?'

'How come we've never been to see your pals before now?'

He flinches. 'Well, that I do regret, and nae mistake. Yeh know how it can be, Hope. The life of a drifter mage takes us all over the Dominion, and our work is never done. I wish I had made the time to come and see Rab when he was alive, but at least I'll get tae say goodbye now.'

He looks away, blinking. As he rubs his eyes, a crack of thunder rings across the landscape, and rain begins to fall.

The cottage sits on the shore of a small loch. When Sandy's caravan pulls up outside, the rain is falling in heavy drops and the black loch water is churning in the swirling wind, which whips against Hope's face.

The stone cottage is pretty, its garden blooming with spring flowers, every shade of grey and black and white. This is one of those times when colour springs into Hope's mind, making her imagine what wonderful shades of blue and yellow and purple might light up this place if the world was suddenly freed from the Emperor's grip.

As they approach the cottage, the door swings open, and there stands a tall, thin, ancient-looking woman. Her face is as lined and cracked as a dried-up riverbed, and her white hair is pulled tightly back in a bun. Hope supposes this must be Effie, and thinks she looks fierce. But when she speaks, all concern melts away.

'Jings, it's good tae see yeh, laddie!' she says in a warm, buttery voice. A smile breaks across her face and Sandy bounds towards her, hugging her tightly.

'Aye, you too, Effie. You too.'

'Crivens, yeh'll pop my ribs, Sandy! Let go and come on in out the rain.'

The cottage is cosy, and the smell of beef stew spills from a bubbling pot on the range, making Hope lick her lips.

'How are yeh, Effie?' Sandy asks. 'We got here as soon as we could. I'm so sorry we couldn't have been here to help when . . .' his lip trembles. 'When it happened.'

Effie smiles warmly. 'Yeh're here now, and that's all that matters.' Her eyes flick towards Hope. 'But surely this can't be wee Hope? My, what a beauty yeh've become! Yeh were just a wee babby last time I saw yeh.'

'I'm eight now,' says Hope proudly. Then she stops and puzzles over something. 'Wait. You've met me before?'

'Aye. Sandy brought yeh here just after he found yeh. A terrible business, what happened tae yehr mum and dad.'

Sandy adds, 'It was Effie who first helped me figure out how to make your medicine, Hope.' Then he looks down. 'Well, Effie and Rab.'

Rab's name hangs in the room like an echo, and suddenly there is a heaviness in the air, like it is filling up with Sandy and Effie's memories.

110

'Aye,' says Effie, dabbing at her eyes. 'Rab was always good at figuring out just the ingredient tae make a spell complete. It was a gift.' She makes a pot of tea and they sit at the dining table, Oliver nestling at Hope's feet, chewing on a ham bone from Effie's soup stock.

'Will yeh stay? I could make up yehr old room,' says Effie.

Sandy shakes his head. 'It's kind of yeh, Effie, but you have enough to worry about without us getting under yehr feet. We're comfy in the caravan.'

'If yeh're sure,' says Effie.

'How did Rab . . .' Sandy begins. 'What happened in the end? Was he unwell?'

Effie sips her grey tea. 'No, laddie. Not unwell. Just very old, and very tired. He fell asleep a week ago and never woke up.' She runs a finger around the rim of her cup. 'Thank yeh for coming.'

Sandy shakes his head. 'There's nothing to thank me for. But, Effie, I don't understand why he chose me tae walk with him. It should be you. You're his wife. You were his best friend and his companion.'

Effie reaches across the table and takes Sandy's deep grey hands.

'As yeh know, Rab and me never had children of our own, but Rab always thought of yeh as his son, just as I do.'

Hope sees that tears are spilling from Sandy's eyes, and she looks away.

'Having yeh walk with him was a decision we made together,' Effie goes on. 'Because, son, if I was tae take this last journey with Rab, I would not be able tae leave him again. It would break me. So yeh're doing it for both of us, yeh understand?'

Sandy wipes his eyes. 'It'll be my honour to walk with him.'

'Thank yeh, laddie.' Effie clasps his hands in her own.

'Tomorrow night?' Sandy asks.

'Aye, that would be grand. He's buried in the village graveyard across the loch if yeh want tae go and see?'

Sandy nods. 'I'd like that.'

The rain falls, heavier and heavier, but despite the weather, Sandy insists on walking to the village graveyard after dinner, as the sky darkens in the west.

'You sure?' Hope asks, staring down from her private little mezzanine in the caravan. 'You'll drown in all that rain.'

Sandy slips on his wax coat and hat. 'Need to clear my heid.' He looks over at the floor by the wood burner, where Oliver is sprawled in the warm glow of the white-grey flames. 'What do yeh say, doggie? Yeh want to go walkies?'

Oliver yawns and opens one eye. 'As you know perfectly well,' he says in his dry tone, 'I have never in my life gone "walkies". I prefer a bracing stroll, or, in the case of a night such as this, an evening by the fire with a good book.'

Sandy stares at him for a long moment. 'Sometimes,' he says with a shake of the head, 'I wish I had a normal dug.'

Oliver shuts his open eye again and rolls over towards

the fire. 'Yes,' he says. 'I'm sure you do. If you did have a normal dog, you might actually win a game of chess now and again.'

Sandy ignores him and turns his attention back towards Hope. 'I'll no be gone too long, lassie. Effie is going to check in on yeh soon. She could do with a bit of company.'

He opens the door to the howl of wind and roar of rain, and then he is gone, and the caravan is quiet.

Barely ten minutes pass before there is a knock at the door. Hope invites Effie inside, and they sit in the caravan's two small armchairs, the old mage smiling as she looks around, her gaze sliding over the grey spines of the many books hanging in the impossible bookcase above her head.

'Well, that's new.'

'What is?'

'The bookcase. Very clever of him. But he was always a talented mage. He built most of this caravan himself, yeh know – with a wee bit of help from Rab and me.' She taps her pale grey fingers on the sides of the chair. 'So, my wee lamb, how's our Sandy treating yeh?'

Hope smiles. 'He's brilliant.'

'Aye. He's a good laddie,' says Effie proudly, and it tickles Hope that anyone could think of Sandy as a laddie.

'Mrs McCabe?'

'Call me Effie, lassie.'

'All right. Effie?'

'Aye?'

'Have you known Sandy since he was a wee boy?'

Effie shakes her head. 'He was a young man when Rab and I met him. Twenty or so.'

'Oh. So where was he before that? I've always wondered about his past.'

A pause. Heavy rain drums on the caravan roof. 'Have yeh never asked him?'

'I have. Lots. Sometimes he talks in his sleep. And when he does, he sometimes sounds different. Posh almost. Like he's turned into someone else. I've asked him, but all he'll ever tell me is he was born in the City and his parents died. Any time I try to get any more out of him, he treats it like a joke, or else shuts up tight as an oyster.'

'I'm sorry, Hope,' says Effie. 'It's not my story tae tell. It's up tae Sandy tae decide when tae share.'

Hope is disappointed, but the fact Effie isn't willing to spill Sandy's secrets makes Hope like her even more. 'I wonder why he hasn't ever brought me to visit you,' she says, frowning. 'Apart from when I was a baby, I mean.'

Effie drums her fingers on the chair again. 'Ah. That I can answer. I think it might be down tae me and Rab.'

'What d'you mean?' says Hope. 'You didn't want to see us?'

Effie's eyes widen. 'No, lassie, that's not it. We wanted tae see yeh very much. Both of yeh.'

'Then what?' said Hope.

'When Sandy first rescued yeh,' Effie says, 'he brought yeh here. He didn't have a clue how tae look after a wee babby, so yeh both stayed in the cottage for a while and we all figured it out together. Yeh were a funny wee thing, always laughing and smiling! And yehr colour lit up the house and brought us joy.' She pauses, shakes her head. 'And that's where we made our mistake, my dear Rab and me. Yeh see, we wanted tae spread the word that a child had been born in colour. We thought that it would give people in this grey world a wee bit of hope tae cling onto, yeh see? We would never have told them any details, never have said anything that might give yeh away, but we hoped the story of the girl born in colour might show folk that the Emperor and his Necromancer could be beat.

'Sandy did not agree. We had a furious argument with him one night, and in the end, he decided tae leave, and tae take yeh with him. Of course, we tried tae convince him tae change his mind, but yeh know what Sandy is like. Stubborn as a mule. Before yeh both left, we helped him invent a potion that would hide yehr colour and protect yeh.' She leans over and takes Hope's hand. 'The day Sandy left, I kept expecting him tae change his mind, tae stop his horse and bring his caravan back. But he didn't. He kept going, until yeh were out of sight. And we never saw yeh again until today.'

'And you never told anyone about me?' Hope asks.

'Never,' says Effie. 'We couldn't go against Sandy's wishes like that. But we did feel the time had come tae take action. So we founded the Rainbow League.'

'What's that?'

The old mage looks taken aback. 'Yeh've never heard of

it? Jings, he did well tae hide it from yeh. I suppose yeh could call the Rainbow League a resistance movement. It started small, but now we have members all over the Dominion, folk determined tae let the Emperor know that we haven't forgotten about colour, that we'll never forget about it, and that, one day, we'll find a way tae bring it back.'

'So Sandy knows about the Rainbow League?' Hope asks, impressed.

'I should hope so,' chuckles Effie. 'He's a member!'

Hope blinks. 'He is?'

'Aye. But I'll let him tell yeh about all of that some other time. No arguments, lassie! Like I said before, Sandy's stories are his tae tell and his alone.' She suddenly becomes quiet, and her old eyes linger on Hope's hands.

Hope looks down and gasps. Her fingertips are beginning to glow with rich brown tones, and the colour spreads, warm and tingling, up her fingers and into her hands. 'I'm sorry,' she says, grabbing for her potion, but Effie holds up a finger.

'No. Don't do that, lassie. Just once, instead of being frightened of who yeh are and hiding it away, I want yeh tae let it out, tae show the world what yeh are made of. It will be good for yeh.'

Hope shakes her head. 'I don't know if I can.'

'Of course yeh can. Close yehr eyes. Feel it. Accept it. Welcome it. Make a sad old woman happy, lassie. I haven't seen colour for such a long time, except in little bottles.'

How can Hope deny such a request? Not sure at all

what she is doing, she closes her eyes, feels the warmth of the colour in her hands, and for the first time in her life she thinks, *It's OK. It's who I'm supposed to be.*

The warmth floods through her, her arms and body, her head and feet and toes, and when she hears a sharp intake of breath, she opens her eyes and sees . . .

Colour.

Colour everywhere, painting almost the entire inside of the caravan! It spreads across the dark brown wooden floor, and up into the bookcases, into the spines of the books, gold and red and blue and green. Oliver is fast asleep by the warm orange-red flames of the wood burner, and she sees for the first time that his coat is not simply black but streaked with dark brown. And there, in the armchair opposite, is Effie, staring at her hands, which are now pinkish white, with eyes that are icy blue and filled with tears.

'Thank yeh,' she whispers. 'Oh, thank yeh, Hope.' She continues to stare about for a long moment, her face filled with childish wonder, until she blinks and wipes her eyes, and says through a sniff, 'Right. I think that's enough now. Better take yehr potion.'

Hope takes a last look around at the bright colours of the caravan, and then takes the bottle and lets a few drops fall onto her tongue. The colour recedes, the warmth of it growing colder, until it is completely gone.

Quite soon after, Sandy comes home to find Hope and Effie laughing as Effie tells old stories of her dear, late husband.

'Yeh're half drowned, laddie!'

'Don't make a fuss,' Sandy tells Effie, taking off his hat and coat. 'What have you two been up to then?'

Hope glances across at Effie and winks. 'Oh, nothing much.'

Later, when Hope is fast asleep in the caravan with Oliver curled up at her feet, Sandy and Effie sit at the dining table in Effie's cottage. Effie puts two glasses on the table and pours them each a dram from Rab's favourite bottle of whisky.

'To Rab,' Sandy says, raising his glass.

'Aye,' says Effie softly. 'Tae Rab.'

They sip the fiery liquid, sucking air through their teeth as it burns their throats.

'I should have come back before now,' Sandy says.

Effie shakes her head. 'Yeh did what yeh thought was right tae protect the wee one. It was our fault for driving yeh away, son, and for that I will always be sorry. We were thankful when yeh joined the Rainbow League, though — and we enjoyed any letters yeh sent us.'

'Letters,' scoffs Sandy. 'Letters are nae substitute for watching such a dear wee lassie growing.'

Effie smiles. 'And I'll say it again, it was our fault. When we saw her colour, we believed we had been sent a miracle.' She pauses. 'I still believe that, laddie.'

'She's getting stronger,' says Sandy.

'Aye, I know. I saw that for myself tonight while yeh were away.'

Sandy takes another sip from his glass. 'I'm worried. I don't know how strong her colour might get. What if it gets tae the point I can't protect her any more?'

Effie considers this. 'I think there's still a while tae go before we get tae that. But when it happens, they'll come for her.'

'I know I cannae hide her away forever. I know the time will come, one day, when she'll have tae face the Emperor and his dear old auntie. But I want tae let her live carefree as long as I can until then, yeh understand?'

Effie reaches across the table and places her old hand on top of Sandy's. 'Aye. I understand. But when the time comes that yeh cannot control her magic any more, bring her tae me. I will help yeh both prepare.'

Sandy raises his eyebrows. 'Yeh will?'

'Of course. She's family after all.' Effie pours one more drink into the empty glasses, takes a sip, drums her fingers on the tabletop. 'Have yeh still never been back tae the City?'

Sandy shakes his head. 'Yeh know I can't go back there. Not after what happened.'

'Whatever debt yeh think yeh owe the world,' says Effie, tapping her finger on the table to emphasise every word, 'yeh have repaid it a hundred times over by now.'

Sandy stares across the table into Effie's grey eyes. 'I will never be able to repay the debt I owe,' he says in a choked voice. 'No if I live tae be a hundred.'

'No even if yeh help Hope bring colour back? No even then?'

Silence, except for the snap and pop from the fire.

'I think I've found something interesting,' Effie says.

'Aye?'

'Aye.' She seems to gather her thoughts, getting them in the right order. 'There's a farm on the outskirts of the City.'

'A farm?' Sandy raises his eyebrows.

'Aye. Gwendle Farm. The woman who runs the place, Mrs Gwendle, is an old acquaintance. She's helped us a couple of times. Yeh remember the fireworks we let off a couple of years ago.'

Sandy is a little confused. 'Lots of folk have helped us. What's so special about Mrs Gwendle?'

'It's not her,' says Effie, shaking her head like she's being bothered by a fly. 'It's the connection her family has with the land itself. The Gwendles have mage blood in the family tree. They have farmed that land for generations, and somewhere along the line, I think the land and the people have become one. It's almost as if the land is alive. Maybe it is. That farm . . . there's nowhere else like it. Even the Necromancer won't go near, and yeh know how strong she's getting. When the time finally comes tae make a move, that farm might be key.'

'Sounds promising,' says Sandy. 'Ye'll keep me posted?'

'Aye, of course.'

Sandy drains the last of his drink and stands. 'I'd better get tae bed.'

'Aye. Are yeh ready for tomorrow night?'

He mulls this over. 'As ready as I can be.'

Chapter Thirteen
In Which We Meet Death and Her Friend

The night is calm and clear when Hope, Sandy and Effie arrive in the graveyard of the village across the loch from the cottage. The village is fast asleep, and the only sounds are the hoots and scratchings of the night-time things as they go about their business.

The graveyard is small and built upon the steep slope of a hill behind the village. It looks like an overgrown garden, the worn headstones jutting from the long grass like rotten teeth, many of them hidden among branches or covered in creeping climbing plants.

At the far side they come to a drystone wall, and there, last in the row, is Rab's grave.

Sandy removes his hat and clutches it to his chest, while Effie places her hand on the plain little gravestone. 'We're here, my love, for yehr final journey.' She carries a hemp bag over her shoulder, and from it she brings a single, tall black candle and places it carefully in front of Rab's gravestone. Then she looks at Sandy. 'Are yeh ready?'

Sandy pops his hat back on and says, 'Aye.'

'Before yeh begin,' Effie says, 'I was wondering something. Might yeh take Hope along with yeh, Sandy?'

Sandy seems taken aback, and Hope feels like someone has just spun her around and around at great speed. '*Hope?* Yeh never mentioned this before.'

'Aye, I know,' says Effie. 'But I've been thinking about it, and I believe Rab would be fair pleased if he had both of yeh tae walk with him and saw Hope one last time. It would be a good thing for her education as a mage too.'

Sandy ponders this. 'I'm no sure . . .'

'Well, then,' says Effie. 'Let's ask the girl.'

Sandy turns his head towards Hope, looking doubtful.

Hope's initial reaction had been fear, but that has quickly subsided, leaving her head a-spin with questions and curiosity.

'Is it safe?'

'I've never known a mage tae go and not return,' says Effie. 'It's the rules. The living must come back.'

'But back from where?' Hope asks, imagining some dark void filled with screaming souls.

'From the Desert of Bones,' Effie answers.

Hope squints at her. 'Have you ever done it?'

'Me? No. But I've known mages who have. I wouldnae ask yeh tae do this if I thought there was any risk.'

'Yeh don't have to,' says Sandy.

'I know,' she says. 'But . . . I think I'd like to meet Rab before he goes.'

Sandy and Effie share a look, and both say, 'Yeh sure?'

'Yes.' There are flutters in Hope's belly. She does not know exactly what is about to happen, but she is sure that she wants to go with Sandy, as much to make certain he comes back as to meet Rab.

'I suppose, if that's what yeh both want, I can't say no,' says Sandy. He looks to Effie. 'And you are certain you don't want to go?'

'I can't,' Effie says. 'As I've told yeh, son, saying goodbye tae Rab again would break me. Naw, I'll see him soon enough, when it's my turn tae cross the river.'

With that, Effie takes a match and lights the black candle, the flame leaping to life in a blaze of colourless fire. Thick smoke belches out and thickens into a swirling grey fog, so dense that Hope loses sight of Effie and Sandy. She feels Sandy's calloused hand grabbing hers.

Then the smoke-fog thins out a little, revealing a woman in a long black coat. She steps towards them, and the light from the burning candle blazes, lighting her face, showing them her long black hair and her pointed chin, her high cheekbones and her skin, white as bone. She stands with her hands in her pockets, looking Sandy and Hope up and down.

'Are you . . . Death?' Sandy asks.

'I'm the personification of death,' she answers in a cheery voice. She cups a hand to her mouth and whispers to

Hope, 'If he saw what I really look like, his brain would melt and run out of his nose.'

'You're in colour,' says Hope, staring into Death's eyes, which are like polished amber.

'Of course I am,' says Death. 'My rules here.'

It is then that Hope glances at her hands and sees that her own skin is brown, her dress green. Sandy is in colour too, his leathery skin golden and his eyes apple green. 'Are we supposed to bow or something?' she asks, stunned.

'You can dance a sailor's merry jig if you like,' says Death. 'Just make it quick. I really want to get back to a card game with Time and Nature. I'm winning this time.'

'Right,' Sandy says, looking puzzled. 'What happens now?'

Death brings a book out of her pocket. 'Who are you walking with tonight?'

'Rab. Rab McCabe.'

Death opens the book and begins flicking through the pages. 'Rab McCabe,' she says to herself. 'Rab . . . McCabe. Let me see. Ah, yes. Here we are.' She snaps her fingers and, instantly, another man is standing with them. He is short and round, his skin a darker brown than Hope's and his head completely bald. For a long moment, he seems to be clueless as to what's going on. Then he looks at Death, and at Sandy, and his eyes widen. He lunges forward and grabs Sandy into a tight embrace, and they are both laughing and sobbing.

Death inches closer to Hope, and Hope gives her a polite smile.

'Why do they squeeze each other like that?' Death asks.

'It's just what people do,' says Hope. 'It's comforting.'

Before she knows what's happening, Death has pulled her in and is hugging her awkwardly. Hope feels a great chill in her bones, and her head spins and she sees stars flashing past as she hurtles through a great infinity.

Then Death releases her and she is back in the fog.

'Did you find that comforting?'

'Um. Yes.'

Death seems pleased by this.

Sandy and Rab have been speaking, but whatever they have said has remained private, and now Rab turns towards Hope and smiles a dazzling smile upon her.

'And here she is,' he says. 'Wee Hope. Jings, last time I saw yeh, yeh were in nappies!'

'Hello,' says Hope, then, for some reason, she adds, 'I'm sorry you died.'

This makes him laugh, hard, and he shakes his head and says, 'Oh how I wish I could have known yeh better in life, Hope. But it's my own fault that didn't happen. And I'm very happy yeh're here tae see me off.'

'Speaking of which,' says Death. 'Let's get going, shall we?' She snaps her fingers again, and in a blink, they are standing on the white sand of a vast desert. This place, wherever it is, is in colour too. The twilight sky is vast and cloudless and red, and a yellow half moon sits directly overhead.

They walk.

Death leads the way, her long black coat fluttering behind her.

'Is this desert really made of bones?' Hope asks. 'Or is it just a name?'

'If you want to get philosophical about it,' Death says, 'it's not really made of anything.'

Hope does not know what she means by this. She changes her line of questioning. 'How come mages get to walk each other across this desert and normal people don't?'

Death looks at Hope thoughtfully. 'A long time ago, a mage offered me help when I was in a sticky situation.'

'You needed help?' Hope asks in disbelief. '*You?*'

Death nods. 'My influence is great. But there are other forces in the many planes of existence, and some of them like to cause trouble. Anyway, when it was all over, I asked my new friend what she might like as a reward. I expected her to request great riches, or perhaps eternal life. Most mortals ask for those things. Instead, the mage simply asked that when she died, she might say a final goodbye to the person she loved most. I agreed, and in tribute to her, I offer the same gift to every mage who crosses my desert. And they all do, eventually.'

On they walk, and Hope finds it strange that she is neither hot nor cold, nor do her legs become tired despite the great distance they cover.

Sometimes, Rab asks her questions, lots of them, and no matter how many she answers he always has another one lined up, his ears ravenous to learn more about her.

And sometimes, during this long walk, Sandy and Rab drop into deep, serious discussion, or decide to regale Hope with long-ago memories that make everyone laugh.

Everyone except Death, of course, who smiles politely.

At one point in the journey, Rab says to Sandy, 'Yehr accent is pretty good now, laddie. Crivens, remember how terrible it used tae be? Ha!'

Hope's ears prick up, but Sandy quickly changes the subject.

At last, they come to the place where the desert meets the water. The river is black and calm. It is not possible to tell how wide the river is, because a short distance out, a dense silver mist shrouds everything.

Nearby there is a wooden jetty, where a rowing boat is moored. A large figure sits in the boat. His wide face is mostly hidden behind a wild brown beard. His hair is pulled back in a ponytail and he wears a wax coat like a fisherman. A pipe is clenched between his teeth, and the smoke from it drifts out and feeds the mist over the river.

'Time to go,' says Death, placing a hand on Rab's shoulder. He nods, turns to Sandy.

'Look after yehrself, laddie. And look after that wee miracle.' He motions towards Hope and gives her a smile.

'Are you coming aboard or not?' booms the man on the boat.

Death rolls her amber eyes. 'Don't mind the Ferryman. He's in a huff because he reckons someone keeps stealing souls from the other side of the river.'

'It's the truth,' says the Ferryman. 'You don't know a thing about what goes on over there. You've never been across the water.'

'Quite so,' says Death, examining her fingernails.

'Someone is stealing souls?' Sandy asks, frowning.

'Aye,' says the Ferryman. 'Plucking them away from the other side of the river like flowers in springtime.'

'But why? Why would someone do that? And how could they do it?'

'I don't know,' the Ferryman goes on, balling up his huge fists. 'But if I ever get my hands on the scoundrel who's responsible, they'll pay. Oh, they'll pay, all right.'

'And how will you get your hands on them?' Death says. 'You aren't allowed to leave your little boat, just as I'm not allowed to cross the river.'

'Everyone must cross the river eventually,' says the Ferryman. He waves for Rab to come forward, takes his hand to steady him as he climbs into the rowing boat and sits. Then the Ferryman takes up the oars with his great hands and puts his muscles to work, rowing the boat out over the river.

'Rab!' yells Sandy, tears running down his face.

Rab turns around and calls back, 'Aye, laddie?'

'Thank you for saving me. Thank you for everything.'

Hope squints at him, wondering what he means. *Saving him? From what?*

Rab smiles. 'It wasn't us that saved yeh,' he says. Then he does something strange. He looks to Hope and gives her a conspiratorial wink. After that, he waves and turns back round. With a peaceful breeze brushing their faces, Hope and Sandy watch as the rowing boat is swallowed by the mist.

Rab McCabe is gone.

Hope continues to stare at the place where the boat disappeared. 'What's on the other side of the river?'

Death raises a perfect eyebrow. 'Didn't you hear old grumpy knickers? I've never been.' Then she winks. 'In any case, I wouldn't ever spoil a surprise like that.'

She clicks her fingers.

Reality spins.

Hope and Sandy are back in the graveyard. The mist is gone and, it seems, Death is gone with it.

For now.

'Well?' Effie stands at Rab's grave, wringing her hands. 'Did yeh see him?'

'Aye,' says Sandy. 'It's done.'

Being eight years old, Hope is not used to staying awake until such an hour. Around the halfway point of their walk home, Sandy scoops her up, and she falls asleep in his arms.

Back in the caravan, he tucks Hope into bed, kisses her forehead and goes back to Effie's cottage, leaving Oliver curled up in the blankets at Hope's feet.

Effie has poured them both another dram from Rab's favourite bottle. She is eager to hear the details of Sandy's walk across the desert, and he tells her as much as he can recall, assuring her that Rab is happy and that he will be waiting there for her when it is finally her time to cross the great river.

After a while the conversation becomes easy, familiar silence, and it stays that way until Sandy says, 'I realised something while I was watching Hope earlier.'

Effie looks intrigued. 'Aye?'

'Aye. She met Death tonight. She walked the desert of bones, and do yeh know what? She never once looked frightened. She asked questions. She asked questions of Death, Effie! I doubt there's many folk alive who could do that. Certainly not me! Jings, and that Ferryman is something else!' His glass is almost touching his lips when he becomes suddenly very still. His mouth opens and his eyes sparkle with realisation. 'Of course,' he whispers. 'Of course!'

'Yeh feeling all right, laddie?'

'The Ferryman!' Sandy says. 'Before he took Rab across the river, he said something . . .'

'What? What did he say that's got yeh all jangling like this?'

Sandy stares across the table at her, his face lit softly by colourless lamplight. 'The Ferryman told us that somebody is stealing souls from the other side of the river.'

Effie's hand goes to her mouth. 'Stealing them? Stealing spirits from their resting place? But who'd do such a thing? And how?'

Sandy gives the old woman a grim stare. 'I don't know about the how,' he says. 'But I'm sure I know the who. It's the Necromancer. Yeh see, Effie? It must be her! All this time we've been thinking that her Black Coats are demons. But I don't think that's true. I think she's using necromancy to tear peaceful souls out of the afterlife and drag them back here to do her work.'

Effie looks horrified. 'But that's monstrous. It's against every law of nature and decency!' She pauses, and another thought strikes her mind like a bolt of lightning. 'If the Necromancer is taking souls from the afterlife, that means . . .'

'Rab,' says Sandy, finishing her thought. 'Rab is there now. What if she takes him?'

Effie trembles with disgust and anger and fear.

'This has tae end,' Sandy says, reaching over the table and taking her hand. 'We have tae act.'

'Act how?'

Sandy empties his glass. 'Hope is stronger than I ever believed. Or maybe than I allowed myself tae see. Her power will grow until I can't hide it any more, and there's not a thing I can do tae stop it. At some point she'll have tae face her destiny. And I have to stop running away from that. I think the time has come, Effie, to do what you and Rab wanted all those years ago.'

Effie sits forward. 'Yeh mean, tell folk about her?'

Sandy nods. 'Not about Hope specifically, of course. Just that there's a person out there who is stronger than the Necromancer's spell. Hope will need help when the time comes, and the Rainbow League will be stronger if we start spreading the word now.'

'And what about the Emperor? And the Necromancer? They'll search far and wide for this special person, just as yeh always feared.'

'It's time tae stop being afraid,' he says. 'I'll keep her safe until she's ready.'

Effie releases a long, low breath. 'Will yeh tell her?'

'Tell her that one day it'll be up tae her to free the world from the Necromancer's grip? No. I'll not tell her that. Not yet. She deserves a few more years of childhood innocence before that responsibility lands on her shoulders. But I will tell her what the Necromancer is doing. How she's wrenching poor spirits out of their afterlife. She deserves to know what we're up against.'

Effie pours them one last drink, raises her glass.

'To Hope,' she says.

'Aye,' says Sandy, clinking his glass against hers. 'To Hope.'

The following day, after Effie has said a tearful goodbye to Hope and Sandy and watched the caravan disappear around the loch, she sits at her table and proceeds to write a series of messages on small slips of paper. When she is done, she rolls the papers up, carries them outside and gives a sharp whistle.

In moments, a dozen ravens have landed in her garden.

'Hello, my beauties,' she says, and she takes each message and ties it gently to a raven's leg. 'Fly safe.'

They fly, each carrying a short message to a different

part of the Dominion, to trusted lieutenants in the secret Rainbow League.

In a matter of days, word begins to spread. The story lives in the whisper of the breeze. It moves between towns and villages, carried on the tongues of believers, passed on in hushed conversations, in taverns and workhouses.

Before long, the story is a living thing.

A child has been born in colour, they say. A child stronger than the Necromancer. A child who will one day free us all.

Hope. Hope sparks to life in their hearts.

Darroch Gwendle first hears the tale of the Rainbow Girl as it is whispered between workers on his grandmother's farm at harvest time.

'Just a story,' Gran tells him later. He wonders if she means this, or if she is trying to protect him, to keep him away from talk of colour and the danger it might bring.

But the possibility of a girl in colour burns bright in his mind and his heart. That night, as he works on the wall mural in his room, he wonders what she might look like. Perhaps he will paint her somewhere in the mural. But how could he? He does not have coloured paint. It never seems to be finished, this mural. All the time, Darroch is adding and changing, and it seems to him that the painting has become a living thing.

He stops again, shakes his head. A girl in colour. That would be a wonderful thing. And if she is real, if she's out there somewhere, it's a sign, isn't it? A signal that the Necromancer's spell can be broken.

Darroch wants to help break it. He feels that so strongly now.

His pulse quickens as he puts down his palette and brush and goes to his messy desk. There he finds the leather pouch that holds his brushes. And something else. Opening the pouch, he slowly brings out the candle that the woman from the Rainbow League gifted him two years before.

One day you'll want to help, she had told him.

And he does. He wants to help so much. He stares at the candle, his breath trembling. But what about Gran? What about the farm? What if he joins the league and brings danger here? But the farm is a safe place, isn't it? Even from the Necromancer.

So many thoughts swirl in his mind, fight each other, make his head spin. And yet, at the centre of it all is something anchored deep, something immovable. He wants to do what he feels is right.

And so, after what seems like a very long time, Darroch takes the candle and lights it.

The wick smokes for a second, before a bright grey flame leaps to life. The flame grows, and Darroch holds the heat and dazzling light away from himself. The flame grows wider, flickers, and in the centre of it, a familiar face appears.

'Hello, Darroch,' says Beth, the woman from the Rainbow League. 'I was wondering when you'd be in touch.'

PART FOUR

THE COLLECTOR

(Ten Years After the Wish)

CHAPTER FOURTEEN
IN WHICH THERE IS A SECRET DELIVERY

Darroch Gwendle stands on the upstairs landing of the farmhouse, still as death in the darkness. Holding his breath, Darroch listens intently. Loud, ripping snores emanate from his grandmother's room and echo all about.

It sounds like she is in a deep sleep. Darroch suddenly feels a rush of guilt at what he is about to do. Gran has spent her entire life keeping him safe. And he appreciates that. But he is growing up quickly, and determined to find his own place in the world, to leave his footprint.

Taking a deep breath of the cool farmhouse air, he moves swiftly and silently through the house and down the stairs.

The back door creaks a little as he slips through, making him wince and become still again. He waits. After a minute, there is no movement from upstairs, and he sighs with relief and moves on, stepping out into the fresh night. The stars wink and shine in their thousands. Two thirds of the huge silver moon is on display.

The smells of the farm wrap around Darroch as he moves. The sickly-sweet stench of the sheep muck; the dry, summery smell of the hay; the fresh, clean scent of the pine trees on the edge of the farm, where he stops and stares into the darkness between the trunks. Somewhere out that way, the farmland ends, and the great forest begins.

It is from there that his visitor will come tonight.

He paces as he waits, full of nervous energy, looking back down the hill towards the farmhouse, half expecting Gran to show up any minute and give him what-for.

'Hello, Darroch.'

The voice comes from above, and it surprises him so much that he ducks, as if someone has thrown something at him. When he has composed himself, he looks up. 'How long have you been there?'

Beth drops down from her branch, landing softly, brushing pine needles from her sleeve and collar and short, dark hair. 'Long enough to see your head's all in a fankle.'

'I'm not in a fankle,' says Darroch, folding his arms. 'I've just never done anything like this before.'

The woman raises an eyebrow. 'You haven't told your gran then?'

'I want to.' Darroch shrugs. 'But she'd only worry sick about me.'

The woman nods. 'Are you sure you want to do this, Darroch?'

'Course I do. I'm here, aren't I?'

'Yes. You are. But you can still change your mind. I

would never try to force you into anything. This must be your choice.'

'I want to do this,' Darroch says, almost pleading. 'It is my choice. I got in touch with you, remember?'

She studies him for a long moment, her large eyes almost seeming to look *inside* him. 'Right,' she says at last. 'We'll do this.' She is wearing a canvas bag over her shoulder, and she slips it off and offers it to him.

'When you first explained your idea to me,' she says with a smile, 'I wasn't sure it would be possible. I mean, I knew we could get the *paint* . . .'

Darroch's hands shake as he opens the bag, but it is too dark to properly see the contents.

'Here,' says the woman, bringing a wand out of her coat, lighting the end like a giant match so that the spell casts light in a soft white sphere around them. Darroch investigates the bag again, and this time he sees.

He almost drops it.

'Careful!'

'Sorry! I just . . .' Slowly, he reaches into the bag and lifts out a small glass jar filled with dark grey paint. Upon the lid, someone has painted the word *RED*.

'The Rainbow League has many friends,' the woman tells him. 'Some are powerful mages. Strong enough to create colour in flashes, to break the Necromancer's spell briefly. You remember the fireworks from the night we first met?'

'I'll never forget them,' says Darroch.

'Well, this is the same sort of thing. The fireworks broke the spell in quick bursts. This paint isn't as big or flashy, but it'll last a bit longer.'

Darroch examines the bag once more, seeing pots marked with other labels. *BLUE. YELLOW. INDIGO.* He frowns at them. 'But these paints, they're not actually in colour.'

She smiles. 'They will be when you're done.'

'They'll turn to colour?' he asks.

'Yes.'

'But won't the Ripper Dogs know? I've heard they're getting stronger as the Necromancer's power grows. I talk to the workers who pass through the farm. Some of them have told me about raids in magic markets. They say the Ripper Dogs can sense colour from miles away now. I've heard anyone caught with colour gets turned into a Black Coat by the Necromancer personally!'

'That may well be true,' says the woman. 'But this paint is special. It won't break the Necromancer's spell and turn colour until daylight. By then you'll be long gone. And there's something else. An extra bit of protection.'

She indicates the bag and Darroch looks again, this time fishing out another object, a long, thin stick of wood with a dried glob of sparkling grey substance at one end.

'A wand?'

'Indeed. Light it, and as long as you stand in its light, nothing will be able to see you.'

'I'll be invisible?' Darroch whispers.

140

'Until the wand burns out, yes.'

Darroch slips the wand back into the canvas bag. He tries to look confident, but his insides are in tangled knots. 'When should I do it?'

The woman shrugs. 'That's up to you, Darroch.' She shakes her own wand and the light goes out, leaving Darroch half blind in the night. 'Remember, Darroch,' her voice says softly, 'nobody will think less of you if you decide not to go ahead with this. You must do what's right for you.'

'I'll do it,' he says, hoping he sounds more confident than he feels. 'I will.'

But he realises that he is now talking to nobody. She has gone.

Chapter Fifteen
In Which Hope Learns a Spell

'Crivens, lassie! Are yeh trying tae blow my eyebrows off? I'd prefer to keep them, if it's all the same tae you!'

Hope is lying on her back, her head foggy and spinning. She stares up at the cloudy sky for a minute, until her head stills, and then props herself up on her elbows and looks across the craggy hilltop towards the campfire.

Sandy is standing over the lashing white-grey flames, staring into his pewter cauldron, which is belching rings of foul-smelling black smoke.

'How much chimney soot did you put in there?' he asks.

Hope gets to her feet and brushes her dress down. 'A pinch, just like you said.'

'A pinch!' Sandy says, looking to the sky. 'A pinch! Jings, lass, I said HALF a pinch!'

'Well how do you tell the difference?' Hope asks, edging back towards the cauldron, which continues to vomit the occasional splash of dark grey gloop onto the surrounding rocks.

Sandy picks up the jar of chimney soot, dips his thumb and index finger in, and brings out a pinch of the black powder. 'You take a pinch, sprinkle half into the cauldron and the rest to the wind.'

'Oh,' says Hope. 'I didn't think it would make much difference.'

Sandy closes his eyes and shakes his head. He tries to remove his hat, and then realises that it's no longer on his head. 'Where's ma hat?'

Hope points behind him, where Oliver is lying on his belly, taking great delight in chewing on the brim of Sandy's hat. When he realises that Sandy is staring at him, Oliver stops, gets up and brings the hat to him, clutching it in his mouth. 'Sorry about that, old boy,' he says. 'Couldn't help myself.'

Sandy snatches his hat back, shakes the drool from it and pops it back on his head, all the while glaring at Oliver. 'Magic spells and potions are not things to mess about with,' he says, turning his attention back to Hope.

'I know, I know,' she says. Then she folds her arms and thinks, *Maybe if you hadn't waited until now to start teaching me properly, I'd be better at this stuff. I've been asking to learn since I was a wee girl and now I'm ten years old and starting from scratch.* But she knows that talking back to Sandy will only send him further into a huff, so she says, 'I'll try to be more careful.'

He nods. 'Aye. I hope so. Spells have tae be treated with respect. You cannae be all loosey goosey with your ingredients or yeh might end up blasting yehrself halfway tae the moon. We're lucky this was just a wee laughter potion and nothing more unstable or we might have been sitting in a crater the size of a house.'

'Can I try again?' Hope asks. 'I'll do it right this time.'

Sandy sighs, and she sees him look at Oliver, who nods his shaggy head and says, 'Oh, go on. Give her another chance, Sandy.'

Sandy tilts his head and narrows his eyes. 'Right. Fine. Sort your ingredients and I'll empty the cauldron.'

Ten minutes later, Hope is crouching beside the empty cauldron again, a series of jars and bottles spread out beside her. She has checked and re-checked the recipe in Sandy's spell book and one by one she begins to place the ingredients into the mix.

One cup of moonlight
Half a cup of silly goose feathers
One short joke
One teaspoon of ink from a giggling squid
One teaspoon of honey
TWO DROPS EXACTLY of hyena drool (any greater quantity
than this may result in prolonged hysterical laughter)
Half a pinch of chimney soot

She holds her breath as she sprinkles in the chimney soot, but this time, thank goodness, there is no explosion. Instead, the potion shifts from black to light grey and the pleasant, thin smell of watermelon hangs in the air. The potion begins to bubble, and to Hope's astonishment, every bubble releases a single burst of laughter.

Ha!

HAA!

Heee!

HO!

'Did I do it?' she asks.

Sandy cranes over the cauldron, takes the long wooden spoon and stirs. 'I believe yeh did.' He glances at her. 'But there's only one way tae test it before we can take it to market.'

Before Hope can even blink, Sandy has raised the spoon to his mouth and taken a sip. Hope stands back, biting her lip. At first nothing happens. Then Sandy's shoulders begin to quiver a little, and then to move up and down in bigger jumps, and that is when the chuckles start escaping him. They grow bigger and bigger, until he throws back his head and sends a series of great bellowing laughs out over the rocky grey hilltop.

One thing everyone knows about laughter is that it is highly infectious. Soon Hope and Oliver are laughing too. Hope laughs and laughs until her stomach hurts and her eyes stream, and she sees Oliver rolling around on his back, his four bony legs kicking and his belly popping in and out.

At last, Sandy staggers to the caravan, where his horse stares at him with dignified bewilderment as he leans on a wheel arch and clutches his belly until the laughter finally subsides. Then he straightens up, turns around and says as he wipes his eyes, 'Aye, there's nothing raises your spirits like a good laugh!' He walks back to the cauldron and stirs the sweet-smelling potion again, then claps Hope gently on the back. 'That,' he says, 'is a fine laughter potion, lassie. Get it bottled up and put it doon in the store. We'll take it tae market tonight.'

Hope smiles up at him, happiness almost lifting her from the ground. She takes a box of little empty potion bottles and carefully fills each one. As she works, Oliver plops himself down beside her and begins grooming the fur on his front paws.

'The old man is very pleased,' he says. 'Proud, actually.'

Hope puts a stopper in the final bottle and places it in the box with the others. 'You really think so?' She glances over at Sandy, who is now sitting on a rock sipping on a hot cup of nettle tea and staring out over the forest below. He does this sometimes, just sits and stares, as if his eyes are peeling back layers of the world to uncover the buried memories of the past. He always looks so serious during these lonely periods of reflection. Serious, and sad.

'He likes to think he can hide what he's feeling,' says Oliver, 'but I can always tell. Humans are very emotional creatures, you know – and terrible at disguising it. Trust me, Hope, he is very happy with how you're turning out.'

146

The thought of grumpy old Sandy being proud of her makes a smile spread across Hope's face. 'I'll get these to the store,' she says, picking up the box. She carries them into the caravan, puts them on Sandy's desk and then crouches and grabs the hooped metal hatch handle on the wooden floor. With a heave, Hope pulls the hatch open, revealing rungs of a wooden ladder.

Hope grabs the box of laughter potions, sits on the floor and swings her legs down into the impossible hatch. Her feet find the rungs, and she grabs the box in one hand and the ladder with the other and climbs down into the dark.

The moment her head dips below the floor, two lamps flicker magically to life in the darkness, lighting up the store. Almost every inch of space is stocked with magic. There are potions by the hundreds, standing in bottles that gleam in the grey lamplight. Transformation potions, elixirs to mend broken bones, antidotes for poison. But not all magic comes in potion form. There are magic wands too, like oversized matches, thin sticks of wood, their tips dipped into powerful spells – the sort used to duel or to momentarily command fire or wind – that have dried out and will lie dormant until a mage sets them alight. And there are spell candles, poured into candle moulds directly from the cauldron. When lit, the smoke from these candles might help people communicate over great distances, or relive important memories, or let them predict a number of possible futures.

With great care she labels the new potions and sets the bottles on one of the few spaces on a shelf. Then she puts one foot on the ladder.

But she does not climb.

Not yet.

Slowly, she turns back towards the store, butterflies flitting around her belly. She casts a glance back up to the hatch, sees nothing but the spines of the many grey books staring down at her from their bookshelf on the caravan ceiling.

The coast is clear.

Hope worries her bottom lip, stares at her hands, wonders whether she should . . .

Four years have passed since the day in the forest when her colour first appeared. Since then, Sandy has had to alter her medicine time and again, make it stronger and stronger to keep the colour at bay.

But these past few lunar cycles, there have been . . . developments.

Hope has begun to learn a quite remarkable skill. A secret skill, of course. She could never tell Sandy. Or Oliver. They'd lose their marbles if they found out – and she supposes they'd be right to do so. What she's been doing . . . what she's about to do again . . . is dangerous, and selfish.

But it calls to her.

One more look to check the coast is clear, and she closes her eyes.

She concentrates on her heartbeat, on the blood pumping

around her veins. She remembers the feeling of colour in her fingertips, the warmth and life.

The joy.

And here it comes, that same warmth, buzzing in her fingers, her arms, her shoulders. It overcomes the defences of Sandy's potion, bursting through. It spreads to her head, her face. Even her hair feels alive. Then, when her entire self is thrumming with magic, she holds out her hands and opens her eyes.

And there it is.

Colour.

The warm brown of her skin, the blueish green of her coat sleeves, the red of her boots. The sight of these lights a fire in her soul, makes her heart light and full.

Beneath her feet, a circle of colour has painted the floor around her too, the yellow brown grain of the floorboards shining in the light. Hope takes a step forward, and another, each one colouring a different spot on the floor, and then reaches out her hand and brushes her fingers down rows of spells, the grey bottles and candles and wands coming to life with brushstrokes of dazzling colour as her fingertips touch them. Greens and blues, reds and pinks, purples and violets shimmer before Hope's eyes, and the sight of them makes her feel like she is flying.

'Hope? Have yeh fallen asleep doon there?' Sandy's voice calls from above. 'We're leaving. Get a move on!'

She gasps, and the power of the colour fades. She fumbles in her pocket and takes a swig of the colour-hiding potion Sandy has been giving her since she was a baby. At once the warming, cheering, glorious hug of colour releases its grip, leaving her skin dark grey, her coat off-white.

All is cold once more.

As she climbs the ladder back to the caravan, she is left with a familiar ache of loss in her heart. Colour is life, and life without colour is a half-life.

Maybe one day things will be different.

She hopes so.

Chapter Sixteen
In Which the Ripper Dogs Come

A few hours later, on the other side of Thunder Valley, the caravan comes to the tranquil village of Crab Apple, nestled in a wooded glen on the outskirts of the great forest. The village is little more than a handful of drab streets centred around a little town hall, but it is not the village of Crab Apple itself that has drawn Sandy and Hope here. No. It is the market that takes place once every lunar cycle in the rolling grey meadow behind the village.

As Sandy's horse pulls the caravan into the meadow, there are already a dozen or so other mages parked up. Some of the caravans and wagons are much bigger than Sandy's, and Hope recognises a handful of them from their journeys around the Dominion's far-scattered moon market circuit.

'Sandy Burns!' calls a freckle-faced woman from her campfire. 'Jings, how are yeh?'

'Grand, Flora, just grand,' Sandy answers with a tip of his hat.

'Hoy! Burns!' comes another call, this time from a very old man brushing his horse. 'I've got you beat this time, boy. Been workin' on ma dishwashing spell and I say it'll beat yours five ways from Sunday!'

'Aye, very good, Walter,' says Sandy, glancing at Hope, raising an eyebrow.

They stop in a spot beside a gurgling stream and Hope helps Sandy set up a fire while Oliver sniffs around, splashes in the water and chases a fat tortoiseshell cat, which brings a few choice swear words from the cat's owner.

As the sun falls lower in the sky, many more caravans arrive, until the colourless meadow is packed, alive with chatter and music and bright, flickering white firelight. The smells of last-minute spells drift through the darkening grey twilight, mixing with the aromas of fire-grilled meat and vegetables, and simmering pots of spiced stew and mulled cider.

All about the place, mages unpack their wares and set them out on stalls that magically unfold from suitcases or small wooden boxes, their black and white and grey canvas canopies fluttering in the gentle breeze.

The night marches on and the music intensifies, grows arms and legs and dances around the blossoming market as mages bring out their fiddles and drums and banjos and join the living chorus. The place crackles and thrums with energy. Hope feels the music burrow into her bones, making her feet tap and her head bob. As she sits at the small campfire and eats salted ribs, she wonders what all of this might look and feel like in colour. She imagines the brightly painted wagons, the leaping orange flames, the multitude of spells and potions all glistening with different hues. Now *that* would be a sight to behold.

'I think I'll dig out my old chanter,' says Sandy, cracking the thin shell of Hope's daydream and filling her world with black and white once more. She sucks the last of the rib juice from her fingers and tosses a bone to Oliver, who is sprawled out on his belly on the grass. He begins to gnaw on it greedily.

'I thought you'd lost that thing,' she tells Sandy, hopefully. Sandy's chanter playing has been assaulting her ears for as long as she can remember, but he hasn't seen fit to torture her for a while.

'Lost?' says Sandy with an incredulous wave. 'I would never misplace my old chanter. Naw, it's here somewhere . . .' He gets up and hurries into the caravan. Soon the clanging and thumping sounds of his search drift out of the door. 'Ah! Here it is! See?'

'Oh good,' Hope replies flatly.

Oliver looks up from the rib bone. 'I should have chewed that blasted thing up years ago.'

Hope suppresses a giggle as Sandy comes bounding back out from the caravan, the chanter grasped in his hand. It is a thin cylinder of hollow wood, with a mouthpiece and a row of finger holes down its length. Sandy cradles it in his hands for a moment, staring at it in doting fashion. Then he raises it to his mouth, presses his lips to the mouthpiece and begins to play.

Even before the first notes spill out, Hope is cringing. When the music (can you actually *call* it music, Hope wonders?) does begin to leak into the air, she feels herself shrinking into her seat, trying to disappear, while Oliver buries his face in his paws.

Hope has always been sure that the chanter, if played properly, must make a pleasant sound. Why else would someone make such an instrument in the first place? It's just that, however a chanter is supposed to be played, it seems nobody has ever told Sandy.

Painful.

That's the word that occurs to Hope as spluttering, goose-honk belches escape the dreaded instrument. Sandy's dextrous fingers dance between the holes, his cheeks puffed and red, his eyes wide as he forces gusts of air through the chanter, producing note after flat, unrelenting note.

In the immediate surroundings, mages who have never met Sandy stop what they are doing to stare. The unfortunates who *have* previously experienced this tuneless assault simply roll their eyes, try to ignore him and get on with playing their own music, or eating, or stocking the shelves of their stalls.

When he finishes his rambling tune at last, Sandy's hands drop to his sides. He stares, out of puff and misty-eyed, up at the night sky and says, 'Aye, that was grand. Music is good for the soul, eh?'

'I think my soul climbed out and ran away ten minutes ago,' Hope mutters, to which Oliver almost chokes on his bone.

A short while later, the chiming of many clocks heralds the arrival of midnight, and the last notes of music are carried away on the breeze.

It is time, under the pale light of that silvery disc in the sky, for the moon market to do its business.

'Dinnae go far. And stay with Oliver!'

Even as Sandy's words leave his mouth, Hope is away from their stall, into the elbowing bustle of the market crowd, Oliver close at her heels. How she loves their visits to market, where the wares on display can surprise and delight even the most worldly-wise of mages. Why, she's even seen Sandy himself bowled over by some incredible spell or other from time to time – like the old lady whose stall was stacked with candle dreams last year in a market on the other side of the forest.

'They're sweet dreams,' she had told Sandy as he examined the many different-sized wax sticks. 'Aye. Not a single nightmare to be found among them, son. Just light the wick and drift into a deep slumber, and the candle will do the rest.' She had leaned closer, lowered her voice. 'You'll dream of your deepest desire every night, the thing that will make you happy and content.'

Sandy had been so enchanted by this idea that he had traded half his potion stock for just a handful of dream candles – this is how mages do business after all, trading spells instead of coins. Those spell candles had seemed to make Sandy happy for a few days. But then he'd begun to spend more time asleep than awake. Only when there was nothing left in the larder for Hope to eat had he finally come to his senses and thrown what was left of his dream candles away – and even then, there had been a moment when Hope had thought that Sandy wasn't going to be able to do it. She has often wondered what dreams the candles brought him. He has never told her, of course. It's not in Sandy's nature to share feelings. He can do so many things. He can hunt, and fight, and make all sort of spells. He can cure illness and deliver babies. But talking about the past seems beyond him. She has wondered, often, if the dreams those candles brought him had something to do with the way he sometimes talks in his sleep, with the strange voice that comes out of his mouth during those dreams.

Back in the here and now, Hope flits from stall to stall, catching snippets of bargaining chatter, smelling a hundred aromas, from sandalwood to trout gills, and eyeing jars of pickled dead things. Non-magic folk have come from the village too, to seek treatments for ailments, or magics to help bring a spark of imagination to their grey lives. One stall trades spell candles as tall as a man, while another displays racks of clothes that the owner claims to have magical properties.

'Those there are clever clogs,' the stall owner tells Hope as she runs a finger along a shining wooden shoe. In this colourless world, the clogs are light grey, but Hope fancies that they might be dazzling yellow, or the pink of a blossom petal – and she knows blossom petals are the prettiest pink

156

because she recently stowed some in her pockets in the forest and brought colour to them in a secret moment later.

'They'll make me clever?' she asks, picking one clog up. It's heavy.

'Smart as a schoolhouse owl,' says the owner. 'You fancy slipping them on, pet?'

'Thank you,' says Oliver, 'but we're not interested.'

The woman's eyes grow saucer wide. 'A dog that can talk!' she says, putting her hands on her wide hips. 'Well knock me over with a fox's tail! I've seen a talking cat before of course – those things are ten a penny in some parts. And I've met a talking owl or two. But I've never seen a talking dog, not before tonight. Never thought a dog had the brains to talk – even with magic to help it along.'

Hope stifles a laugh.

'I beg your pardon?' says Oliver, his voice dripping with indignation.

'Oh, I didn't mean to offend,' says the mage. 'But dogs are well known to be dense as potato stew.'

'Potato stew?' gasps Oliver, his hackles rising. 'Can potato stew compose poetry, madam? Is potato stew capable of navigating the world using the stars? And, pray tell me, have you ever seen potato stew—' He stops dead in his tracks, because the same fat cat he chased earlier comes sauntering out from underneath a nearby caravan, casually sits down and aims a hiss at him. Oliver's entire body quivers. His back arches. 'Um. Excuse me for one moment,' he tells the stall owner. Then, with a bark, he tears off after the cat,

157

which screeches and darts into the busy crowd. Hope hears the startled calls of many mages across the market as the chase unfolds between their feet.

She turns back to the stall, shrugs and says, 'He fell into a cauldron when he was a pup and came out like that.' Then she pops the clever clog back in its place, wheels around and begins dodging through the bustle, knowing that she'd better find Oliver before he gets himself into real trouble.

'Oliver!' she calls. 'Oliver?'

She hears a distant bark over the haggling rabble, makes a sharp left, passing wagons and caravans and stalls trading all manner of spells and ingredients. In one, a man is weighing out scoops of shining, dried black beetles. In another, a skinny woman is showcasing the effects of a strength spell by juggling huge iron weights.

'S'cuse me,' Hope says, ducking between two mages arguing over the best way to make a raincloud spell.

When she hears the first scream, she thinks that Oliver must have startled someone, or maybe got tangled in a mage's feet and tripped them up. But then there is another scream, and another. There are scattered cries of shock and fear, and Hope feels a heavy ball of dread forming in her stomach as her gut tells her something is awfully wrong.

She is not tall enough to see over the crowds, but something is drawing the attention of every mage in the market. They turn as one, and cover their mouths, and mutter to one another. The atmosphere of the market, so full of bright life only moments ago, has become eerie and still.

Hope pushes through the crowds, eager to catch a glimpse of what has caused such a fuss, and when she finally squeezes to a place where she can properly see, she freezes mid-step. An involuntary whimper escapes her lungs.

The market throng has parted to make way for a pack of horse-sized dogs. Their coats are matted masses of thick, knotted black fur. The flesh of their mouths is peeled back to show rotten fangs the size of daggers. Their huge heads swing around, their white glowing eyes flicking all about the crowd. As they move, their heavy paws leave deep prints in the trampled grey meadow.

These are the Ripper Dogs.

Chapter Seventeen
In Which an Example is Made

Upon the backs of the Ripper Dogs are their dark riders, the Black Coats, swaddled in ragged black material, their faces hidden deep in the shadows of the folds of their hoods. The smell that comes from this nightmarish pack is ancient and dry and, at the edges, decaying. Hope knows why this is, of course. Sandy has explained to her that the Black Coats are the spirits of the dead, ripped from their resting place across the river in the afterlife.

'Can they remember who they were?' she asked him once. 'Do they remember their lives? The people who loved them?'

Sandy had shaken his head. 'I don't think so, lassie,' he had said. 'I think her magic strips them of all of that. I don't even think they know that they were alive at all.'

From the market crowd, Hope stares at the Black Coats. There are more of them than ever now, or so they say, their numbers growing as the Necromancer's power increases.

A lump of dread rises in her throat as she wonders, as she does sometimes, if her parents have become Black Coats, if the Necromancer has ever taken them from their peaceful afterlife.

'No good can come of wondering that,' Sandy has told her. 'They are not the people they were in life. They're only energy now. Another reason, as if we needed one, tae break the Necromancer's magic.'

Presently, the Black Coats stop their dogs and stand still, and from the back of the pack comes something that steals away Hope's breath. A white bear bigger even than the Ripper Dogs comes padding to the front of the pack. It is a beautiful, frightening thing, with a sleek coat as pure as tundra snow against the darkness of the night, and black eyes and a black nose. On the bear's back rides a woman. She wears a dress of a strange, shining silvery material that seems almost to glow in the grey lamplight of the moon market. Her hair is dark and tumbling over her shoulders, her face stern and coldly beautiful, with pointed cheekbones and large grey eyes. There is something familiar about those eyes, Hope thinks. The sight of this woman both enchants and troubles her. She cannot tear her gaze away as the woman rides the bear to the very head of the pack, stops and looks out over the market.

This is the moment that Hope feels the familiar, tingling warmth of colour in her hands. Perhaps it has been sparked by fear, or shock. She takes a sharp breath, looks down and sees that the skin of her fingers is turning brown, and the colour spreads up her hands and paints the sleeves of her coat.

'Not now,' she whispers. 'Please not now!'

She stuffs her trembling hand into her pocket, brings out the medicine bottle and takes a swig, sagging with relief as the colour stops in its tracks and then recedes. Her heart beating like a kingfisher's wings, Hope looks up at the woman on the bear, and then at the Black Coats and Ripper Dogs, and to her horror she sees that a few of the dogs are sniffing at the air and growling. Is it too late? Can they follow the echo of colour to her?

She takes a feverish look around, scouting an escape route, wishing she could see Sandy. Her eye catches the eye of a light-grey haired woman in the crowd, and her heart gives a jolt. The woman is staring not at the Ripper Dogs or the woman on the bear, but at Hope. And there is wonder in her eyes.

She saw, thinks Hope. *She saw my colour . . .*

The uneasy silence suddenly breaks as the woman on the great white bear speaks.

'For those of you who have never seen me, I am known as the Necromancer. I am aunt and advisor to the Emperor.'

Hope's head swivels away from the woman in the crowd and she stares up towards the woman on the white bear. The Necromancer! This is the woman who stole colour from the world! And when people speak of her, which is rarely, they can barely spit her name out quick enough, such is its poisonous taste. But what is she doing here? She's never been to a moon market before, not so far as Hope knows at any rate.

'I am here,' says the Necromancer, as if reading Hope's mind, 'to deliver a message from the Emperor.' She sits tall on her white bear, stares all around, and continues. 'There are whispers of a rebellion. Whispers of colour. Whispers of the Rainbow League.'

A muted murmur ripples through the market crowd. Rebellion? Hope listens intently. Fear is gripping her tightly around the chest, but that word, rebellion, pushes it back a little.

'I have no doubt,' the Necromancer goes on, 'that there are people here tonight who would like to take a shot at me. To fire an arrow into my heart and bring colour back to the world. Well, my friends, let me assure you that there are forces protecting me that you cannot begin to understand or imagine. Death is my friend, as she is your enemy, and I promise you this: if any of you try to interrupt me, then every breathing thing at this market will be slaughtered.'

Silence. Stony, frightened silence.

Death isn't your friend, Hope thinks, remembering her walk across the desert. *She isn't anyone's friend. And you, Mrs Necromancer, would not at all like to meet Death's friend. But the Ferryman would like to meet you.*

'Now,' says the Necromancer, 'to the Rainbow League I say this: colour is gone, and it will stay gone. A colourless world is a pure world, and anyone who tries to infect it will pay the price.' She looks around the market again. The night is calm and still, and the only sounds are the snap of the campfires and the night birds in the trees. 'There are some gifted mages here,' the Necromancer says. 'Indeed, a few of you may even be strong enough to break the great spell for brief moments, to bring tiny flashes of colour to reality in spell bottles or fireworks. But do not be tempted. Do not test me.' She strokes the fur of her great bear's shoulder blades. 'I feel an example must be made. There is colour here, in this market, tonight.'

A collective gasp. Hope's heart forgets to beat. Fear chokes her.

'Find it,' the Necromancer tells her pack of hunters. The Black Coats dig their heels into the sides of the Ripper Dogs, and the enormous black creatures let out growls and start sniffing feverishly around, at the air and the ground.

People scream as the Ripper Dogs enter the crowd, sniffing at people, at stalls and caravans, knocking mages over, forcing them to scramble away before they are trampled under massive paws.

Terror now has Hope in its icy clutches. It blinds her, brings on a brain fever that makes her tremble, makes her want to throw up. She backs up a step, and another, ready to wheel away and run – for all the good that'll do with the Ripper Dogs chasing. Then her eyes lock with those of the woman in the crowd who had been staring at her earlier, who had seen her colour appearing.

The woman gives Hope a calm shake of the head and

puts her finger to her lips. The message is clear. Don't run. Stay still. Stay quiet.

Everything in Hope, every instinct, every muscle, wants to run. But she fights to stay rooted to the ground, even as one of the Ripper Dogs comes closer and closer, even as it sniffs at the ground near her, and then swings its great head towards her. She stares into its glowing eyes, hoping, praying that it will go away. It comes closer. Its head is the size of Hope's torso, its great wet nose as large as a melon, and it pushes its snout into her side. She almost loses the strength in her legs as the Ripper Dog sniffs her hands, and then her face. The stench of its breath buckles her knees. She closes her eyes, knowing that the end will soon come, that the dog will seize her in those jaws like a rag and tear her to bits.

The Ripper Dog grunts, blasts a gust of putrid breath and drool over her face, and then moves on.

Hope opens her eyes, dares to breathe again. She watches the Ripper Dog padding off into the crowd. The woman is staring at her again.

A thunderous bark rings out from somewhere across the market, followed by a screech and a scream. Soon after, one of the Ripper Dogs returns to the Necromancer, dragging a mage by the hood of her grey coat.

'Put me down!' the mage yells. She kicks and struggles and spits. Hope recognises her. It is the woman who shouted a greeting to Sandy when they first arrived in the meadow.

Upon the Ripper Dog's back, its Black Coat rider holds

something out in a scabbed hand. A magic wand, like a giant grey match, with a glob of dried magic on one end.

The glob of magic is bright blue.

There are murmurs from the crowd. Is this mage smuggling colour? Is she working for the Rainbow League? The dogs must have found the colour in her caravan. Oh, she's in trouble now.

'Drop her,' the Necromancer says. The Ripper Dog lets the mage go, and she gets up and stands straight-backed, staring up at the Necromancer.

'What do you have to say for yourself?' the Necromancer asks.

The woman juts out her bottom lip. 'I have nae got a thing to say to you, except your time is coming to an end, lady. You cannae keep us locked up in a colourless world forever. We'll take it back.'

'Is that right?' says the Necromancer, climbing from the bear's back and dropping to the meadow. 'With silly wee sparklers like this?' She snaps the wand in two, drops it, stamps on it. Then she looks around at the onlooking crowd. 'I said an example must be made, and this is it.' She takes her index finger and touches it to the forehead of the mage.

'Gerroff!' yells the woman. Then she stops struggling, her eyes growing wide. 'Our time is coming!' she calls out in defiance. 'The Rainbow Child is out there, and she will free us!'

Hope gulps, and her throat makes a clicking sound. The Rainbow Child. She knows that's what they call her. But suddenly she realises that maybe the stories about her have become living things and turned her into something she isn't. She's not a great hero. She doesn't have power to match the Necromancer. She's just . . . Hope.

Just Hope.

The Necromancer's finger is still pressed to the captured mage's forehead. She presses harder, looks around. 'Would you all like to see a new trick I've learned? It's taken me a while, but I think I've got the hang of it.'

She pushes the woman back with her finger, making her stumble. Next moment, the captured mage stares around, as if a horde of ghosts are closing in on her, and her face contorts into a terrible mask of agony. Black, inky smoke leaps up from the ground and envelops her, swirling quicker and quicker in a circle. Hope can see glimpses of the poor mage, of her skin rotting and peeling off, of her eyes becoming cloudy marbles . . .

Then the smoke settles and becomes dark clothes, a long coat and hood, swaddling the mage.

What used to be the mage.

She is now, Hope realises with dawning horror and disgust, a Black Coat.

The new Black Coat stands motionless, until a new Ripper Dog comes padding to the head of the pack, sniffs at her, and in one fluid, unnatural motion, she is upon the great creature's back.

'Wherever you go,' calls the Necromancer, 'tell the story of what you have seen tonight. Spread the message. My power grows every day. If you go against me, against the Emperor, this is the hell that awaits you. If you are caught with colour, you won't just face death. You will become death. Your soul will not travel on the Ferryman's boat to the lands beyond.' She points to the new Black Coat. 'This will be your beyond. This will be your forever.'

She mounts the white bear again with graceful ease, urges it forward. As she passes out of sight, Hope hears the Necromancer say to her Black Coats, 'Wreck the market.'

There are shouts and screams as the Ripper Dogs snarl and bark, and suddenly the market erupts into a chaos of charging feet and screaming, of growling and crashing and smashing glass.

Her head all a-spin, Hope begins to dodge and weave through the stampede, ducking flying bottles, watching in horror as a Ripper Dog tips someone's caravan onto a campfire.

'Sandy!' she calls, tears blurring her vision. 'Sandy, where are you?'

Something hits her hard on the back, and she falls, the weight of an adult on top of her, pressing her into the ground. Pain shrieks in her ribs. She cannot breathe. Then whoever knocked her over is gone, leaving her winded on the ground, hot agony stabbing her sides every time she tries to take a breath. A horse bursts past her, inches from trampling her head. Then there is a hand gripping her arm, helping her up.

'Sandy!'

But it's not Sandy. It is the woman who was staring at her earlier. The woman who knows her secret. Another poker-hot lash of pain strikes Hope's chest and back, and she falls into the woman.

'Take it easssssy,' the woman says. 'I've got you. I've got you.'

'I can't breathe . . .'

The woman supports Hope's weight, puts Hope's arm over her shoulder, making Hope cry.

'I'm sorry,' the woman says.

'I need,' Hope sputters, 'need to find my friends.'

'What you need is to get to safety,' says the woman.

'But—'

A thunderous explosion rocks the entire market, and a plume of black smoke erupts into the sky over the meadow. Someone screams. A baby cries out for her mother.

'No arguments. Come with me. We'll find your friend when all this calms down – unless you want a Ripper Dog to trample what's left of your guts out?'

Hope shakes her head, lets the woman guide her through the market, ducking behind upturned wagons and burning stalls, until they are out of the meadow and into the edges of the grey forest. There Hope stops and looks back at a terrible sight. The moon market is a blazing ruin, and from that ruin she sees the pack of Ripper Dogs leaving the scene, tearing away across the meadow like shadows.

Black billowing smoke has blanked out the stars, and somewhere among the chaos is Hope's family.

Chapter Eighteen
In Which Hope is Collected

'You thirsty?'

'What?'

The woman has taken Hope a little further into the shadows of the forest, away from the meadow and the burning wreckage of the market. Hope sits with her back resting on a tree, gasping for breath, sharp, hot pain scratching at her innards. The woman lights a lantern and places it on the ground, illuminating a sphere of darkness with pale white light, casting the grey tree trunks into columns of light and shadow.

'Are you thirsty?'

'I . . . I need to get back to Sandy. And Oliver. Oh, I hope they're safe!'

'I'm sure they're fine,' says the woman. 'The Ripper Dogs and Black Coats are gone now. Try to relax. Your ribs are busted. Must've been from when that big fella landed on you. They'll need fixing.'

Hope shakes her head. 'Sandy can do that.' She grimaces, tries to get up, then, exhausted by the pain, leans her head on the trunk of the tree and closes her eyes. White spots dance in front of her eyelids.

'Nope,' says the woman. 'Needs fixing now. Hold still.'

The woman's hands press into Hope's ribcage. There is an instant of blinding, unbearable pain, and then cool relief, as if a fire in her bones has been put out. The pain is gone.

Hope stares into the woman's face. It is an unremarkable face. Forgettable and plain. 'How'd you do that?'

'I know a thing or two,' the woman says. She narrows her eyes. 'I might ask you how you did that fine trick of yours back in the market.'

Hope swallows. Her body tenses. 'I don't know what you mean.'

'You know I saw you,' the woman says. 'I saw the colour coming into your hands. I saw you panic. I thought you were going to run, and that would have been the end of you, because those Ripper Dogs would have caught you in two bounds and ripped you to pieces and fought over the scraps. I couldn't have that, not something as precious as you going to wasssssste.'

Wasssssste. That's how she says it, with a long, drawn out hiss.

'Right,' says Hope, beginning to feel uneasy. A memory is fighting against the current in the river of thoughts in her mind, but it hasn't reached the surface quite yet. 'I really

171

should be getting back. Sandy will worry I've been hurt. He's probably searching through the wreckage now.'

'Do you like the moon markets?' asks the woman, ignoring Hope's line of conversation.

'Um. Aye. I mean, yes.'

'I find them tiresome,' says the woman with a dismissive wave. 'When you've been around as long as me, most things become tiresommmmme.'

Hope finds this a strange thing for the woman to say, because she doesn't look very old at all. Come to think of it, it's difficult to tell what age she might be.

'But I keep going back. Keep looking for treasure. I must wear a disguise, of course. But it's worth it. Because sometimes, just sometimes, a shining wonder will turn up that I simply must have.'

'Right,' says Hope, standing up, taking a step back. 'Thanks for everything. I'm going to go now.'

'Go?' says the woman. 'You're not going anywhere. How could I let you go when you'll look so fine as part of my collectionnnnnn?'

Hope's eyes bug wide.

Suddenly the memory breaks the surface, shining bright. Clear as day, she recalls a wyvern lying wounded in the dark forest. Remembers a tall thing standing over the stricken creature.

As these thoughts come to Hope, the woman *changes* before her eyes.

With a sickening, twisting series of bone snaps and

clicks, her skin stretches and thickens. Her face grows lopsided, her shoulders rounded and hunched. She grows taller, taller, taller still, her arms becoming nightmarishly long, her bony fingers almost brushing the forest floor. A black ragged dress appears around her, and a light grey shawl smeared with dark stains wraps around her misshapen, oversized head.

Hope has been frozen with fright, but her senses return with a sudden rush, and she wheels away and tries to run. One of those long, long arms reaches out, and iron-strong fingers close around her waist, lifting her from the ground, turning her around so that she is brought close to a face that belongs in bad dreams. Watery, bloodshot eyes fix on Hope from beneath a jutting brow of thick bone, and the sloping gash of a mouth becomes what might be a smile.

'No more running, dearie,' the monster says, her rancid breath sticking in Hope's throat. 'Come on with me now. Come on hommmme with old Baba.'

Hope tries to scream, tries to fight, but Baba's grip is strong and cold and crushing, and Hope cannot gather enough air in her lungs to make a squeak, or find the strength to wriggle. Every one of Baba's steps takes her further from Sandy and Oliver, further from the safety of her home. The dark forest moves around her, a sea of colourless shadow. Sometimes they pass through a pool of moonlight that has broken through the canopy, and Hope catches a glimpse of Baba's huge, bare feet as they softly tread through the fallen leaves. The sight of those lumpy, claw-like toes makes her shudder.

After a while, Baba slows, and the lights of a shack come into view high among the branches. The shack is suitably large enough for a creature of Baba's size. By the soft spills of light from the windows, Hope can see that it is made of wood. It sits high among the branches, and she wonders if this is all a nightmare, or if Baba is squeezing her too tight, because she realises that the shack is standing on a pair of scaly chicken legs, half as tall as the surrounding trunks.

Baba stops, crouches, and then takes them whooshing through the night with an enormous leap. They land with a creaking groan on the porch of the grey shack. Baba opens the door, and they are inside, where the air smells like animals and hay and dust.

In three strides they are at a tall wooden table. Baba drops Hope onto the tabletop and Hope sits up and looks around. A huge pot on a stove catches her eye.

'Are you going to cook me?' she asks, trembling.

'Cook?' says Baba, standing over her. 'No, not cook. I donnnnn't eat what's in my collection, dearie. I look after it forever.' She indicates upward, and Hope tilts her head back and gasps at what she sees.

Hanging from the high, high ceiling, and stacked on shelves and cabinets and tables, are cages. Hundreds and hundreds of cages, like the sort you might keep a pet bird in. Only, in these cages, instead of birds, Hope's eyes are met with a dazzling array of varied life. In one cage, a leather-skinned, monkey-like creature with white wings clings to the bars. In another, what looks like a living lump of rock slowly rolls over. She spots what she thinks must be a faery, a glowing little thing with buzzing grey wings. Over here is a black dog with three heads, and there a white unicorn, shrunken down to the size of a child's toy. Everywhere there are fluttering things and shadowy shapes, creatures she has only read about in the many books in Sandy's caravan, and others she does not know at all.

Baba spins away from the table and yells in a thunderous voice, 'Odd? Odd, come down here this instant!'

Hope's eyes flick to the ceiling when she hears light, hurried footsteps from above. Down a leaning wooden staircase comes a boy, jumping each large step, rushing to meet Baba. He is dressed in tattered rags, from which his legs and forearms stick out, and he is about the size of an average boy of ten or eleven. There is, however, nothing else average about him. Hope leans to get a better look, and she gasps and covers her mouth. Her stomach turns. This boy, it seems, has been sewn together from many mismatched parts. A huge scar runs across the top of his bald head and down under one eye. The left eye is light grey, while the right is a black marble. His arms are different colours. The right is pale as milk, the left a few shades darker. His left hand is altogether darker again, almost black. His legs are similarly mismatched. He is a patchwork of flesh and bone.

'Yes, Baba?' he says.

'Fetch one of my threadssss,' she hisses. The boy, Odd, nods and runs off upstairs again. When he reappears a minute later, Hope can see that he is clutching something in his closed black hand.

'There you go, Baba,' he says.

Baba glares down at him and, with one of her long grey hands she snatches the thing from him.

'Who's she?' Odd asks, staring up at Hope with his eerie eyes.

'Never you mind,' Baba snaps. 'She's special. Not like you.'

A look of hurt flashes across Odd's face. Then he shrugs. 'She doesn't look special.'

Hope frowns.

'Well, she is.' Baba shoos him away from the table. 'You'll seeeeee.' She turns back to Hope, leans over her, and Hope scrambles backwards. 'Nowhere to go, dearie,' Baba tells her with an ugly smile. 'Nowhere else you'd want to be either. You're home.'

Baba reaches out. Cold, clammy, elongated hands come towards Hope. 'Give me your arm.' This is not a request. Hope holds out a shaking hand. Baba takes the thing in her hand – Hope realises it is a fine silvery thread – and ties it around Hope's wrist. No sooner has the knot been fastened than a swimming rush fills Hope's head. The room spins, and shifts, and everything seems suddenly to grow around her, becoming not just huge, but gigantic. Baba towers over her like a giant, and as she stares all about, her guts in knots and her heart thumping, Hope realises with a start that the world around her has not grown. It is Hope who has changed.

She has shrunk.

She stares around the tabletop, hardly able to believe her eyes. She supposes she must be no bigger than a fieldmouse.

With a ragged breath, Baba sits down upon a chair, leans her bony chin on the table and stares at Hope. 'Do it,' she says.

'Do what?' asks Hope, trying not to gag on Baba's breath.

'Show me colour.'

Hope stares into Baba's giant, watery eyes. How can she refuse? Baba might get angry and squish her like a bug. She closes her eyes, concentrates as much as she can in the circumstances, tries to calm her mind. She thinks of the feeling of colour flowing through her, the life of it, and soon that familiar warmth spreads through her, until she feels like she is shining as bright as the sun.

She opens her eyes and sees Baba's twisted face full of wonder.

'I haven't seen colour for so lonnnnng,' she says. 'Haven't smelled it. Haven't felt it.' She claps her hands like thunder, reaches down and snatches Hope up from the table, the flesh of her hand turning sickly, scabbed, greyish-green at Hope's touch. The giant hand lifts her up, high through the air, and before she knows what is happening, she is lying on the straw-scattered floor of an empty cage and the door is shut and locked. And there she hangs from the ceiling, looking down over the room.

'My, that is a pretty thing,' says Odd, staring up at her.

'Told you,' says Baba. She yawns, her squint jaw seeming to dislocate with a loud snap. Ropes of drool hang from her rotten, blackened teeth. 'Sleeeeep. I must sleep now.' She looks up at Hope's cage again, tapping the bars, making the cage gently swing, and then she turns away and shuffles to the stairs. 'Sort things out downnnnn here,' she snaps at Odd, clipping her hand across the back of his hairless head when she passes.

'Yes, Baba. I will, Baba. Sweet dreams, Baba.'

She waves him off, climbs the stairs. When she is gone, Odd makes his way around the room, putting out the lamps and using a long, rickety stepladder to check each of the animal cages. When at last he reaches Hope's cage, he stops and, by the light of the lantern in his hand, gazes at her.

'Last time I saw colour,' he says, 'a different king sat on the throne, and my old dad was still alive.'

'Let me go,' says Hope. 'Please let me go.'

'Can't,' he says. 'Baba collected you, and once Baba collects something it stays collected.'

'I don't belong here,' Hope pleads.

'Oh, but you do,' says Odd. 'Don't you see? Everything in this house is different, or rare, or unique, and every single creature is safer in here than they would be out there.' At this he wiggles the fingers on one of his stitched-on hands.

'I saw how you looked at me when you first saw me. I know how I look. If I was on my own, the world would tear me up for being a monster, just like the Ripper Dogs would tear you up because of all that lovely colour. But not here. Not in Baba's house.'

'But my friends . . . my family . . .'

'Baba's your family now. We all are.'

Before Hope can speak again, Odd's head has ducked out of sight. She runs to the bars of her little cage, high above, and gazes down as the patchwork boy climbs into a nest of dusty covers in the corner of the room, puts out the lantern and closes his eyes.

Hope sits in the darkness, hugging her knees, listening to the fluttering and snoring from the many other cages. She wonders what Sandy and Oliver must be thinking right now. Are they searching through the charred remains of the moon market, calling her name? No answer will come. And they'll never find her, not here, not in this place.

Somehow, she knows that to be true. She can feel it.

For the first time in her life, she is on her own.

In her cage, she starts to cry.

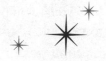

Chapter Nineteen
In Which the Ragged
Boy Seeks Help

The shack's giant chicken legs carry it far across the grey land over the next few days, cutting a wedge through the forest.

The house moves at night and stops each morning to rest, and it is during these daylight hours that Baba goes off into the woods to collect eggs and berries, and to look all day for more treasures for her menagerie.

While Baba is gone, Odd is left to clean and cook and look after the many creatures. This is the way of things in Baba's house on legs.

Every day the same.

By the fourth day, Hope has no tears left to cry, so she sits in silence and watches the ragged boy go about his chores.

'You're her slave,' she tells him as he mops the floor.

His mop keeps sloshing from side to side. He does not look up. 'Think what you will,' he tells her. 'I'm not the one in the cage.'

'Aren't you?'

She sees him falter only for a moment, but then the swishing of the mop resumes. He does not so much as glance at her for the rest of the day.

In the twilight of the fifth day, Baba comes back from foraging in a foul mood, slamming the door and stomping to the table.

'Food!' she snaps, bumping her fist down on the tabletop.

'Yes, Baba.' Odd scurries around to the stove, climbs a short wooden ladder and stirs the bubbling, foul-smelling contents of a huge iron pot. He ladles a few scoops of viscous grey slop into a bowl, turns and pops the bowl on the table. Baba reaches out a long arm and snatches it up, and Hope catches a glimpse of a bobbing fish head in the stew, its milky, unseeing eyes staring up at her cage. Baba leans over the table and sticks her face into the bowl. The slurping, gurgling, smacking sounds that follow make Hope's stomach turn. When Baba is done, she slides the bowl back towards Odd.

'More.'

'Yes, Baba.' Odd refills the bowl, and Baba drains it again, spatters of greasy, stinking stew landing all over the table and floor.

'More?' asks Odd.

'No. Done.'

'Did you have a good day in the forest, Baba?'

'Ha,' she says bitterly. 'No. I did not, idiot boy. I found

no humans to trick, no creaturesssss to collect, and no little children to frighten.'

'Oh well,' says Odd in a cheery tone, 'I expect tomorrow will bring better things.'

Baba grunts. 'Oh, you do? And what would you know, fool boy? Hm? You're nothing but an ugly, brainlesssss rag doll. Pah!' She stands up, sweeping the bowl off the grey table, and it spins through the air and smashes on the floor. 'Clean that up!' she orders. 'I'm going to rest.'

Baba shuffles away from the table, her short legs and freakishly long arms dragging her jerkily up the stairs in a creepy, crawling movement. When she is gone, Odd stares after her for a long moment, his shoulders sagging and his mismatched hands clenched. Hope watches him closely as he grabs a broom and sweeps up Baba's mess.

Is he crying?

'Why do you let her treat you like that?' Hope asks.

Odd does not answer. His sweeping intensifies.

'She shouldn't talk to you that way,' Hope goes on. 'Calling you all sorts of names. Saying you're useless.'

'It's true though,' Odd says in a soft, hardly there voice. 'I *am* useless.'

'I don't think that's true at all. You cook for her, don't you? Clean up after her and look after all the poor creatures in these cages? That's not useless.'

He does not answer, just opens the door and sweeps the fragments of broken bowl out, where they fall to the forest floor far below.

'What gives her the right to lock up all these things anyway? Who does she think she is?'

'I told you,' he says, 'they're better off in here.'

Hope shakes her head. 'You don't mean that.'

'You don't know what I mean,' he says. 'And you don't know anything about me, so why don't you keep your trap shut?'

Hope frowns. She has been locked up in Baba's house for days, and she has watched very carefully for the merest glimmer of potential escape. She has come to the conclusion that this ragged, patchwork boy may be her only chance. He has the keys to the cages, after all. And Baba treats him like a skivvy. It is important, then, to gain his trust. That's what Sandy would do. He can be a silver-tongued old devil when he wants to be, and even though he's a very powerful mage, he much prefers to talk than fight.

'You're right enough,' she says. 'I don't know much about you at all. But I'd like to learn.'

Not once has Odd looked at her during this conversation, until now. His eyes flick up towards her. 'You don't want to know about me. There's nothing good to say.'

'Well, how did you end up here?' Hope asks.

'Baba collects rare things,' he shrugs. 'And I'm as rare as you'll find.'

'Aye,' says Hope, 'but you had a life before this?'

'I did. If you can call it a life.' He stands with the broom forgotten in one hand, examining the deep, knitted scars around his other wrist. 'Doesn't matter now anyway. The past is the past.'

Hope is standing in her little birdcage, her hands gripping the bars, the colour spreading from her fingers into the rusted, flaking reddish brown metal. 'Are you happy here?' she asks.

Silence.

'I'm safe,' Odd says at last.

'That's not what I asked.'

'What's all the jabbering when I'm trying to get my beauty sleeeeep?' comes Baba's grating voice from the top of the stairs. Odd jumps almost a foot into the air and immediately starts sweeping again. The stairs creak as Baba comes halfway down, her lopsided face full of suspicion. 'Who you talking to anyways?' Her eyes find Hope. 'Ah. The neeeeew one, eh? What's he been saying to you, dearie? He been telling you all about olllllld Baba? Gossiping? I'll bet he has, the useless bag of bones!' She comes down the rest of the stairs with deceptive speed, aims a kick at Odd, and her massive, bony foot connects with his backside, sending him flying across the room.

Hope shrinks back in her cage as Baba flashes towards her, reaches up and slaps the cage with a long hand, making it swing wildly, sending Hope crashing and rolling about the straw-littered floor.

'I hope we haven't got a troublemaker herrrrrre,' Baba breathes, grabbing the cage and settling it. 'You a troublemaker?'

Hope sits up and shakes the cobwebs from her head. 'No.'

Baba runs a hideous fingernail down one of the cage bars. 'I've had troublemakers before, you knowwwww. An ice wolf that scratched and bit and clawed. A golden phoenix that burned itself up over and over again, trying to escape. But they all come round in the ennnnnd. Sooner or later, they realise that once old Baba has collected them, they're here until they take their lasssst breath, and they calm down.' She indicates the many cages scattered around the room. 'My treasures. All unique, or very rare, and mine to share with nobody.' A long, stained fingernail disappears up her nose and digs around until she brings it out, examines the tip and slips it into her lopsided mouth. 'I've never collected a human being before,' she goes on, chewing whatever she sucked off her finger. 'Human beings are usually dull as ditchwater, and they have a nassssty habit of thinking they are cleverer than they really are. There's never been a humannnnn being special enough to collect, not until you. And now that I have you, with your shining, pretty colour, I'm never going to let you go. You'll learn to like it here in time. You'll give up your little dreams of esssssscape, and you'll enjoy beinnnnnngg part of Baba's family.'

Hope gets back up and stares into Baba's eyes, praying that she looks braver than she feels. 'I won't ever give up.'

'Hm. We'll see.' Baba wheels around, shakes a finger at Odd, making him cringe. 'Don't you be talking to little miss sunshine here any more, you hear? Not until she adjusts her attitude.'

'Yes, Baba.'

'And clean out the unicorn cage. I can ssssssmell it from upstairs. Fool boy.'

'Yes, Baba.'

She peers around the room again, her rotten mouth all puckered up like she's sucked on a lemon, then she smacks her lips and, with a final 'pfft', she goes back upstairs. A few minutes later, loud snores echo all about the place, frightening some of the caged miniature creatures.

'You see what I mean?' Hope half whispers. 'She's horrible to you! You haven't even done anything wrong. If I was you, I'd tell her I'd rather take my chances out there in the world than stay another second in this prison running about after her like a scolded dog.'

'Please don't talk to me,' Odd says quietly. He has gone to the unicorn cage, and Hope watches how gentle he is with the tiny, shrunken animal as he picks it up so that he can clean out the muck and change its bed of straw. When the job is done, he doesn't put the unicorn back right away. Instead, he lets it trot around in his open, mismatched hands and along the length of his arms. A peaceful smile plays on his lips.

Hope can feel kindness in him, and hurt, and sadness. Knowing how to read people is something you have to learn to do when you are a travelling mage, and Hope fancies she's become almost as good at it as Sandy. This boy, this strange, locked-away, patchwork boy is hurting badly.

And she finds all of a sudden that she doesn't just want to escape this place, but to help Odd too.

'I'll leave you be,' she whispers. 'But I'm here when you do need to talk. And when the day comes you want to get out of here, I'll help you do it.'

He does not reply.

Back at the moon market, in a large tent near the centre of the meadow, Sandy Burns walks to the opening and gazes out across what is left of the many stalls and caravans. All about, mages are still helping each other with repairs, fixing wheels, replacing wooden beams, treating wounds. And the village folk help too, supplying materials and food and firewood.

Sandy looks beyond the meadow, to the darkness of the forest, and in the darkening twilight he sees movement coming from the trees. His chest tightens as he walks out to meet them, two mages on horseback, and with them, Oliver the dog.

'Well?' he asks. 'Anything?'

Oliver shakes his shaggy head. 'I'm afraid not, Sandy. It's the same as the last four nights. Hope's scent leads some way into the forest, but then it disappears.'

Sandy grits his teeth in frustration. 'She cannae just have dropped off the world!' he yells at no one. 'She has tae be somewhere.'

'We'll go back out again at first light,' says Oliver. 'We'll keep looking until we find her.' He sits at Sandy's feet, paws his leg gently. 'We won't give up on her, Sandy.'

Sandy looks at the ground. He nods. 'I know.' He addresses the mages on horseback. 'Thank you.' They nod and canter away, leaving Sandy with his loyal little dog. He reaches down and scratches Oliver behind the ear.

'She's out there, Sandy,' Oliver says. 'I can feel it.'

Sandy does not answer. He simply looks out towards the forest again and whispers to himself, 'Where are you, Hope?'

By now, word has spread far and wide that the Rainbow Child is missing. It is the talk of every hushed conversation in every tavern, and soon it reaches Gwendle Farm, where Darroch overhears two farmhands discussing it.

'I reckon the Necromancer got her,' says one.

'Nah,' scoffs the other. 'If she had caught the Rainbow Child, you think she wouldn't be crowing about it from the rooftops?' She shakes her head. 'More likely it's all part of some clever plan by the Rainbow League.'

'Excuse me,' says Darroch, causing them to stop picking strawberries. 'Is what you said true? Is the Rainbow Child missing?'

They nod. 'So they say.'

Darroch does not hang around. No sooner has the woman answered him than he is off. See him go, fast as a flash, across the farm and into the empty house. Up the stairs he rushes, tripping, and into his room, slamming the door. He drops to the floor and reaches under his bed, bringing out the canvas bag the woman from the Rainbow

League left in his possession. Still out of breath, he sits on the edge of his bed and opens the bag. The glass jars of magic paint clink as he reaches in to touch them.

He has been wondering, these past weeks, if he will ever gather the courage to use the paints, to execute the plan in his mind. But just now, in the field, something in him has changed. If the Rainbow Child really is gone, then the people who believe in her will be frightened, and worried. They will, he concludes, be grateful for a sign. A reminder that they are not alone.

Darroch closes the bag, hugs it to his chest.

It's time.

More days go by. How many is difficult to say. Hope is beginning to realise that a cage does funny things to time, stretches it and ties it in knots and makes it seem less real. The monotony is only broken up by two meals a day, usually a crumb of bread and cheese or a few flakes of rubbery fish. There is a little wooden hutch in her cage, in which she sleeps and is afforded privacy when she needs it. Sometimes, in quiet moments, she brings the little bottle of colour-hiding potion out from her pocket and considers taking a few drops. Might she persuade Baba that living in captivity has drained her of her colour? No, probably not. Baba is smart, and would surely catch on to the trick. She certainly wouldn't set Hope free or show any sympathy.

One day, while Baba is out in the forest as usual, Hope is pulled from an uneasy daytime slumber by the sound of gentle sobbing. She rubs her eyes, sits up and comes out of her little wooden box, looking around the room.

'Odd? That you?'

No reply. The sobbing goes on, interrupted by the occasional wet sniff. It's coming from somewhere she can't see, a corner of the room hidden by a tall cabinet stacked with cages.

'Odd?' she tries again. 'What's the matter?'

The crying suddenly stops, and the only sounds are the muted scratchings and snuffling and fluttering from the many cages, and the breeze in the branches of the tangled forest trees.

Then, in a thick, sorrowful voice, Odd says, 'He's sick.'

'Who's sick, Odd?'

'Elmo.'

Hope pushes against the bars, tries to see him, but catches only a glimpse of his back as he sits on the floor behind the tall cabinet. 'Who is Elmo?'

Odd sniffs, then slowly leans back and pops his head around the corner. His mismatched eyes are puffy and wet, and the deep patchwork scar on his face glistens with tears. 'One of Baba's creatures. He's my friend.'

'Maybe I can help?' says Hope.

'You? How?'

'Well, I'm learning to be a mage. At least, I was before Baba snatched me. I know a wee bit about animals. My best friend is a dog and I'd hate it if he ever got sick.' She pictures Oliver, and her heart aches to rub his belly, to feel him curl up in the crook of her legs while she sleeps. Tears gather in the corners of her eyes, but she wipes them away and swallows them back. 'Will you let me look?'

Odd casts a desperate glance towards the door. 'All right. But quickly.'

He disappears again, and Hope hears the gentle creak of bars as he lifts one of the cages. When he reappears into the open, he is carrying a birdcage, and in that cage . . .

Hope looks closer, her heart picking up the pace.

She knows this creature instantly. Four years ago, she rode on its back, flew so high that she could reach out and brush the stars with her fingers. Sometimes she still dreams about that night.

In the little cage, Elmo the moon wyvern lies on his belly, wings splayed awkwardly. Even from such a distance, it's obvious to Hope that the poor creature is suffering.

'Can you bring him closer?' she asks.

Odd hesitates, then puts the cage down and fetches his wooden stepladder. In a few moments he's climbed four or five rungs and placed the cage atop the ladder, holding it steady with patchwork hands.

Hope decides, for the moment at least, to keep her previous meeting with Elmo to herself. She looks closer. Elmo is a shadow of what he once was, half wasted away and emaciated. She can clearly see his ribs through his scaly flesh, and the black scales are dull and lifeless.

'Elmo is a moon wyvern,' she tells Odd. 'How long has he been kept indoors?'

'Let me see,' says Odd. 'About four years, I think.'

'Four whole years inside? Jings, no wonder he's in bad shape. A moon wyvern needs strong moonlight to survive, Odd. I'll bet poor Elmo has been feeding on little scraps of moonlight that sometimes come through the window and fall on his cage. It's been enough to keep him alive, but only barely.' She balls up her fists and bangs one of the bars on her cage. 'This is what happens when you take things out the wild and keep them locked up. It's no good, Odd.'

Odd's eyes are wide and innocent. 'What should I do?'

'You need to get him out in the moonlight,' says Hope. 'Soon as you can.'

'How am I going to do that? Baba won't let me take Elmo out. She doesn't let any of her collection out the door, not even for a second. And I can't tell her what Elmo needs. If I suddenly seem to know all about moon wyverns, it'll be obvious to Baba that I've been talking to you and there'll be big trouble for us both!'

'Well,' says Hope, 'you better sort something out quick, because from the look of him, poor Elmo won't last much longer.'

That evening, when Baba comes home, her mood is unusually happy. In fact, when she comes through the door, Hope is amazed to see that she is downright cheerful.

'Good day, Baba?' asks Odd, busy at the stove.

'Yes, idiot boy. Good. Very good indeed.'

'Did you find something else to collect?' asks Odd,

scooping ladles of grey, congealed eel stew into a bowl. It smells like rotten fish guts.

'No. But I did come across something almost as good.' Baba grabs the bowl and slurps and dribbles as she pours the eel stew down her gullet, then slides the bowl back to Odd. 'More.'

He refills the bowl. 'So, what did you find?'

Baba smiles. It is not a pretty sight. 'A little village,' she says, pointing towards the door, 'filled with silly little people who are frightened of the darrrrrk. Frightened of what monsters might come out of the forest to get them.' She drains another bowl of rancid eel stew and licks her lips with a watery smacking sound. 'There are children in the village,' she says, and her lopsided mouth contorts into another hellish smile. 'Lots of little chilllldren.'

'What are you going to do to them?' The question has spilled out of Hope's mouth before she can think properly about it.

Baba's head snaps in her direction, and Hope takes a backwards step away from the bars of her cage.

'Oh,' Baba says, coming slowly towards Hope. 'This one's a nosy parker, isn't she?' She comes closer, and closer still, until her face is almost pressing against the cage and Hope can do nothing but stare, frightened half to death, into Baba's giant, watery grey eyes. 'You want to know what I have planned for those little childrennnn? I'll tell you. Tonight, when the night is darkest, I'm going to sneak into the village. I'm going to climb through the windowsssss,

193

into the rooms where those itsy children are peacefully asleep, and I'm going to frighten themmmm. I'm going to make their teeth chatter and their blood turn to ice. I'm going to make them wet the bed and scream for their parents. And I am going to eat all of the fear that spills out of their little heartsssssss.'

Hope covers her mouth, shocked. 'Will you hurt them?' she whispers.

Baba sneers. 'There's no sport in that. No challenge. No funnnnn. Fear is tastier than flesh and blood and bone. Fear is nourishing and dellllllicious. And chasing little children through their nightmares is the best way to taste the purest fear of all.'

Hope's mind shows her a frightful vision of Baba contorting herself, squeezing through windows into the rooms of sleeping children, standing over their beds and poisoning their dreams.

'We'll stay put for a few nightsssss,' Baba says, going back to the table, where a third bowl of steaming eel slop is waiting for her. 'No longer than that. A few nights of feasting on the fear of little children will attract attention, and we don't want any mages coming looking for us, thank you very much.'

Hope wishes more than anything for Sandy to come and find her. But that is not going to happen. If she wants to stop Baba, to save the children of the nearby village and free all of the poor trapped animals in the cages of this house on chicken legs, then she must do it alone.

Unless . . .

Her gaze finds Odd.

Somewhere in a back room of her busy mind, the first sparks of possibility leap to life.

CHAPTER TWENTY
IN WHICH ODD TELLS HIS STORY

That night, the house does not move through the forest as usual. Instead, the great legs rest, and under the cover of darkness, Baba creeps out among the trees and disappears into the shadows towards the village.

The wooden house is still and cold and dark. Many of the creatures in Baba's collection are asleep, but not Hope. She sits by the bars of her little cage and watches Odd, who as usual, is lying beneath his blankets on the floor.

Hope waits.

At last, Odd comes out from his nest, hurries to the door and goes out to the porch. There he takes great care in looking all about.

'Baba?' he calls into the night. 'Baba, are you there?'

There is no answer. Somewhere in the forest a wolf howl echoes.

Odd comes back into the house, rushes upstairs, and reappears a moment later carrying what looks, in the dim colourless light of his single lamp, like a huge spool of yarn. The yarn is fine and silvery, and it seems to glow. Hope holds up her wrist, where Baba tied the length of string that magically caused her to shrink. In contact with Hope's skin, the yarn is rich and golden, but she is sure it is the same, that it has come from this enormous spool.

She stays quiet as Odd puts the spool down, dashes over to the corner of the room and comes back into view holding the little bird cage in which Elmo, the moon wyvern, is resting.

'What are you going to do?' she asks at last, unable to hold her curiosity any longer.

Odd glances up, though only for a moment. 'I'm going to get him some moonlight,' he says.

Hope gets up from the straw-littered floor of her cage, grasps the bars. 'How are you going to get down from here?'

Odd does not answer. He is too busy with his hands. He takes the cage and puts it down, then he goes back to the enormous yarn spool and ties the end of the glowing silvery string around the top of Elmo's cage. When he's satisfied with his knot, he takes a knife from the kitchen, cuts the other end of the string from the spool and ties that loose end around his waist.

Hope begins to understand what he's doing. But . . . 'How come you're not shrinking?' she asks. 'That yarn made me shrink.'

Odd tightens the knot around him. 'Baba spun the yarn on her magic wheel, so it only works for her.'

'Where are you going to take Elmo?' Hope asks. 'Not down to the ground? We're fifty paces up!'

'Don't be daft,' says Odd. 'The moon is up, isn't it? So, I'll take him up.'

Before Hope can say anything else, Odd picks up Elmo's cage again and carries it out of the door. The front door of the shack creaks shut, and Hope is left staring at the grey walls and grey ceiling and listening to the scratching, scuffling noises of Odd climbing the house. Then, it seems, he is on the roof. Hope listens to uneasy footsteps clunk-clunking overhead, followed by the unmistakable sound of rustling branches and feet on tree bark.

He's climbing the trees, she realises, to get Elmo's cage up into the moonlight.

For a long time, all is still. Hope sits in her cage, listening intently, hoping that the sky is clear so that Elmo can bathe in the light of the moon, and also hoping that this will be enough to make him a little stronger. What he really needs is to find a moonpond, like the one Hope was visiting with Sandy when she first met Elmo. There he could drink the moonlight and regain his strength completely.

When she hears Odd coming back at last, Hope goes to the bars of her cage and peers out at the door, which swings open, and there stands Odd, holding the cage.

He is smiling.

'It worked!' he says. 'At least, it worked a little. I couldn't risk any longer. Don't know when Baba will be back.' He comes into the house, shutting the door behind him, and climbs the stepladder so Hope can get a closer look.

She can see right away that there is a lustre in Elmo's scaly armour that was missing before. Also, he is now awake and sitting up, though he looks sleepy and the silver glow of his eyes is dim. As the cage comes closer to Hope, Elmo sniffs at the air and looks around, finally seeing her. He snorts and fidgets and shuffles to the edge of his cage, so that he is pressing against the bars, trying to get to her.

'He likes you,' says Odd, sounding a little hurt that Elmo's attention is on Hope.

Hope reaches through the bars of her own little cage, stretching, and manages to gently brush the horny skin of Elmo's snout with her fingertips.

The effect of Hope's colour is instant. Where there was only grey and black, a darkest red shine now fills up the scales of Elmo's head, and the glow of his eyes turns silvery blue.

'Oh my,' breathes Odd, and there is wonder and amazement in his eyes as they drink in the sight of Elmo's colour. 'Aren't you a fine sight, eh, Elmo?'

The miniature wyvern gives a tiny trumpet call and stretches out his wings.

'He still needs more moonlight,' Hope says. 'This is a start, but he's in pretty bad shape. Jings, look how thin his wings are! I can nearly see through them.'

'I'll take him back out tomorrow,' Odd agrees. 'And the next night, and every night from now on. I'll find a way.'

Hope gives him a smile, and he looks away shyly. Then she lets her face become serious. 'You see why this is wrong, don't you, Odd? You see why Baba shouldn't be keeping all these beautiful creatures locked away from the world. It's hurting them. You keep saying that they're safer in here than they would be outside, but I think that's just a story you tell yourself to make you feel better about things.'

Odd's mismatched eyes, one dark, one light, stare at Elmo. 'The world can be a bad place,' he says, and there is darkness in his voice. 'I know. I've seen it.'

'I have too,' says Hope. 'But I've also seen how wonderful a place it can be. I'll tell you this: I'd rather live just one day out there, free, than live a hundred more years in this cage.' She takes her hand away from Elmo's snout, and the wondrous colour leaves him. The tiny wyvern lets out a moan of dismay.

Odd frowns. 'I better get him back in his place. Baba might be back any minute.'

As it turns out, Baba does not return for several hours. When she walks through the door of the shack, Hope jolts out of a restless sleep. Down on the floor, Odd rushes to greet his mistress. Baba's belly is swollen, her face twisted into a look that might be contentment.

'There is nothinggggg more delicious,' she says, her long hands resting on her full belly, 'than the fear of little childrennnnn.'

'Did you have a good night, Baba?' Odd asks, taking Baba's lantern from her.

'Of course I did, idiot.' Baba goes to a cracked mirror on the wall, removes her stained grey veil and preens her thin, greasy grey hair. 'Oh, look at my skin! Look how much younger and more beautiful I look than yesssssterday!'

'Beautiful, Baba. It's done you the world of good.'

She spits on the floor. 'What would you know, idiot boy?' She looks around the room, sniffs, and her eyes lock on Hope's, making Hope feel an icy jolt down her spine. Baba raises an eyebrow, smacks her lips and then turns away. 'I'm going to work on my spinning wheel for a while. Don't wake me for breakfast, idiot boy. I need my beauty sleep.'

With that she is gone, and the house fills with the click-clicking of her spinning wheel as she spins her magic thread.

Next night, after Baba leaves for the village, whistling in anticipation of scaring more children in their beds, Odd once again brings Elmo's cage out of the corner and prepares to take him to the treetops.

This time though, before he leaves, he makes another stop, climbing the stepladder to Hope's cage, bringing out a key and opening the door. She can only stand and stare at him.

'What's happening?'

'I thought you might like to come with us tonight,' says Odd. 'You were the one who suggested it, after all. If it wasn't for you, who knows what would have happened to Elmo.'

Hope knows very well what would have happened. 'Is this a trick?'

Odd shakes his patchwork head. 'No. No tricks. You don't have to come if you don't want.'

Hope edges to the door. Odd holds out a hand and she steps onto his open palm.

'Don't do anything stupid,' he says. 'If you try to get away, I won't give you another chance.'

'You don't have to worry,' Hope says. 'I don't fancy being out in the forest on my own when I'm this small anyway. I wouldn't last a night before a hawk or an owl gobbled me up.'

Odd gently lifts her down and slips her into his pocket. It's dark in there, and smells of dust and mud, but it is soft and warm. Hope pokes her head out of the top of the pocket as Odd climbs back down the ladder. He lifts Elmo's cage, ties it around his waist again with the magic yarn, and walks out to the porch. There he hoists himself up to the porch roof, showing great strength.

'Sorry,' he says, as Elmo's cage clangs off the side of the shack and Hope rolls around head over feet in his pocket. 'Hang on. Almost there.'

They are climbing in the trees now. Hope can hear the swoosh of the leaves and creak of the branches.

'Here we are,' says Odd at last. Hope pokes her head out of the pocket, breathing fresh, sweet forest air for the first time in ages. Odd is sitting on a thick, knotted branch with Elmo's cage on his lap. The sky is vast and clear and filled with points of starlight, and the moon is half full and shining brightly.

Elmo stretches his wings and raises up his head, his eyes closed as he lets the moonlight rain down on his scales and armour. Hope is happy just to be out of her cage, in the open night air. And she has never seen the world like this before. At her size, every leaf could float her down a stream like a boat, and there are knots and grooves in the branches that she could hide behind, or inside.

They sit in silence for a while, listening to Elmo's soft little sounds as he bathes in the light of the moon. There are also the wider sounds of the forest, the breath of the breeze in the trees, and the occasional hoot of an owl, howl of a wolf or lonely call of a troll.

Odd opens his mouth to speak a few times, and then seems to think better of it, until Hope can stand his indecision no longer.

'Is there something you want to say to me?'

Odd seems startled by her voice. He looks down at his pocket, and Hope stares up at him. 'I was wondering,' he says, 'if you really meant what you said last night. Would you really rather live just one more day free than live a hundred years with Baba?'

'I would,' she says. She can see the puzzlement in his eyes. 'Before Baba took me, I travelled all over the Dominion with my family, free as a mountain eagle. I miss that. I miss my family.' She feels a lump forming in her throat and swallows it back down. 'I think you'd like my family, Odd. First, there's Sandy. He's a mage, a good one. He helps people all over the Dominion. I've seen him treat sick little babies, and rid villages of bullies and robbers. I've seen him collect moonlight from magic ponds. Sandy knows what it means to really look after someone, Odd. Not like Baba. Sandy has been keeping me safe my whole life. And then there's Oliver.' She chuckles. 'He's a talking dog. He got a voice from a magical accident when he was a pup and he's never shut up since!'

Odd smiles briefly, but soon becomes serious again.

'But it's so dangerous out there.' He seems to be nodding to the world in general. 'There are so many things that can hurt you. They can hurt you with fists or claws or teeth. They can hurt you with words.'

'What happened to you,' says Hope, 'to make you so frightened? What happened to you that you'd rather spend your life serving a monster than live free?'

Odd looks up to the black-grey sky, blinks his mismatched grey eyes and curses the grey world.

'I wasn't born, you know. I was made.'

Hope blinks up at him from his coat pocket. 'What?'

Odd gives her a sad smile. 'I know how I look. I know you must be wondering how I came to be this way. It began with my papa. He was a fishing boat captain in a village called Rock.'

'I know that place,' Hope says. 'It's on the Eastern Sea coast. I've been there!'

'There you go,' says Odd. 'Then you'll be able to picture it right. This all happened years ago – long before you were born – but Rock has always looked much the same, houses all stacked and crooked on the jagged cliff. So, my papa was a captain, and one day they got caught up in a great storm. He said the waves were a hundred paces high that night.

'During the storm, papa spotted someone in the water, clinging to a big bit of driftwood. He pulled the drowning man from the sea. This was before the colour was gone from the world, and papa used to say the man he pulled from the water was so pale he was blue, and his eyes were yellow like a cat's. When the man woke up, he told my dad he was an explorer coming home from an expedition to the Eastern Lands, that his boat got chewed up by the storm and he was the only survivor. Papa said he never could figure out whether that was the truth, or whether there was another reason for the man being out there, but he always suspected there was more to it than that. He said that the man had strange tattoos on his hands and arms, and if you watched them carefully, they'd move around on his skin.

'Anyway, when they got back to Rock, the man – he never told Papa his name – he said, "I owe you a great debt. If you ever need anything, no matter how impossible it might seem, burn this parchment and I'll come and see you."

'He left Papa with this enchanted parchment and off he went. Papa never expected to see him again. But he kept that parchment.

'A few years went by. Papa and his wife had a baby girl,

and she was a beauty. Hair the colour of fire, Papa always told me, and a smile that could melt a glacier. Then, when the little one was only three years old, a sickness came to Rock. A lot of people died. Papa lost his wife. He lost his wee girl.'

Hope takes a sharp breath and covers her mouth. 'Oh, that's terrible. His heart must have been shattered.'

'Worse than shattered,' says Odd. 'Papa became a shadow. He might have kept breathing, and his heart might have been pumping, but he wasn't alive. Not really. Just there. Just existing. One night, after a fight in the pub, he went home, and he fell to his knees and screamed and screamed and cursed the world for taking his wee girl and leaving him behind. And that's when he remembered the parchment.

'"If you ever need anything, burn this," the man had told him, remember? "No matter how impossible it might seem." Papa was desperate. So that's what he did. He burned that parchment.

'Well, sure as Death, the man Papa had saved from the sea came knocking on his door the next night. Papa begged him to bring back his family, but the man said some things were beyond his power. "What I can do, though," he told Papa, "is bring you a new child, one who'll never leave you."

'And poor Papa was so desperate, so lonely, that he said yes.'

Hope is open mouthed. She has been around with

Sandy, and she likes to think she knows a thing or two about the world, even at ten years old, but she has never heard anything like this. 'And that was you?' she manages to ask. 'You were the new child.'

Odd is staring off into the dark sky. 'The first thing I can remember in this life is waking up, exactly as I look now, on the floor of Papa's cottage, and Papa was at the door, yelling after the man, telling him he didn't want me, that he'd made a mistake. But the man kept going, and soon it was only Papa and me.

'Well, you can imagine, I suppose, in a little place like that, nobody can keep a secret for very long. Soon everyone knew about me, about the monster who lived with the fishing captain. A lot of people stopped talking to Papa. People blamed me if things went wrong. If the winter was bad, it was because of me. If there was a summer drought, it was my fault. "The monster is cursed," they whispered to each other.'

Odd stops here to draw breath, and Hope can tell that he is reliving it all as if he is back in the village at this very moment.

'That's the sorry story. That's how I came to be, just the way Papa would tell it to me every single night when he was drunk.' His voice wavers. 'Then he'd tell me, every night, how I was a curse on his life and how he wished every day he hadn't asked for another child.'

Odd looks down at Hope, and there is so much sorrow and trouble in his eyes that it makes her heart ache. 'But it wasn't my fault, was it?' he says. 'I never asked to be made this way.'

'It wasn't,' says Hope, her eyes filling with tears. 'It wasn't your fault, Odd.'

He nods, wipes his eyes.

'So how did you end up with Baba?' Hope asks. 'Did you run away? I could hardly blame you if you did!'

'No. I didn't run away. I might not have been useful for much, but I'm strong, so Papa put me to work on his boat. You can imagine how the crew felt about that! But Papa insisted. One day, after we went a few weeks without a good catch, the crew mutinied. They grabbed me, and called me a jinx, and said the world would be better off without monsters like me in it.' He is breathing heavily now. 'The crew threw me overboard, into the sea.

'At first,' Odd continues, 'when I was in the water, I kicked my arms and legs and tried to swim. But then something occurred to me.' His ragged brow knits together. 'I realised that when the crew were throwing me overboard, Papa wasn't fighting to stop them. Wasn't trying to save me. He was just . . . watching . . .'

Hope's hands are clenched, her jaw tight.

'Nobody in the world was willing to fight for me,' says Odd. 'And so, I thought, what's the point in fighting for myself? And I shut my eyes and stopped kicking and thrashing, and I just let the waves carry me away. I went under, and after a while everything just faded to nothing.

'I woke up on a beach down the coast. Don't know how

long I was in the water or how far it took me. I just got up and began walking. I don't eat or drink, you see, so I didn't need to worry about that. I walked into the forest, and I walked and walked until the day I walked right into Baba. I told her my story and she said I'd be safe with her, that she'd look after me.'

Hope shakes her head. 'Only, it ended up the other way around, didn't it?' she says. 'You're the one who looks after Baba. That house is your cage, Odd. It might not have bars, but it's a cage just the same.'

He stares into her eyes, and he is crying. 'We best get back inside,' he whispers. 'No telling when Baba might come home.'

Hope does not push Odd to talk more. She can see that telling his story has left him exhausted, and no wonder, reliving a thing like that. She stays quiet in his pocket as he makes the awkward climb back down through the branches, with Elmo's cage swinging on the length of yarn tied around his waist. An hour or so in the fresh air and moonlight seems to have improved the wyvern's condition again. His grey-black scales are gleaming, and the cold glow of his eyes is a notch or two brighter. He is more alert too, looking around in fascination as they drop back onto the roof of the wooden house on legs, then onto the top of the porch. From there, Odd is careful to lower Elmo's cage before sitting on the edge of the porch roof and dropping nimbly down.

Odd has picked up the cage and is reaching for the door handle when the door swings open.

There, filling the enormous doorway, staring down at Odd and Elmo and Hope with burning fury in her colourless eyes, is Baba.

'Come back insssssside, my dears,' she says, and the ice in her voice freezes Hope's blood. 'There's some things we need to sort out.'

Chapter Twenty-One
In Which Hope Formulates
a Plan

Baba is lightning quick. She reaches down and grabs Odd by the scruff of the neck before he can blink, and with effortless strength she drags him into the cabin and slams the door shut.

'This is what you get up to whennnnnnn old Baba is away, is it?' she screams, slapping Odd repeatedly across the back of his bald, scarred head.

'No, Baba. Stop. Please!'

She wrenches the birdcage from his grasp and sneers, 'This wyvern belongs to me. Everything here belongs to me, and nothing moves from its place!'

'But he's sick, Baba. He needed moonlight.'

'I think I know better than you what my collection needsssssss.' Baba's voice has become a crazy, shrieking scream. Threads of drool fly from her rotten mouth and her lopsided eyes are wide and mad.

'You're wrong.' Odd's words are quiet, but they make Baba freeze.

'What did you say?'

She is holding Elmo's cage in one hand, and Odd by the back of the neck with the other. Now she sets Elmo down and turns her full attention to Odd, grabbing him roughly by the lapels of his ragged fisherman's coat. 'WHAT DID YOU SAY TO ME?'

From Odd's pocket, Hope stares up at the angry giant, huge globs of stinking drool narrowly missing her as they spray from Baba's lopsided mouth.

Don't push her too far, Odd, she thinks. *Not tonight.*

Perhaps he is still filled with anger and resentment from reliving his sad life story. Perhaps he feels emboldened somehow after talking with Hope. Or perhaps he has simply had enough. Whatever the reason, Odd chooses this moment to finally talk back.

'I said you're wrong.'

Baba lets him go and draws back. She staggers as if she has been stabbed, and clutches at her chest, and for the briefest of moments, the thought occurs to Hope that maybe Odd's words have actually harmed Baba in some way, broken a spell, or been enough to strip some of her power.

Then Baba's misshapen, twisted, ancient body begins to shake with fury. She opens her mouth and expels an inhuman roar, a sound that Hope has never heard, or ever wants to hear again. She knows without doubt that it is the true voice of a creature that does not belong in this world.

Odd staggers back, but Baba lunges at him, grabs him, picks him up so that her massive face is in his. 'This is how you repayyyyy Baba? I take you in and keep you sssssafe and you pay me back with sharp, hurtful words? Pah!' She shakes him hard, making Hope roll around inside his pocket. Then she rears back and throws Odd across the room. He hits the floor with a crash and somehow lands without crushing Hope, but the impact rattles her bones and makes flashes of light dance before her eyes for a few moments. Dazed, she crawls towards the pocket opening and peeks out in time to see Baba striding towards Odd.

'Look out!'

But Odd is stunned. Baba grabs him, roughly lifts him up again so that their faces are level. 'I knew you were up to no good soon as I got innnnn last night,' she spits. 'Could smell missssschief in the air. And I was right. Baba is always right.' She shakes him again, making his teeth bang together, and Hope flies helplessly about the pocket once more, her thoughts scrambled.

'Sneaking out of the house with one of my possessions!' Baba screams. 'I should tear your armsssss off. I should pull out your teeth with my fingers. Pop out your eyyyyyes and use them as marbles.'

'No!' Hope screams as loud as she can manage. 'Don't hurt him!'

Baba becomes still again. Her face is still stuck in Odd's, but one of her eyes swivels downward and finds Hope. Then, slowly, a bony, twisted hand comes down towards

213

Odd's pocket and plucks her out. Gigantically long fingers wrap around her, the skin turning sickly whitish green with Hope's touch, the nails thick and yellow and caked with grime. The hands lift her up until she is in line with Baba's face. Baba drops Odd to the floor with a thud, and her other eye now swivels to meet Hope too. Blasts of rancid breath stun Hope. She imagines how easy it would be for Baba to simply pop her into that horrible mouth and swallow her whole.

'Please,' she says, finding courage deep inside that she did not know she had. 'Don't hurt Odd. It was all my fault. My idea. I tricked him.'

Baba frowns. 'Tricked?'

'Aye. I told him the wee wyvern was sick and needed moonlight, that there was a special way of feeding him and I knew how. Odd was only trying to look after one of your collection. I thought if he took me outside the house I could escape, but he kept a close eye on me. He was too clever.'

Odd is picking himself up off the floor, his face a mix of pain and confusion. 'No, that's not what happ—'

'Shut up, idiot boy!' Baba squeezes Hope a little tighter, and she feels her ribs ready to pop. 'There was no trouble in thissss house before you arrived. If you were not such a preciousssss thing I might be tempted to take you to the village tomorrow night and feed you to a cat.' She sniffs Hope's hair, and Hope looks up the huge nostril and sees a nightmare she will never forget. 'But colour is such a rarity.

Such a treasure. You might be the greatest treasure in all of this little world, and you belonggggg to me.'

Baba lifts Hope and deposits her back in the cage, slamming the door. 'From now on, keep your yap shut.' Then she spins around and says to Odd, 'What are we goinggggg to do with you, eh? Can't have you talking to my collectionnnnn if it ends up like this. No, can't have that at all. I'll have to shut your trap for good.'

She lunges at him, grabs his collar and drags him off upstairs.

Hope sits in her cage, hugging her knees. All around, she can feel the keen eyes of the other creatures on her, and so she tries not to cry. She prays that Odd will be OK, but her mind imagines all sorts of terrible things.

Eventually footsteps echo upstairs, and then the small, shadowy figure of Odd descends the staircase.

'Odd,' whispers Hope, unable to keep quiet. 'Are you all right? Did she hurt you? Odd? Odd, please let me know you're all—'

She freezes when he looks up at her and she sees his face. It takes every bit of strength left in her body not to scream. But the shock soon gives way to seething, scorching anger.

Odd's mismatched eyes are overflowing with tears. He does not speak.

He cannot speak.

Baba has sewn his mouth shut.

'There,' says Baba, clapping her hands together as she

comes back downstairs, 'that'll teach you, idiot boyyyyy. No more gabbing to your little friend now. No more gossip. If you can't ssssspeak, you can't get yourself into trouble. I've done you a favour, really.'

Hope's anger is boiling, in danger of spilling over, but she knows that causing any more of a scene will do more harm than good. She breathes slow, shaky breaths, clenches her jaw and squeezes the bars of her cage tight.

'I am going to the village,' says Baba. 'Still plenty of darknesssss left in this night. Lots of time to scare the little childrennnnn while they dream.' She smiles, rubs her hands together and shuffles to the door. There she stops in the doorway to look back. 'A word of warning to you both,' she growls, pointing a long, crooked finger first at Odd and then Hope. 'I will know, when I come back, if you have been up to no good. Baba alwaysssss knows. And next time, I won't be so nice.'

She leaves with a thunderous slam of the door, and Odd rushes over to his little nest of blankets, buries himself away and begins to sob.

Hope sits for a while, feeling heartbroken and frightened and livid. She is surrounded by the gentle sounds of the many creatures in their cages. Some are already asleep again after the night's drama, while others, like the flower dragon and the rust bird, scrabble about in their sawdust beds and pick at their food. Everything in this awful place is a prisoner, and every one of them will eventually die without seeing the sky again, or feeling the outside air on their skin, if Baba is allowed to continue.

A nebulous idea has been forming in her mind these past couple of days, but Hope's anger seems to be sharpening her thoughts. She decides, at last, that she will not wait a moment longer. She must make a move.

'Odd,' she says, going back to the cage bars. 'Odd? Please come out.'

His muffled sobs and sniffs stop, but he does not appear.

'Please, Odd. I can't imagine how frightened you are, but surely you realise now that you can't stay here any longer. If you do, Baba will eventually kill you.'

Still nothing. Hope decides to try a different tack.

'Well, if you won't think about yourself, think of all the creatures in this rotten house. Think of what happened to Elmo. And he won't be the last, I can promise you that. In every single one of these cages a poor living thing is wasting away. You're the one who cares for them, Odd. You care *about* them too – I know you do. You love them, I think. And if you do, then you'll know deep in your heart what you must do. You must help me free them.'

A pause. Hope holds her breath. Then the nest of blankets shifts, and Odd comes out.

'There now,' she says, smiling, her eyes wet, 'that wasn't so hard, was it?'

He goes to the table, lights a lamp, and a soft white glow illuminates part of the vast room. Hope can barely bring herself to look at him, but she must. The last thing she wants is to make him feel like more of a monster than he already does.

He casts a worried glance towards the door.

'I think she's really gone this time,' Hope tells him. 'She's hungry, and she thinks she's got us beat.'

Odd's eyebrows raise up, and he gives Hope a look that says, *Hasn't she?*

'We're not beat,' Hope says. She stands as tall as she can manage. 'I think I can get us out of here, Odd. I think we can save all these creatures. Do you want that?'

He is still staring at the door, as if he expects Baba to come crashing through any moment. Then he tears his gaze away and looks up at her, the yarn that seals his lips shut giving off a weak grey glow. He nods.

Hope's shoulders relax a little and she exhales a slow rush of relief. She had been frightened that Odd would be too scared to help. But he is brave.

'I'll need your help,' she says.

He nods again, then raises his eyebrows, waiting to hear what she has to say.

Hope gathers her thoughts. She raises her hand, points to her wrist. 'This yarn. You said it only works for Baba because she makes it, right? On a spinning wheel she keeps upstairs?'

Another nod.

'I know you clean up there,' says Hope. 'You must have watched her make yarn a thousand times.' She pauses, her heart beating fast. 'Do you think you could work the spinning wheel, Odd?'

At first, he seems puzzled by the question. Then, as he begins to realise what Hope might be getting at, his eyes widen and flick about the place, like he is trying very hard to remember. After a little while, those mismatched eyes narrow, and he looks up at her and nods, slowly at first, and then faster.

Yes, he is trying to tell her. *I think I could work the wheel.*

Hope's heart is fluttering. 'We wouldn't need much yarn,' she says.

Odd holds his hands a little apart, palms facing each other, indicating a length.

'Maybe just a wee bit longer.'

He widens the gap between his hands.

'Aye,' says Hope. 'I think that will be grand.'

He drops his patchwork hands to his sides and takes a deep breath in and out.

'You sure you want to do this?' Hope asks.

He shoots her a sharp look.

'OK,' she says, her hands up. 'Just checking. Do you think you can make the yarn before she gets back? Last night she was away most of the night, and I reckon we still have a good few hours of darkness ahead of us.'

Again, he nods, before hurrying away up the stairs, almost tripping in his rush. Hope listens to his footsteps clomp overhead, hears a door creak open, and then quiet.

She begins, after a time, to think that Odd cannot get the wheel to work, but then a soft *click, click, click* drifts through the ceiling, and never has a sound been so welcomed by her ears.

She has seen a few spinning wheels in her travels with Sandy, and though she has never heard of an enchanted one, it makes sense. She can picture Odd sitting at the wheel, the patchwork boy's feet working the treadles, up and down, up and down, driving the wheel around, making it twist the yarn into being.

As she waits, every sound from the forest makes her jump, and she looks frequently towards the door, praying that Baba will not come home early. If she were to find Odd working her spinning wheel, then Hope supposes that would be the end of Odd completely, and the thought of that fills her belly with a heavy ball of dread.

Clickety, clickety, click goes the wheel.

And then the clicks are gone.

Footsteps echo through the ceiling once again, and as Odd comes downstairs, Hope squeezes the bars of her cage so tightly that her fingers cramp.

'Well?' she asks breathlessly. 'Did it work? Did you get some?'

Odd looks up, triumph sparkling in his eyes, and holds aloft a ragged-looking short length of silvery grey yarn.

Hope punches the air in delight. 'I knew you could do it,' she says. 'And you called yourself useless. Ha!'

Odd looks at the bit of yarn in his hand, and then at Hope. He holds out his hands, open palmed, and she knows what he is asking.

So? What's the plan?

Hope beckons him closer, and he climbs the stepladder

and brings his face close to her cage, making her wince at the look of the rough stitches sealing his lips shut.

Then, in a hushed voice, she tells him her plan.

Odd listens intently, nodding along with every detail. When Hope comes to the end, Odd holds his hand up and looks at the yarn sitting on his palm. It all comes down to that bit of string. And Hope can tell from the look in Odd's eyes what he is thinking.

What if it doesn't work.

'It'll work,' she says. 'I believe in you.'

CHAPTER TWENTY-TWO
IN WHICH DARROCH MAKES
HIS MARK

Darroch slips out of the farmhouse under cover of darkness, closing the door silently and moving across the yard to the shadow of the barn. There he stops and glances back, a pang of guilt flashing in his chest as he looks up at Gran's bedroom window.

Is he really going to go through with this?

Steeling himself, clenching his fists, he decides that, yes, he is.

Away he turns, into the night, down the dirt road to the edge of the farm and following the main track towards the City. See him there, a speck on the dark landscape, moving by the light of the moon? He passes no one at this hour, no carriages or caravans the entire way along the sweep of the sea cliffs. When the City comes into view, he stops, takes the canvas bag from his shoulder and brings out the wand and a box of matches. He strikes a match, lights the glob of magic on the end of the wand, and waits. The head of the wand sparks to life, and the glow of its flame forms a warm sphere of colourless light around him.

Nothing else happens.

Has it worked? Is he invisible?

He doesn't *feel* any different.

He throws the bag back over his shoulder, stands in the cool darkness and breathes the fresh, salty sea air, thinking things over. The only way to check if the spell works, he figures, is to try it out.

Ten minutes later, he approaches the City walls.

He swallows as he comes to the huge gates. They are open, as they always are, with one guard standing either side of the entrance. These guards, he knows, are ceremonial more than anything else. No one has dared attack the City in hundreds of years. But still, he thinks they might be suspicious of a young lad travelling on his own in the dead of night. If they see him, they might stop him. Might ask questions.

Might look in his bag.

On he walks, his feet silent on the road, his fingers clutching the wand tight. Beads of sweat form on his forehead. His heart races.

Closer to the gate he comes.

The guards continue to look straight ahead.

Closer still.

The guards do not react.

He steps through the gate, and they do not so much as blink. They have not seen him. The spell works!

This knowledge gives Darroch confidence, and he

smiles at the wand as he sweeps into the City proper to begin his task.

A few hours later, Darroch hurries back out of the City. As he passes the guards, his eyes are fixed on the wand. It is burned almost completely away. He should not have cut it this close. Is there enough life left in it to get him safely away from the City?

The guards do not see him as he goes, and when he is far enough away to be out of earshot, he breaks into a run. The flame wobbles and flickers.

'Just a little further,' Darroch pleads with it.

He makes for the cliff tops, and there he stops and drops to his knees, exhausted from his night's work. Here, at last, the spell fizzles out, but he is far enough away from the City, and it is still dark enough that he knows he need no longer worry. He lies on the grass for a while, catching his breath, smiling up at the stars.

He can't believe what he's just done. It feels strange, like a dream, like he was someone else for a few hours, someone brave and bold and daring.

At last, he gets up and walks wearily back along the road, smiling to himself as he climbs the track to the farm. Through the yard he walks, his legs heavy with tiredness. He opens the front door expertly, silently, and moves to the foot of the stairs, up one stair, then another, already imagining the warmth of his bed . . .

'Would you care to explain to me,' comes Gran's voice from behind him, 'where you have been?'

Darroch freezes. He swallows hard, then squeezes his eyes shut.

'Well?' says Gran.

Slowly, Darroch turns around. And there she is, standing at the front door, her arms folded and furious fire in her eyes.

The interrogation doesn't take long. Darroch cracks quite quickly, spilling his guts. He tells Gran about his meeting with Beth from the Rainbow League, about how, for a long time, he has wanted to help in the fight against the Emperor and Necromancer. How tonight was the night that he finally did something.

'How could you be so reckless?' she yells. 'After all I've done to protect you, to keep you out of it!'

'I don't want to be out of it!'

Stunned silence fills the kitchen. Gran's eyes are wide. It is the first time in Darroch's life that he has raised his voice to her, and they are both shocked.

'I'm sorry,' he goes on, quietly this time. 'But I can't stay out of it any more, Gran. Something inside me wants so bad to be part of the League. To put things right.'

She has been standing, but now she sits across from him at the table and puts her head in her hands. When she speaks, there is resignation in her voice. 'What did you do tonight, son?'

This time, Darroch doesn't crack so easily. 'I think it would be better if you saw.'

She looks up. 'Saw? What d'you mean?'

Sunup is a couple of hours later. The main road is not near as dead as it was in the middle of the night, and as Gran drives the horse and cart towards the city, they pass several other travellers.

'What a commotion!' one woman on horseback calls to them as she passes in the opposite direction. 'What a bloomin' commotion!'

Before Gran can ask, the woman is gone.

As they draw nearer the gate, they soon hear the echoing calls of Ripper Dogs from across the city. Gran glances suspiciously at Darroch, but he says nothing.

'What's happening?' she asks the guards at the City gate. Darroch recognises them from his adventure during the night. They look tired and frightened.

'Rainbows,' says one.

Gran raises an eyebrow. 'What?'

'Rainbows,' says the other guard with a gulp. 'Some beggar has only gone and painted bleedin' rainbows all over the City. On buildings, on the roads . . . even on the outside of the castle!'

'And what's more,' adds the other guard. 'They're in colour!'

Gran gasps. 'Colour?'

'I know!' says the first guard. He bites his bottom lip.

'It's terrible. Oh, the Emperor will be livid. And the Necromancer . . . who knows what she'll do!'

Gran urges the horses on, and the cart trundles through the gate and into the streets. Usually, at this time, the City would still mostly be asleep. Merchants and street sellers would be setting up for the day, and other early risers might be up and about. But this morning, only a short time after sunrise, the streets are buzzing. All about, people are huddling and chattering, and as they pass in their cart, Darroch and Gran catch snippets of excited conversation.

'They're everywhere! Rainbows all over the place!'

'It's the League that's done it!'

'Ripper Dogs are going crazy, sniffin' about, tryin' to find the culprit. They haven't found anything at all, I've heard.'

'The Emperor will be spitting feathers!'

'Never mind him, it's the Necromancer who should be worried.'

'Yeah? How d'you figure that?'

'Well, this is the work of the Rainbow Child, isn't it? Must be! She's back!'

Gran stares across the street to a place on a stone wall where a rainbow has been painted. Its colours are bright, dazzling, and her eyes drink them in, feeding her soul. A frightened-looking man is scrubbing madly at it with a wire brush, which is having no effect at all. When she turns to Darroch, she is holding back tears. 'You?' she whispers.

He nods, and is amazed when she reaches over and

squeezes his hand. She stares at him as if he is brand new, and there is such pride in her face.

'I'm still bloomin' angry with you,' she says.

'I know. I'm sorry.'

'No more secrets,' she demands, pointing a finger at him.

'OK, Gran. I promise. No more secrets.'

Chapter Twenty-Three
In Which Baba Tastes
her Own Medicine

The first splashes of dawn are painting the forest in lighter shades of grey when Baba comes home. Up in her birdcage, Hope lies on the straw and pretends to be asleep, though she is watching Baba through half-shut eyes.

At the sound of the closing door, Odd's nest of blankets moves, and out he comes, rubbing his eyes sleepily. He hurries to the table, pulling a chair out for Baba, and then goes to the stove.

'No,' Baba tells him. 'Leave it, idiot boy. Why would I be hungry, when I've been out feasting on the fear of little childrennnnn?' She smacks her lips and drums her nightmarishly long fingers on her swollen belly. 'I ate like a queen tonight, and now I am going to sleep like a baby.'

The sun comes up, and the grey tones of the world brighten. It is the sort of morning Hope imagines would burst with colour, if colour were ever to come back. But even as the birds sing their dawn chorus, and the grey flowers open up and drink the light of the colourless sun, Baba slips into a deep, contented sleep, her snores and grunts spilling downstairs.

Hope stands at the bars of her cage, listening. Far below, Odd stares up at her and opens out his hands. *Well?*

She worries her bottom lip and then says, 'Check she's properly asleep.'

Odd nods and creeps silently up the wooden stairs, knowing exactly the spots to avoid. He is only gone a minute or so, but the time stretches out before Hope, and her chest tightens with nervous anticipation. And fear.

At last, he returns and stands below her cage, giving the thumbs up.

'Did you leave her room door open?'

Another thumbs up.

Hope takes a slow breath in and out. 'Then I suppose it's time.'

Odd fetches the stepladder, unfolds it as quietly as he can beneath Hope's cage. He unlocks the little door and Hope steps onto his waiting palm, and the skin of his hand fills with darkest brown, the palms pink. On the other side of the deep scar around his wrist, the skin is pale and freckled, and disappears into the ragged sleeve of his dirty blue shirt. Hope's colour spreads up Odd's arm, over his shoulder, before fading out around the top of his neck, only just painting the point of his chin, which has a yellowish pink tinge.

'Let's go,' she says.

Odd's fingers close gently around her, so that her feet and head stick out from the thumb and little finger sides of his fist. He carries her down the stepladder, and as they move she is afforded a view into a number of cages, seeing inmates that she has been unable to from her own cage.

There is a dirt-streaked glass tank, in which a swarm of tiny, winged, golden things move as one undulating, flickering cloud. In another cage sits a ball of light grey, shivering fur. And in yet another, she spies a leathery little bag of bones with a yawning mouth of sharp teeth.

Behind a tall cabinet, in a dark corner, sits Elmo's cage.

Odd places Hope gently on the floor and she approaches the cage, where the shrunken wyvern is curled up. Already she can see that the lustre of last night's moonlight is fading from his scaly armour.

'Hello, boy,' she says in a soft voice.

The creature stirs, and sniffs, and gets slowly up. He comes towards her, and she reaches through the bars and rubs his snout, turning the grey-black scales many shades of darkest, pearlescent red. He closes his silver blue eyes, presses against her, and makes rumbles of pleasure at the colour she is transferring to him.

'I know,' she says. 'I'm scared too. But it's going to be all right. We want to get everyone out of here, but we need your help to make it happen. Will you help us?'

Elmo opens one eye and emits a soft series of low clicks.

Hope smiles. 'Remember the night we met?' she asks him. 'At the moonpond? The night you flew me to the stars? Will you let me fly with you again, Elmo?'

The wyvern opens both eyes and bows its head.

'I think,' Hope says, 'that means yes.' She can see confusion dawning on Odd's face as he realises what she's said, that she has met Elmo before. 'I'll tell you about it some other time,' she says.

Odd shrugs. He unlocks Elmo's cage and lifts the miniature wyvern out. At first Elmo seems bewildered, as if he does not remember life beyond the bars. He sits on the floor and looks from Odd to Hope and back.

'Fly,' Hope tells him. 'Fly, Elmo.'

The wyvern stretches his wings out gingerly, flexes his neck, and lets out a soft moan.

Odd gives Hope a doubtful look, and she can tell what he is wondering, because she is worried about it too. Has Elmo been in the cage too long? What if he can't fly any more?

She pushes the doubt away. 'He just needs to warm up,' she says. Then, to Elmo, 'Go on.' She moves towards him, a girl the size of a fieldmouse approaching a wyvern the size of a cat, and she pushes at his backside, trying to budge him. He yawns, stretches his wings again, and inches forward. Then he tries an experimental flap of his wings, the force of them blasting Hope backwards.

'Aye, that's it!' she says, channelling Sandy. 'Get up in the sky, yeh great silly galloot!'

This seems to do the trick. Elmo takes a few hesitant

steps. Then a few more. Then he breaks into a short run and, *whoosh*, his wings lift him off the ground.

He flaps once, twice, tumbles over in mid-air and comes crashing down onto the floor, rolling under a nearby cabinet with a thud.

Hope and Odd freeze. They stay perfectly still, straining to listen upstairs.

Thankfully, Baba's snores continue to come uninterrupted.

Elmo scrabbles back out from beneath the cabinet, shakes himself off, and tries again. One step. Then another. Then another.

Then a burst of speed, and a jump, and he is up, every beat of his wings taking him higher.

Flap

Flap

Flap

'Yes!' whispers Hope, punching the air as Elmo soars around the room, first in level circles and then adding swoops and spins and dives. After a dozen or so laps, he comes back down, but it seems he has yet to fully remember how to land, because Hope has to dive out of his way as he goes skidding into the side of his cage.

She rushes to him, hugging against him, the colour from her hands blossoming in his grey side, his scales and part of his belly, turning them shining, blackish red.

He swings his long neck around and, just as he did four years ago, he lifts her and sends her rolling into the nook on his back between his great wings.

'Wait for a minute,' she tells him, rubbing his back, seeing her colour paint each of his scales, spreading down his neck to the top of his horned head.

She nods at Odd, and away he goes, to the kitchen table, where he takes a long length of Baba's magical yarn and ties one end around the heavy table leg at roughly knee height. Next, he takes the other end of the string, walks to one of the tall cabinets across the room, pulls the line tight and ties that end around the handle of a drawer, so now the yarn stretches tautly between the two.

'It's time,' Hope whispers to the Elmo. 'Let's go see Baba.'

She pats his back, and the wyvern bursts forward and takes off with a few wingbeats. Hope holds on tight, a rush of great happiness coursing through her as the wyvern carries her up and up towards the ceiling, gathering speed, and makes another few laps of the room. From up here she can see the many creatures watching from their cages and pens. Even those that are usually asleep have awakened, maybe sensing something different in the air.

Then, with a wave to Odd, who is staring up in wonder, Hope pats Elmo once more, and he carries her up the staircase and through a massive door and a curtain of cobweb to Baba's room.

The room is dim, because the curtains are drawn, and the smell is thick and heavy. The only pieces of furniture in the room are a crooked wooden wardrobe and an enormous iron bed.

And upon the bed, beneath a mountain of filthy covers, lies Baba, fast asleep.

'OK,' Hope says, filling with self-doubt now that the moment has arrived. 'Take us down. Right on her pillow.'

Again, Elmo does as she asks, taking them down towards the bed, hovering over Baba, and coming down as softly as he can manage on the pillow just inches from her giant face.

Hope sits still on the wyvern's back for a long moment, taking in the hideous details of Baba's terrible features. Her mouth lolls wide, and from that stinking cave come blasts of breath that make Hope cross-eyed. From her nose sprout long, wiry white hairs and wispy whiskers stick out from the grey skin above her top lip.

'Jings, what a sight,' Hope whispers. Then she rubs Elmo's back and asks, 'Ready?'

He bows his head in answer.

Hope takes a deep breath, lets it out slowly, takes another and shouts, as loud as she can, 'Baba!'

Baba snorts and opens her eyes a fraction.

'Baba! Wakey, wakey! Rise and shine!'

Baba's eyes crack open more. She yawns, showing rotting teeth that, to Hope, are the size of tombstones. Her eyes are hazy and unfocussed, and Hope can tell that Baba is still in that place between sleep and awake.

Then Elmo raises a wing and slaps her across the cheek with a loud clap.

That does it.

Baba snaps awake. Her cloudy grey eyes fix on the wyvern, and then on Hope, and Hope can see realisation dawning in them. They stretch wide. The brow knits together. The lopsided mouth curls in a sneer of shock.

'I've decided I've had enough of this place,' Hope says. 'I'm leaving, Baba. And I think I'll take your collection with me.'

'What's this?' Baba sputters. 'WHAT. IS. THIS?'

'Now!' Hope yells.

Elmo takes them into the air just as one of Baba's great hands shoots from under the covers and grabs at the place they used to be. Up they fly, and Baba spews out a screech and falls out of bed, then scrambles up and stares in disbelief, before spitting a horrible scream of anger and flapping her too-long arms around, her hands swatting at the wyvern.

Elmo dodges and spins, dives towards the door, out into the hall, then turns back and hovers in the doorway.

'Come on then!' Hope shouts. She feels invincible on the wyvern's back. 'Come and get us!'

Baba stands in the centre of the room, her twisted body shuddering with fury.

She throws her head back and charges.

Elmo waits until the last moment, then spins away from Baba's flailing hands, takes a sharp right and dives down the staircase. As they go, Hope glances back just in time to see Baba skidding to the top of the stairs and then following, leaping after them, her eyes wild and mad.

'I'll get you! I'll get you both and you'll suffer!'

Hope holds tight as Elmo reaches the bottom of the stairs and takes a hard left. His wings beat, once, twice, three times, and they arrow across the room, Baba in hot pursuit.

'Nobody gets away from Baba!' she screams. 'Nobody takesssss my collection away from m—'

In her hurry, Baba has not seen the length of twine Odd tied across the room earlier. Her foot catches as she runs, and with a yelp of shock she tumbles, her arms windmilling around, and crashes chin first to the floor. There she lies, her twisted body sprawled awkwardly, until Odd appears from the shadows and, quick as a flash, takes the short length of yarn he made on the spinning wheel and ties it around Baba's wrist.

Hope looks on from the air.

Come on, she thinks. *Work. Please work, or else we're in deep trouble.*

But even as she wills Odd's twine to come to life, it seems that deep trouble is upon them. Baba has shaken off the fall and is getting back to her feet. She towers over Odd, a giant, twisted thing, and growls, 'I'm goinggggg to pick you apart, idiot boy. I'm going to pluck the wings off that leathery little bird up there.' Her eyes flick to Hope. 'And YOU, girl. You, I'm going to . . .'

She stops.

Her thick brow dances up and down. Her eyes cross and uncross, and her fingers twitch.

She starts to shrink.

237

Smaller and smaller she becomes, until she is no bigger than a small rat. She looks around the place, and then she notices the yarn tied around her wrist, and she begins to tug at it, to pull it and bite it. 'Get this off me! How dare you!'

Odd crouches over and picks her up in his patchwork hands. She wriggles and struggles but can't escape his grip. Hope urges Elmo down, and he lands on Odd's shoulder.

'Let me go, idiot boy!' Baba screams. 'I'll make you pay for this!'

'Aye?' says Hope. 'And how will you do that, indeed?'

'I'll get you. I'll . . .'

'You'll do nothing,' Hope says. 'Odd made that yarn around your wrist, made it on your own spinning wheel. He's the only one who can free you.'

Baba wrings her hands and wails and throws her head back. 'Oh, let me go, Odd. You were allllways a good boy. A smart boy. And old Baba treated you right, didn't she? Old Baba took you innnnn. Here, I'll show you how much you mean to me . . .' She waves a hand, and the yarn holding Odd's lips shut vanishes, leaving his mouth free. He wiggles his jaw experimentally.

'There now,' Baba says in what is supposed to be a sickly-sweet voice. 'Isn't that better? You mussssst understand, Odd, that old Baba only sealed your lips for your own good. So you couldn't speak to that devious girl. She's dangerous. She wants to break up our happy hommmmme.'

Odd shakes his head, indicates the many cages. 'All these creatures are suffering, Baba. I suppose I've always known that. But I ignored it, because I thought they were safer here than they were out in the world. But then Hope arrived, and she reminded me that life isn't just about being safe or hiding away. It's about living. I want to live again. I want everything in these cages to live. Set them free, Baba.'

Baba looks like she's tasted something disgusting. 'I won't! Not ever! They're minnnnne!'

'Then this is what's going to happen,' says Odd. 'I'm going to start a new collection. There's only going to be one thing in it. You. And you're going to find out what it's like to live in a cage.'

He reaches down with his free hand for Elmo's old cage.

'No!' Baba wails. 'Don't put meeeee in a cage! I'll die in a cage!'

'Then you know what you have to do,' Hope says from Odd's shoulder.

Baba stares up at her, hatred burning in her grey eyes. 'I wish I'd never set eyes on you, girl. Ten days, you've been with us, and that's all it's taken for you to poison everything. I. Hate. You. You're a curssssse.'

Hope smiles. 'No. I'm a mage. And I've been taught by the best. You're just lucky you didn't have to face him.'

Baba spits on the ground. 'I can see glimpses of your life, girl. I can see the man you're talking about. You think you know him? You don't know the first thing. You don't know who he really is. What he's done . . .'

Hope leans forward. 'What are you talking about?'

'Don't listen to her, Hope,' says Odd. 'She's trying to trick you. Set them free, Baba. Or else.'

Baba claws at her face. 'Fine. Oh, my collectionnnnn. My beautiful collection . . .'

'Now, Baba!'

Baba looks desperately around, but it seems she knows she is done. 'I set you free,' she says in a broken voice. 'I set you all free.'

The entire house rumbles, and shakes, and the floor moves. Then the shack starts to lower, the branches pinging and scratching on the walls, until the wooden house is sitting on the forest floor.

Odd bolts out of the door, off the porch, to the carpet of moss and leaves, while Elmo swoops off his shoulder and circles the house. As far as Hope can see, the huge chicken legs have disappeared. Maybe they've dug deep into the ground or folded up into some hidden place beneath the house.

Through the open door, all the cages of Baba's collection float out of the house, into the forest air. There are dozens and dozens of them in a bobbing line, and they float around the place and softly touch down on the ground. When the last cage is down, the bars turn to dust and scatter in the breeze.

A warm feeling starts in Hope's chest, spreads out into her limbs and head and fingers and toes. She is still sitting on the wyvern's back, and he is making low purring sounds, his body vibrating.

There is an instant when Hope feels like she is being stretched, and then a loud *POP*, and in the next moment her view of the world changes as Elmo returns to his regular, gigantic size. Hope stares down at her hands and body, and she sees that she is no longer tiny either, and all around, the creatures of Baba's collection are springing back to the way they ought to be. A tiny ball of fur is now the size of a boulder. A unicorn is bigger than a shire horse. A fanged cat grows and grows until its fangs are like knives and its paws as big as dinner plates.

The creatures begin to form a circle around Odd, and the circle tightens as they come closer, sniffing at the air, and growling. Not growling at Odd, Hope realises from her place on the wyvern's back. He was the one who fed them and cleaned them and looked after them. No. They are growling and spitting and hissing at Baba.

'I've done my bit!' she screeches from Odd's hand. 'I've put you all back as you should beeeee. Now it's time for you to turnnnnn me back too, Odd.' She holds up her wrist, flashing the length of yarn tied around it.

Odd frowns. 'I don't remember saying anything about turning you back, Baba.' He glances up at Hope. 'Do you remember me saying that I would?'

Hope smiles at him. 'Nope.'

Baba grunts and struggles against Odd's grip, but there is no escape.

'Releassssse me!'

Odd shares a look with Hope, and she smiles. It seems they are thinking the same thing.

'OK,' says Odd. 'I will. I'll let you go.'

He crouches and places Baba on the ground, and there she stands staring about, wide-eyed, as the creatures from her collection close in around her, hissing and growling.

'Stay back!' Baba screams. 'All of you! I'm warning you all!'

'I'd start running now if I were you, Baba,' says Hope.

Baba gives her a look filled with hate, and then spits at the ground. The unicorn brays and drags a hoof along the ground, getting ready to charge. Baba jumps in the air, spins and begins to run just as the big cat pounces. It misses her by a whisker, and she screams and goes scrambling up onto the porch and into the house, the door slamming shut.

The great legs explode upward from under the wooden house once more, lifting it up, and the house turns away and runs into the forest. As it goes, it shrinks until it looks like a nightmarish dollhouse. Baba's newly-freed collection stays in hot pursuit, swooping down upon the house, nipping at its legs, swooping down and banging on the windows. Baba's screams and screeches and curses echo away into the distance, until all trace of the house, and of Baba's collection, is gone, and all that remains is a ragtag trio. A girl blazing with colour in a world of black and white, a patchwork boy and a moon wyvern.

And they are free.

Chapter Twenty-Four

In Which there is a Reunion
and a Parting

Look.

See there, that speck soaring across the colourless, cloudless sky?

There they fly, Hope and Odd, on the great wyvern's back, high above the sprawl of forest and river and far off mountain. They fly and fly, Hope using the stars for guidance the way Sandy taught her, until the sun dips below the edge of the world and the moon takes its place in the night sky, and then they land in a glen and drink from a crystal stream as Elmo soaks up the moonlight.

The following morning, they set off again, and they have been flying for a few more hours when at last Hope leans forward, her heart quickening.

'There. On the edge of the forest. That's it!'

The village comes into sight, and behind it, the rolling meadow where a number of caravans still sit, smoke belching upwards from campfires. Hope can't tell from this height whether Sandy's caravan is among them, but she can't imagine that he would leave the moon market while many of his fellow mages need help. There would be much work to do, repairing the damage caused by the Necromancer and her Ripper Dogs and Black Coats. And, if she knows Sandy at all, he will also have stayed to organise searches for her. He will not give up on her, just as she would never give up on him.

'I don't think we should land there,' Hope tells Elmo, patting his back. 'Don't want you scaring the villagers, do we? Maybe down in the trees would be better?'

Elmo takes them down with slow, easy grace, circling lower and lower, until he brushes down through the grey trees and lands on the forest floor, then lowers a wing so that Hope and Odd can dismount.

Hope hurries towards the meadow, but stops when she realises that Odd is not following.

'What's wrong?'

He licks his scarred lips. 'I can't go out there. They'll call me a monster. They'll chase me away, or worse.'

'You don't know that for sure,' says Hope.

'Oh yes, I do. I'll frighten them – maybe not all of them, but enough to make a mob. Look at me, Hope.' He holds his arms open. 'I'm a monster.'

Hope shakes her head, walks towards him and takes his mismatched hands. Her colour floods his skin, a patchwork of different tones, from darkest brown to pinkish white. 'You are not a monster. You're brave and kind, and you're my friend.'

He gives her a sad smile. 'I wish everyone could be like you.'

'Will you wait here while I go look for Sandy?' she asks. 'If he's here, he'll help you. I know it.'

He backs away a step. 'Oh, I don't know about that . . .'

'Please? He's been protecting me since I was a wee baby. He might be able to help you too.' She's sure Sandy will be able to help somehow. He can fix anything. She watches Odd closely. He takes a deep breath, glances at Elmo, and the huge black-grey wyvern rumbles at him.

'Fine. But I'm not coming out there.'

'You won't have to!' she says, happiness inflating in her chest. She's almost about to wheel away but stops herself when she realises that her vibrant colour is on full display. Her hands fumble in her coat, bring out the little bottle and she takes a few drops of the sweet-tasting potion, and then a few more, just to be sure.

The magic works almost instantly. The warmth of colour in her body fades and chills, and the colour drains from her skin and clothes and hair, until she is all shades of grey once more.

She gives Odd another smile, seeing the amazement in his face at her transformation. Then she is running, as fast as her legs can carry her, laughing despite her tiredness and the cold void in her heart left behind by colour. She bursts from the trees, bolts out over the meadow, drawing looks from mages even as they are busy repairing their damaged caravans, or cooking, or mixing magic.

The sound of the meadow is all hammers and saws and shouts, and Hope dodges through the place, searching, searching, until . . .

There he is.

She stops, hardly able to believe that she is looking at Sandy again. Presently, he is helping to attach a new wheel to a wagon, but, as if he can feel her eyes on him, he suddenly stops and is still for a moment before he turns slowly around.

When his eyes find her, she cannot stop the tears coming. At first Sandy stares at her blankly. He looks exhausted, shattered, broken, and she is afraid that maybe something happened to him in the chaos of the Ripper Dog attack, that he no longer recognises her.

Then his face lights up, joy chasing away the dark shadows under his eyes, and he says, 'Hope? Is that really you?'

'Aye, Sandy.'

He laughs, and bursts forward, and Hope throws her arms around him, crying and laughing at the same time as he lifts her up and twirls her around and hugs her tight. 'I thought yeh were gone, lassie,' he says. 'I thought I'd lost yeh.'

'I'm back,' she says, her eyes closed tight.

The sound of barking, and then Oliver is on the scene too, the little dog jumping up and licking her, his tail wagging madly. 'Oh, Hope! You're back! You're OK!'

'But where have yeh been, lass?' Sandy asks, composing himself. 'We've spent days searching all about here.'

'I'll tell you everything,' says Hope. 'But first there's something you must see.'

Odd is hiding behind Elmo when Hope leads her family into the forest to meet him, but soon the wyvern nudges him out into the open, where he comes face to face with Sandy.

'Don't worry, my friend,' Sandy says softly. 'I'm not going tae hurt you. Hope has told me a little about how you helped her. But I'd like to hear the whole story now, if yeh don't mind.'

Together, Hope and Odd tell him everything, from Baba's collection to her magic spinning wheel, from Odd's sad past to their eventual escape. Sandy listens with great concentration, and when they are done, he takes off his hat and runs his hands though his messy hair.

'My, what a tale. What a tale, indeed.'

'What do you think Baba is?' asks Hope.

'Yeh remember, lassie, me telling yeh that there are other worlds than this? How sometimes things can push through, where the borders are thin?'

Hope nods. 'So she doesn't belong here?'

'I know how she feels,' says Odd, running a finger over the thick scar around his wrist, where the light skin borders the almost black skin of his hand.

Sandy lets out a long sigh. 'It sounds to me, laddie, like you were created by powerful magic from another land, magic that I neither understand nor want to mess with, for fear of doing more harm than good.'

'So you can't help him?' Hope asks, crestfallen.

'Maybe no in the way he'd like,' says Sandy. 'I cannae make him look different, if that's what yeh mean. But why should he have to look the same as everyone else to be accepted in the first place?'

'That's easy for you to say,' says Odd. 'You *do* look like everyone else.'

'Aye,' says Sandy. 'Yeh're right there, laddie. And I can't begin to imagine what it must be like to be in yehr shoes. But yeh are welcome to travel with us, Odd. I can promise yeh my protection.'

'You'd do that for me?' Odd says in a hushed voice.

'Hope could not have made it home without yeh, and for that I'll always be in yeh're debt, son. So? What do yeh say? Will yeh come with us?'

Hope looks from Sandy to Odd, her eyebrows raised.

'It's kind of you,' Odd says after some thought. 'I'm grateful. But ... I don't think I'm ready for that yet. I think ... I think I want to spend some time just being free for a while. Living in the forest, out of the way.' He nods to the great wyvern nestled in the shade of the trees. 'And someone needs to keep an eye on Elmo for a while. I'll make sure he gets back to health.'

Hope cannot help feeling disappointed, but she would never try to change Odd's mind or force him into staying.

'Well,' she says, 'when you are ready, we'll be waiting. Won't we, Sandy?'

'Aye.' Sandy nods, then something seems to occur to him. 'Hold on. Wait here for a minute . . .'

Off he goes, back towards the edge of the forest and the meadow, returning a few minutes later with a pair of identical silver objects in his hands. They look like pocket watches, their shining lids decorated with swirls and flourishes. 'Here,' he says, handing one to Odd and the other to Hope. 'These are bond mirrors. If one of them is open, no matter how far away, the other will glow and sing like a bell. Try it.'

Hope takes one of the objects from Sandy, and Odd the other. The lid clicks smoothly open, revealing a small, perfect mirror. A moment later, the mirror in Odd's hand trembles and glows and lets out a crystal, bell-like note.

Odd's patchwork face fills with wonder when he opens the mirror. 'I can see you!' he says.

'Me too!' exclaims Hope. It is quite an extraordinary thing. Through the instrument in her palm, Hope can see out of Odd's mirror. There he is, his amazed face filling the frame.

Sandy says, 'If yeh ever need anything, Odd, yeh only have to open your mirror and ask for help. But you must remember that the further apart the mirrors are, the more of the spell they'll use up. You might only get a minute or two, so you should keep them until you're in a real fix.'

Hope stares down at this marvellous object, and she thanks her lucky stars that she has Sandy and his magic in her life.

'Thank you,' Odd says, tucking the mirror away.

Musical laughter rings through from somewhere nearby in the forest, and Sandy says, 'It's probably no safe for the wyvern to be here. If the villagers come across him while they're out hunting or picking fruit, there could be trouble.'

'You're right,' says Odd. 'I suppose we'd better go.'

Hope approaches the moon wyvern, places her hand on his side; he closes his eyes and rumbles, and she feels his great muscles rise and fall with every breath.

'Bye, Elmo. Thank you.' Then she leans in and whispers, 'Look after Odd, won't you?' Another rumble from the wyvern lets her know that, yes, he will, and she presses her head against the side of his snout and then turns away towards Odd.

'Well,' he says, 'I suppose this is goodbye. For now.'

'Aye,' says Hope. 'Look after yourself, Odd.'

'You too, Hope.'

She grabs him and hugs him tight, and she can feel from how rigid his body becomes that he is shocked by this. It occurs to Hope that maybe nobody has ever hugged Odd before. Then she feels his arms wrap around her, and he is hugging back.

'Thank you,' he whispers in her ear. 'If you hadn't come along, I'd probably have been stuck with Baba forever, hiding away from the world. I'll never forget it.'

He breaks away from her and climbs onto Elmo's back. The wyvern stands up, rumbles, gives Hope one last look with his glowing eyes, and then, with a couple of steps and a few powerful wingbeats, he is up in the air, brushing through the treetops and into the clear, colourless sky. Hope watches them climb up and up, almost feeling the wind in her hair, imagining that she is with them, until, at last, they are out of sight.

Sandy gives her a sideways look. 'You all right, lassie?'

'Mmm? Oh, aye – I mean, yes, I'm fine.'

'It's good to have yeh back, Hope.'

She smiles. 'It's good to be back.'

And off they walk, towards the meadow and the waiting road, Hope wondering if she'll ever see Odd or Elmo again.

She will, of course.

But not yet.

PART FIVE

THE TURNING TIDE
(Twelve Years After the Wish)

Chapter Twenty-Five
In Which We Meet an Unsavoury Character

The heat of the summer night is stifling as Gloria, Sandy's fine shire horse, pulls the caravan across the creaking wooden bridge of Crescent Canyon in the far south of the Dominion.

'I can't wait to see the caves,' says Hope, sitting beside Sandy on the driver's bench. 'It's been ages.'

'Aye,' says Sandy. 'It will be good tae see the Night Caves again. They're always a sight for sore eyes, so they are.' He pulls on the reins, guiding Gloria around the rocky trail, then turns his attention back to Hope. 'Have yeh taken yehr medicine?'

'Yes,' says Hope. 'Haven't I, Oliver?'

The scruffy little black dog is sprawled over her knees, eyes shut as she scratches his ears. 'Mmm?' he says. 'Oh. Yes. I saw her take it.'

'Well, maybe take another wee drop, just tae be safe. You know how unpredictable your colour is getting now.'

Hope sighs, reaches into her pocket, brings out the bottle and takes a swig of the potion that has hidden her colour for all these years. She is twelve now, growing up, and the world is changing. Sandy's hair is a lighter shade of grey and his face more lined. Oliver is a little slower at bringing back a stick when they play fetch. And Hope herself has been feeling her colour growing stronger, almost by the day.

A year ago, the Emperor saw fit to make moon markets illegal, and oh, how Hope has missed those gatherings. But they have been replaced by secret meetings, in rooms above taverns, and in the cargo holds of boats, and in clearings in the middle of the great forest, because mage magic is made to be shared and traded, and nothing is ever going to stop that.

So, magic itself is under attack, and as they reach the moonpond on the other side of the canyon, surrounded by twisted trees and thorny bushes, Hope sees the reason that Sandy is so keen that she should be taking more colour-hiding potion.

A small caravan is parked on the water's edge.

It is the caravan of a tax man.

The Emperor has decided, in his infinite wisdom, that there shall be a tax on any moonlight collected by mages from the moonponds. It is just another way the world has changed.

Sandy pulls the caravan up beside this other wagon, and the door opens and out comes a small, round man. What little is left of his hair is scraped across a shining bald scalp that reflects the light of the burning white lamps in the window of his little home.

'Good evening,' he says, approaching the caravan, hands clasped over his beer gut.

'Evening,' says Sandy.

'Are you here to collect?' the tax man asks.

Sandy nods.

'How many bottles?'

'Three.'

'You know the price?'

'Aye.' Sandy reaches down and drops a jingling bag of coins into the tax man's waiting grey palm.

The tax man opens the bag, counts, closes it again. He takes a handkerchief and dabs the sweat from his brow. 'Very well,' he says. 'Carry on.'

Sandy gives him a nod and Hope breathes a sigh of relief. As Sandy climbs down from the driver's seat, Hope starts to follow, but he stops her.

'No. Stay inside this time.'

She blinks and is about to argue when she sees the seriousness in his expression and backs off. Maybe he's right. Something in the air feels . . . off.

She goes back into the caravan with Oliver and sits at Sandy's desk.

'You smell frightened,' Oliver tells her, pressing his muzzle against her. 'Are you all right?'

She pulls the curtain aside and peeks out towards

the moonpond, where Sandy is filling his bottles with glowing silver magic. 'I don't know. I have a bad feeling in my gut.'

'Maybe,' says Oliver, 'it's the stew Sandy made for dinner.'

Hope doesn't laugh. She continues to watch Sandy, and then something tells her to look in the other direction, and she realises with a start that the tax man is watching her closely through the window of his own caravan. She shuts the curtain, drums her fingers on the desk, and is horrified to see the first sparks of colour in her fingertips.

'Your medicine,' says Oliver.

She nods, and with clumsy fingers unscrews the lid and takes more of the potion. The colour does not go. 'It's because I'm nervous,' she says, beginning to feel her stomach turn loops. 'It's more unpredictable when I feel scared.'

'Breathe,' Oliver says. 'In and out. Nice and slow. That's it. Nothing is going to happen to you. Sandy and I are here.'

Hope nods, watches her fingers. She feels her heart slow with each deep breath, and at last the potion takes effect, chasing the colour away and leaving her fingers dark grey.

'That was too close,' she says. It seems to take forever for Sandy to come back to the caravan, and when he does, Hope says, 'I've changed my mind. I don't want to see the caves this time. Can we just go, please?'

He nods. 'Aye. Something tells me you're right, lassie.'

Sandy climbs back onto the driver's seat, takes the reins and thanks the tax man.

'Going so soon?' the tax man says.

'Aye. Places tae be, I'm afraid. The work of a drifter mage is never done.'

He urges the horse to move, but she has taken them no further than a few paces when the tax man calls, 'Actually, would you mind waiting for a minute?'

Hope, who has stayed inside the caravan with Oliver, shares a worried look with the little dog as the caravan stops. 'What's going on?'

'I don't know. I'll go and take a loo—'

Oliver becomes very still, rooted to the spot, and the hackles on his back stand up. He bares his teeth, which is very unlike Oliver, and emits a low growl.

'What's the matter?' Hope rushes forward, opens the door. 'Sandy, what's happ—'

The rest of her words get stuck in her throat. A cold veil of fear drops over her. Out in the dark, beyond the edge of the moonpond, two glowing eyes blink in the darkness. They come closer, stalking, until a great black form steps into the light. A dog the size of a horse, with a black matted coat and a faceless, hooded rider upon its back.

Slowly, very slowly, Sandy reaches down towards his feet, to the place he always stashes his bow and quiver of arrows when they are on the road. He lifts the bow, places the end of the arrow shaft upon the string, draws the string tight and aims.

'Tell that thing not tae come any closer.'

The tax man's eyes are wide. He holds up his hands. 'Now, now. Let's not do anything silly, eh? It's just a routine check of your caravan. If you're not smuggling colour, you have nothing to worry about.'

Sandy draws his bow tighter.

'Don't,' Hope whispers to him. She feels like her heart might explode from her chest.

'We cannae risk it,' Sandy whispers. 'I'm no letting one of those things anywhere near yeh.'

Across the moonpond, the Ripper Dog barks thunderously. Its glowing eyes are fixed upon them, and its rider is motionless upon its back.

'Put the bow down,' says the tax man. 'You are only making matters worse for yourself.'

'Oh, aye?' Sandy's eyes do not leave the Ripper Dog or Black Coat, not for a single moment. Time seems to freeze.

And then he lets the arrow loose.

It zips through the lamplit night, explodes into the chest of the Black Coat, which turns instantly to ash and blows away with the summer breeze.

The Ripper Dog howls, bounds forward around the pool, snarling and slobbering, its paws skidding on the dry grass as it tries to get to them.

Sandy lets another arrow loose, but it screams past the great beast's head. He curses as Hope yells out. The Ripper

Dog is almost upon them. It launches itself from the ground, flies through the air . . .

Sandy stays calm, steady handed. He takes another arrow, draws the bow . . .

Thwack!

The arrow pierces the creature through the eye. It makes a horrible, yelping sound and crashes to the ground, skidding to a stop against the tax man's caravan, causing it to rock. The tax man makes a series of unintelligible, frightened sounds. He gags and chokes as the Ripper Dog's carcass starts to bubble.

'Hold on!' Sandy yells. He snaps the reins. Gloria whinnies and starts to move.

'Sandy! Look!' Hope points ahead, her hand shaking wildly. 'There's more of them!'

They are coming up the only path out of the moonpond. Six sets of glowing eyes. Six Ripper Dogs. Six Black Coats.

Sandy heaves the reins, making the poor horse skid to a stop. He looks around wildly. 'Grab yehr bow.'

Hope nods, rushes inside, grabs her bow and quiver.

Sandy has already jumped from the caravan.

'Turn yourself in,' the tax man yells, running for his own wagon, slamming the door shut behind him. 'There's no escape now!' he adds, peering through the curtains.

Sandy ignores him, taking Hope's hand, helping her down. Oliver comes too.

'The caves,' Sandy says. 'If we can make it inside, we might have a chance.'

'OK,' says Hope.

They make a sprint for it, past the moonpond, to the place where a high wall of rock juts out of the dusty grey ground. The howls and barks from behind grow louder, and Hope knows without looking back that the Ripper Dogs are close. Oliver skids, stops running, spins around. Hope looks over her shoulder to see the little dog charging at the nearest Ripper. He yaps and snarls and leaps at it.

'No!' Hope screams as the Ripper Dog bats Oliver away with an enormous paw, and he flies through the night like an insect, hits Sandy's caravan and slams down on the ground, where he is still.

'Come on!' Sandy has Hope by the sleeve, pulling her, dragging her. Then they are at the cave entrance, and with one last look back, Hope follows Sandy into the waiting dark.

Chapter Twenty-Six
In Which there is Deep Trouble

'Sandy, watch out!'

'Hope! Run!'

Sandy pulls another arrow from his quiver, aims his bow and lets his shot rip through the tunnel. The arrow pierces the chest of the charging Ripper Dog, sending the enormous beast clattering to the ground and its rider flying into the rock wall. The Black Coat springs up, spins around just as Sandy lets another arrow loose. His aim is true. The Black Coat falls and turns to dust.

Sandy hurries towards Hope, who is hiding in the shadows. All about them, the roars of more Ripper Dogs echo from adjoining caves.

'What now?' Hope asks.

'Stick close,' Sandy tells her. 'Ready your bow.'

She does as he asks, taking her own bow and an arrow from her quiver as Sandy retrieves his arrows, one from the rocky floor where the Black Coat stood, the other from the bubbling, spitting body of the Ripper Dog.

He leads Hope further into the tunnels. Their way is lit by brightly glowing algae that grows on the damp walls and roof of the caves, their ghostly grey-white light bursting from a million, million star points.

Around a tight corner they creep, and then Sandy stops dead. His arm reaches out across Hope, holding her back. The deep, rumbling growl of a Ripper Dog echoes along the tunnel wall, and then it suddenly ceases.

Hope strains to listen over the crazy drum of her heart.

Nothing.

She looks at Sandy, and he frowns, his eyes darting about as he listens. Then his eyes become wild, and he grabs her and pushes her out in front of him. 'Run!'

An ear-splitting howl blasts down the tunnel, making Hope cover her ears. Behind Sandy, back along the cave tunnel, a huge shadow with glowing eyes lumbers forward in the glow of the algae.

'Go, Hope!' Sandy screams.

'I won't leave you!'

He grabs her by the shoulders. 'RUN!' He spits as he yells in her face, and he pushes her away. 'Get out of these caves and hide. I'll hold them off as long as I can!'

He spins away down the tunnel towards the approaching Ripper Dog and its Black Coat rider. Hope's eyes blur with tears as he draws his bow.

Hating herself, cursing the world, she turns away and runs.

The warren of caves is tangled and labyrinthine, and she does not know which way to turn. Left then right she goes, again and again, hoping that the next corner will bring fresh air and a way back into the night. Praying that she will not run into a Ripper Dog.

The tunnel widens, and she comes out in a natural chamber of rock coated in millions of points of glowing algae, leading to five other caves. Five possible ways out. Or five ways deeper beneath the ground.

'Hope!'

Her heart lifts. She wheels around, listening. 'Sandy! I'm here!'

'I'm coming, Hope!'

She waits, listens. Sandy's footsteps drift along the tunnel, strangely slow and dragging, and when he steps into the clearing and the light of the concentrated algae falls upon him, she gasps. He is limping heavily. His right trouser leg is ripped open, and through the tear she can see a deep, bubbling wound.

She runs towards him as he staggers into the chamber and falls.

'Sandy! You'll be all right. It's going to be fine.' Her head is spinning with panic and fear. The smell from the wound on his leg makes her gag. The skin sizzles, and she can see a huge puncture wound, presumably from one of the Ripper Dog's fangs. 'What should I do?'

'My coat,' Sandy manages to say. 'There's a wee bottle of moonlight in . . . in one of the pockets. Pour it on . . .'

She nods, begins to search his coat, but her hands are trembling badly, fighting against her.

Before she finds the bottle, a cacophony of growls from the surrounding tunnels makes her freeze. The rumbles grow louder as Hope's eyes flick around the chamber, from one cave entrance to the next. Which one? Which way will the Ripper Dog come?

As it turns out, they come from all of them.

Five Ripper Dogs lumber from the caves. They stand around Hope and Sandy, and Hope sits down and cradles Sandy's head in her arms. He coughs and gurgles.

'Ssshh,' she says softly. 'I'm here. We're together.'

The Ripper Dogs edge closer, their lips drawn back over their huge, poisonous fangs. Upon their backs, the Black Coats look down upon Hope and Sandy from somewhere deep in their dark hoods.

As one, the Ripper Dogs throw back their heads. They howl, a terrible, blood-chilling sound. They are hungry, and they are about to feast.

Chapter Twenty-Seven

In Which Colour Shows
its Strength

Hope holds Sandy tight. Her entire body shakes with uncontrollable terror. All around her, huge, snarling, tearing jaws close in.

She knows now that these will be her final moments, that she will die the same way her parents did, and she wonders if this is how they felt at the end.

She wonders, now that it is her turn to cross the river in the Ferryman's rowing boat, if her mum and dad will be waiting for her on the other side of the water.

The hot, rancid breath of the Ripper Dogs brushes her face now.

She closes her eyes, and she waits.

'Colour.' The whisper comes from Sandy and is so quiet she is not sure she heard right.

'What?' she whispers, still cradling his head.

'Colour, Hope,' he manages to say again. 'Colour is our only chance now.'

Colour?

The word floats around in her mind.

Colour. What does he mean it's our only chance?

Colour!

The word flares to life in her brain, and she realises, or thinks she does, what Sandy is talking about.

Colour. These monsters are sensitive to colour. What happens, then, if their senses are overloaded?

The jaws close in.

Hope clenches her own jaw. All the fear and anger boils over inside her. The pressure builds and builds and then . . .

Her body fills with heat, and light, and warmth. She opens her eyes and sees that her hands are brown, her dress blue. This time the colour is fierce, glowing with a dazzling, powerful radiance.

The Ripper Dogs whine and back off from the intensity of the colour radiating from Hope. They buck and shake, throwing off their Black Coat riders.

Hope looks around at them all, and she no longer feels frightened.

When she speaks, her voice echoes powerfully around the chamber.

'Leave. Us. ALONE!'

She clenches her fists as the power in her reaches a white-hot high, and the cavern fills with blazing colour. The glow of every point of light from the algae-covered walls turns from grey-white to dazzling, greenish blue. The colour grows stronger and stronger, brighter and brighter, and the Ripper Dogs and Black Coats howl and wail and try to run.

Then, with one final yell of fury, Hope lights the place up so brightly that she shields her eyes, and screams.

And then all is quiet.

The colour dies down in its intensity, though it does not leave the cavern. Blinking, Hope stares around the chamber, looking for the Ripper Dogs.

But they are no longer there.

Instead, shadows of the monsters have been burned into the walls, as if the scorching power of Hope's colour has left an imprint on the world, a scar where these unnatural creatures used to be.

Sandy coughs, bringing her round, and she gasps and resumes her search of his pockets, finding the tiny bottle of moonlight, opening it, pouring it over the bubbling, festering wound.

Sandy screams. He claws at the air, and his eyes roll back in their sockets. Then he lets out a long breath, and blinks, and his eyes open, apple green and alive.

'Hope,' he says in a barely there voice. 'You did it.'

She helps him out of the cave, taking a large part of his weight. His leg looks better than it did, but she will be surprised if there isn't some permanent damage. They get to the caravan, where Sandy manages to climb onto the driver's seat. Next, she hurries around to the opposite side of the wagon, to the place Oliver fell.

The little dog is lying on his front, awake, looking quite stunned.

'That,' says Hope, wagging a finger, 'was the most stupid, foolish . . . bravest thing I've ever seen!' She picks him up in her arms and kisses his furry head, and he licks her face. 'Don't ever do anything like that again.'

'It was a moment of madness,' he says, his voice a little dopey from the knock. 'Do we have any sausages?'

She laughs, carries him around to the door and places him gently into the caravan. A twitch of light catches her eye, and she spins and sees the curtains of the tax man's caravan close with a jerk.

'I forgot about him. What are we going to do?'

The question is for Sandy, but he is slumped on the driver's seat, massaging his temples. He seems not to hear her, or maybe he cannot find an answer at the moment, and who could blame him for that?

A flash of inspiration hits Hope. She dashes into the caravan, opens the hatch to the spell chamber beneath and hops nimbly down the ladder. It is only when she gets down there, and all of the spells shine many splendid colours in her presence, that she realises her own colour has still not faded.

With no time to spare, she browses the many and varied labels on the bottles until at last she finds the spell she has been hoping for. A potion. She grabs it, climbs back up, dashes out of the wagon and then barges into the tax man's caravan.

He falls back onto his untidy bed, whimpering.

'It's impossible,' he keeps saying. 'Nobody beats that many Ripper Dogs. Nobody.'

'Seems somebody did,' says Hope.

'Please! Don't harm me! I'm only doing my job!'

'Shut up,' says Hope. 'I'm not going to hurt you.'

'You're in colour!' says the tax man, his hand clutching at his chest as if he's only just realising this. 'How?'

'I said shut up! Here. Take this.'

She throws the bottle to him. It lands on his belly and bounces off. He picks it up, squints at the label. 'For memory loss?' he says. Then he looks at her and shakes his head so hard his jowls wobble. 'Oh, no. I'm not taking this. I don't like magic.'

Hope takes one step towards him, and he whimpers again. 'Well, I don't like almost being killed by giant dogs with breath nearly as bad as the stink inside this caravan. Now take it. Just a few drops. Enough to make you forget the last few hours, for a while at least.'

The simpering tax man unscrews the lid, raises the bottle to his wet grey lips. Hope's colour has faded a little more, and it does not reach all the way over to the other side of the caravan.

'That's it,' she says. 'Go on.'

He tips the bottle, closes his eyes and whimpers as the drops fall onto his tongue.

One.

Two.

Three.

The tax man blinks. He looks over at Hope and smiles a dreamy smile. It's quite horrible.

'I'll have four slices of daffodil, please,' he says, raising a finger. 'And a cup of butterflies.' Then he falls asleep.

Hope grabs the potion bottle from him, and runs back to Sandy's caravan. Sandy is still slumped on the driver's seat, looking stunned and out of it. Hope sits beside him, grabs the reins and says, 'Let's get out of here.'

Chapter Twenty-Eight
In Which Sandy Makes
a Decision

'What do you mean you're leaving?' Hope demands. 'We just travelled halfway across the Dominion to get here!'

Sandy stares across the breakfast table in Effie's cottage, a forkful of potato scone halfway to his mouth. 'I don't think there's a simpler way tae say it. I'm leaving. There's somewhere I need tae be.'

'You never go anywhere without me,' Hope says, feeling both hurt and panicked.

Sandy chews on the potato scone and swallows. 'We've never been in this situation before though, have we, lassie? That tax man will have got his memory back by now, and you can bet he's been shouting from the treetops that he's seen a girl who lives in colour. Everyone will be on the lookout for us. There'll be Ripper Dugs and Black Coats all across the Dominion hunting for you.'

'But the potion is working again!' Hope pleads. 'My colour is gone.'

'Aye, for now. But when will it come back, eh? And what if it's too strong next time and yeh're stuck on the road in full colour? Besides, the tax man knows what yeh look like. He's seen yehr face, and mine, colour or no colour.'

'Your leg,' Hope says desperately. 'It hasn't healed right yet. You can't go until it does.'

'I'll thank yeh to let me decide what I can and cannae do,' Sandy says.

Hope frowns. She looks over to the range, where Effie is frying eggs. The old mage shakes her head. 'Don't look at me, lassie. Yeh know he's right. It's best if yeh stay here with me for a while. Yeh'll be safe that way.'

'But I don't want to stay here!'

'Oh,' says Effie, flipping an egg. 'Thank yeh. I'll try not tae take that personally.'

'No, I didn't mean I don't want to *stay* here. I just meant . . . well, actually, I did mean that. But not because I don't like it here. Please, Sandy? Please can I come with you? I'll be good. I'll stay out of trouble!'

Sandy puts down his fork and looks to the heavens for strength. 'Jings, crivens, lassie. I don't know how tae make it any clearer. I am leaving for a wee while. You are not. That is the end of the matter, yeh hear?'

Anger and betrayal are bitter in Hope's mouth. She gets up, storms out of Effie's cottage and runs out of the garden to the shore of the loch. There she picks up a handful of stones and starts skimming them, her mood as dark as the black water, and the grey landscape, and the angry grey sky.

'Leave me alone,' she says when she hears someone approaching, but when she turns and sees that it is Oliver, she sighs and goes back to throwing stones.

'Are you all right?' he asks.

'What do you think?'

'I? I think you have a talent for drama. And I think you will be all right.'

'Drama? He's leaving me in the middle of nowhere!'

'We're not leaving you to fend for yourself, are we?' Oliver says.

'We?' Hope raises an eyebrow. 'So it's WE now, is it? You're going too?'

The little dog sits by her feet and stares out over the loch. 'I don't really have a choice in the matter, do I? Man's best friend and all that.'

'Why is he doing this?' Hope asks.

'Because he's frightened,' says Oliver. 'Not for himself, but for you. And I have never seen him frightened before. He thinks he has failed you, Hope. The Emperor and Necromancer know even more about you now, and they will do everything in their considerable power to find and kill you. Sandy, on the other hand, will do everything in his power to stop them.'

'But what is he going to do?' says Hope. 'I'll bet it's something stupid and dangerous.'

'That's probably the safest bet you could ever make,' the little dog says, leaning into her as she reaches down to scratch his ears. 'But whatever he is going to do, he is doing for you. To protect you. Don't be mad at him for that.'

Hope shakes her head. 'I'm not mad. Not really. I'm scared. Scared he's going to get himself killed trying to . . . I don't even know what.'

'Something stupid and dangerous,' Oliver reminds her.

'Aye,' she says, and she sits beside the scruffy dog and hugs him as the grey sky rumbles.

Chapter Twenty-Nine
In Which a Storm Gathers

Twilight on a fine summer evening three days later. Sandy
Burns guides his horse off the road and stops at the entrance
to a narrow dirt lane that cuts between two fields of grazing
sheep. To the east, the wall and tall buildings of the City
stretch up and cast their shadows all around. Sandy has not
been to this part of the Dominion for many years, and the
sight of the City makes his belly turn.

'Are you quite all right?' Oliver asks.

'Aye,' says Sandy, shaking off the memories.

'Is this it? Is this the farm you're looking for?'

Sandy turns his head away from the City. At the end of
the lane sits a white farmhouse, a tendril of smoke drifting
from its chimney. 'Aye. This is it.'

He snaps the reins, and Gloria the shire horse pulls the
caravan up the dirt lane. As soon as they cross the threshold
into the farm, Sandy feels the air change, become charged

and heavy, the way it does before a great storm. The hairs on his arms stand up, and his skin is all gooseflesh.

'There's strong magic here.'

The track leads to a cobbled yard, where the white house sits, and also a grey barn and stable. Sandy stops the caravan and climbs down. He is stiff after three days travelling, and when he stretches, his bones creak and groan.

'Sandy Burns?'

A stout, white-haired woman stands in the doorway of the white farmhouse on the other side of the courtyard, beyond the stable.

Sandy removes his hat, his unkempt grey hair blowing in the warm evening breeze. 'Aye.' He makes a small bow. 'Mrs Gwendle?'

'That's right.' The woman surveys him with keen, cold eyes. Sandy thinks that, even in a world of colour, those eyes might still be the colour of thunder.

'Thank you for allowing me on your land,' he says.

'Aye,' says Mrs Gwendle. 'I've agreed to listen, and nothing else, mind. As a favour to Effie. We'll see what comes next when I hear what you have to say.'

'Of course. Thank yeh.'

She nods once. 'Well, you better come in.' She shouts over her shoulder. 'Darroch! Come here, boy.'

A boy of seventeen appears behind her. He is tall and untidy, with the awkward, gangly arms and legs of a young man who is still growing into his body. Sandy gives him a smile, and he smiles back, looking a little star-struck. 'Why don't you make Mr Burns's horse comfy in the stable, Darroch,' says Mrs Gwendle. 'Then come and join us in the kitchen.'

'Yes, Gran.' He hurries past Sandy, and Sandy is impressed with the gentle manner the boy has with his horse as he leads her away.

'Come in,' says Mrs Gwendle. 'I'll make some tea.'

'It's really true?' Darroch says. His face is full of wonder as he stares over his forgotten tea mug at Sandy. 'There really is a girl who lives in colour?'

Sandy rests his elbows on the heavy, wooden kitchen table, clasping his mug in his hands. 'Aye.'

An amazed, goofy laugh escapes Darroch's open mouth. 'I knew it! I knew it was true. I've always said so, haven't I, Gran?'

Mrs Gwendle is quiet. She has listened to what Sandy has to say, and it seems that she is mulling it all over. Sandy finds her impossible to read, which has never happened to him before.

'What colour is her hair?' Darroch asks.

'Who?' says Sandy, distracted.

'The Rainbow Child!' Darroch says.

'Oh. It's brown.'

'Brown!' Darroch claps his hands. 'Brown hair! Wow! What about her eyes?'

'That's enough, Darroch,' says Mrs Gwendle.

The boy nods, then asks, 'Um, why haven't you brought the girl with you?'

'Because he wants to protect her,' says Mrs Gwendle.

'Aye,' says Sandy. 'She's innocent in all this. Me? Not so innocent. If I can end this whole mess without putting Hope in harm's way, then I will. I owe her that.'

'If you're so sure you can put an end to the Necromancer's spell, how come you haven't done so before now?' asks Mrs Gwendle.

'Because I wasn't ready. Part of me always thought that Hope and I would take care of the Emperor and Necromancer together. When Hope grew strong enough. But I took my eye off the ball. Now, Hope is in danger, and it's up tae me. It's time to take responsibility for my past. For the damage I've done.'

Mrs Gwendle frowns. 'You talk like it's your spell that's stolen colour from the world, not the Necromancer's.'

Sandy's face darkens. He leans a little further over the table. 'Will you help me? Please?'

Mrs Gwendle frowns. She looks at her grandson. Darroch's eyes plead with her.

'If we don't help,' he says, 'then we're just giving up, aren't we? We're accepting that the Emperor and the Necromancer have taken away our colour, our freedom, our chance to live in a world that's alive the way it should be.'

Mrs Gwendle looks down at the table, taps her fingers on her mug. 'Fine,' she says, and as she speaks, Sandy feels the atmosphere of the farm crackle. 'Send out your messages, Sandy Burns. We will help any way we can.'

Hope sits in Effie's garden, eyes closed, concentrating as hard as she can. 'Come on,' she says, willing her colour to get stronger. The familiar warmth spreads through her, and she opens her eyes to see that her skin is brown, her dress a pretty red, and a patch of grass around her green and lush. But the colour spreads no further than a couple of paces before everything turns to grey. She curses under her breath, closes her eyes, tries again, with the same results.

'What are yeh doing, lassie?'

Hope jumps in surprise. 'Effie. I thought you were out fishing.'

'I was.' She holds up a large, shining fish. 'Trout for dinner.'

Hope gets up, a little embarrassed, and afraid she might be in trouble. 'Sorry. I'll take my potion right away.'

'What were yeh doing?' Effie asks.

Hope shrugs. 'Oh. Nothing.'

'It didnae look like nothing tae me. Yeh can tell me, Hope.'

Hope looks into the old woman's kind eyes. 'I'm trying to bring my colour back.'

'Back?' says Effie with a frown. 'It doesn't look like it's gone away from where I'm standing.'

'I know. But on the night the Ripper Dogs almost killed

Sandy in those caves ...' she holds her hands out, 'the colour in me became so strong, so bright. More powerful than I ever imagined it could be.'

'And why do yeh want that back?' Effie asks.

Hope considers this. 'Because I want to help Sandy, and I can't do that unless I'm strong enough.'

'Aye? Help him do what, exactly?'

Hope puts her hands on her hips. 'Whatever craziness he's off doing right now. I'm not daft, Effie. I know he's planning something big. I'm not a wee girl any more.'

'No,' says Effie, and there is more than a hint of sadness in her voice. 'Yeh are not. But nor are yeh a woman yet. I've promised Sandy I'll keep yeh safe here, and that's exactly what I'm going tae do. No arguments – unless yeh want tae find yehrself gutting this fish for dinner.'

That puts a lid on Hope for now.

Seemingly satisfied, Effie starts to turn back towards the kitchen, then pauses. 'That's not tae say yeh shouldn't try tae understand yehr powers though.' She twitches her mouth to one side. 'In fact, I think it's a good idea that yeh do practise.'

'Really?'

'Aye. Yeh can never tell when yeh might need tae call upon yehr strength – like in the Night Caves. And if trouble comes, yeh're best being prepared. Tell me, what happened that led tae yehr colour growing so strong in the caves?'

'I was scared,' says Hope. 'More scared than I've ever been. I thought Sandy was going to die. Do you think that's

282

it? Do I need to be really frightened for it to work? Like a survival thing?'

'Maybe,' says Effie, but Hope thinks she sees doubt in the old eyes. 'Let me think on it.'

Over the next few days, a constant flow of caravans arrives at Gwendle Farm in the shadow of the City.

Darroch guides them all, dozens and dozens, to a grey field of high corn at the far side of the spread, out of sight, where they can park up among the tall corn stalks and remain unseen. The mages among them have brought what Sandy requested: moonlight. Bottles and bottles of it. The others have brought arrows and bows and blades, and the mages treat the weapons with their moonlight, readying them for battle with an enemy that cannot be beaten by anything else. Mrs Gwendle and Darroch feed the camp with endless pots of hearty stew and vegetables.

'I cannae believe so many came,' says Sandy one evening at the kitchen table. 'I knew the idea of the Rainbow League had spread all around the Dominion, but until tonight I didn't know if folk would be willing to turn up when it mattered.'

'Hope is a powerful thing,' says Mrs Gwendle. 'And stories of your Rainbow Girl have given them just that, reminded them that something precious has been stolen from them, something sacred.'

'Aye,' says Sandy. 'Without her, I don't think any of this would have ever happened.'

Darroch stirs up his grey stew with his fork. 'Once,' he says hesitantly, 'when I was a wee boy, I saw a falling star from my window. And I wished for someone to come along and bring colour back to us.'

'You never told me that,' his grandmother says.

'Oh, I thought it was a silly thing after a while. A wee boy's childish imagination.'

Sandy smiles. 'There is power in imagination, laddie. Just as there is great magic in a wish.'

Darroch looks wonderstruck. 'You think my wish *worked*?'

Sandy looks at Mrs Gwendle, and she smiles. 'I think, laddie, that we are sitting here with an army willing to fight to bring colour back to the world. And somewhere out there is a Rainbow Girl who made it possible. A miracle. If that isn't an answer to yehr wish, I don't know what is. Maybe that falling star heard yeh.'

Sandy stands from the table, goes to the window and leans on the wall, looking out over the grey landscape. The night is fine and clear, and the sun is setting in the west, painting the sky with many silver-grey shades.

'You want to make a move tonight, don't you?' says Mrs Gwendle.

Sandy's brow furrows. 'Aye. I worry if we wait too much longer, we might be discovered, and they'll be ready for us. Besides, tonight is a full moon. I'll take that as a sign.'

Mrs Gwendle rises from the table. 'Darroch, go down

to the camp. Tell everyone to gather in the courtyard at . . .' she looks to Sandy.

'Midnight,' he says. 'Tell them midnight.'

The night is calm as Effie rows the little boat out into the middle of the loch. Hope sits on the bow seat, looking out over the peaceful water towards the twinkling lamps of the village at the far side.

Effie sets the oars down, and they drift, constellations shining down upon them from the vast countryside sky.

They bring out their fishing rods, each putting a glow worm on a hook, and cast their lines into the water.

'Nothing like a spot of midnight fishing tae warm the soul,' Effie says, slowly winding the reel. Then, casually, she adds, 'Did yeh try yehr colour training again today?'

'Yup. It's just the same. It seems like the more I try, the further away it gets. It's infuriating.'

Effie clicks her tongue. 'Well, yeh keep trying, lassie. Yeh'll get it in the end.'

She seems distracted, Hope thinks, always looking up at the moon and fidgeting.

'It's happening tonight, isn't it?'

'What is?' says Effie.

'Sandy taught me to read folk better than that, Effie. I can see it all over your face. Plus, tonight is the full moon. You know Sandy likes to add a touch of drama to everything. Whatever he's off doing, it's tonight. Tell me I'm wrong.'

Effie looks down at her fishing reel. 'Yeh're not wrong.'

'What is he going to do, Effie?'

'Honestly? I'm no sure. But I know he wants tae put things right.'

'Put what right?' Hope looks to the sky and shakes her head. 'Why won't anyone ever tell me anything? It's always secrets and mystery with you lot!'

Effie sets down her rod, swivels around so that she and Hope are face to face.

'Before Sandy left, he asked me tae do something. He asked me tae tell yeh a story.'

'Oh? What story?'

'Yeh've always wondered where Sandy came from,' Effie says. 'Well, now, finally, he wants yeh tae know.'

Hope swallows. She sits forward. 'Why does he need you to tell me? Sandy can tell me himself when he gets back.'

A pause.

'That's just it, Hope. He might not come back.'

Hope's throat seems suddenly to tighten. 'No. No, don't you say that.'

Tears sparkle in Effie's old eyes. 'He asked me tae tell yeh his story, lassie, under the full moon. So that is what I must do.' Her voice is tremulous, and Hope can see that Effie is quivering.

Hope leans forward, taking Effie's hands in her own.

Then Effie stares up at the silver disc of the moon and starts to tell Sandy's story.

Chapter Thirty

In Which the Rainbow League Makes its Stand

Sandy stands in the cobbled yard of the farmhouse, gazing up at the full moon as midnight arrives.

Before him have gathered a ragtag bunch, maybe two hundred people, young and old, mages and non-magic folk, all united in their courage and their desire to see colour and freedom returned to the people of the Dominion.

Sandy holds up his hands and the quiet chatter of the Rainbow League dies away. He looks around the crowd.

'Thank yeh all, from the bottom of my heart, for answering the call. I've no doubt that, if we had more time, our number would be much greater, that the Rainbow League would gather here from the furthest reaches of the land. But time has run out.'

A ripple of anticipation in the audience.

'I look around here and I see familiar faces. Many of yeh I have met on the road, in secret meetings or at moon markets across the Dominion. And many of yeh I have never encountered, but I know we are joined together by a common enemy, and a common desire tae restore the world tae the way it should be.'

Another wave of agreement, this time louder.

'Twelve years ago a miracle came to me. A wee babby in living, breathing colour! I took her in, and I protected her, and I watched her grow. And as she grew, the wee lassie taught me more than I could ever hope to teach her. She showed me what it means tae be brave, tae be loyal.

'Nobody, friends, deserves tae live their life in fear because of the way they look, or sound, or the things they believe in. Nobody should have tae hide away their true self because what they are doesn't fit in with the rest of the world. The wee lassie I speak about, the Rainbow Girl, has suffered her entire life. She's lost her family. She's hidden who she is. But her story has travelled the length and breadth of the Dominion. It has inspired us. It has given us hope, even as the grey fist around us squeezes tighter.

'Now the Rainbow Girl is in danger. Now they know about her, know that the stories are true. And if we do not stop them, if we do not fight them, they will find her and kill her and all memory of colour, all hope of a free world, of a world where our children can imagine and create and feel the glow of a golden sun on their faces, will die with her. Now, who is with me?'

A roar from the crowd. They throw up their hands, and clap, and whistle.

'Ready yourselves,' Sandy yells. 'We leave within the hour!'

After the meeting, Sandy takes a short walk with Oliver to a secluded spot on the west side of the farm, under cover of tall chestnut trees.

'Are you sure about this?' Oliver asks.

'There's nae other choice,' Sandy replies. 'We're out of time. I can't keep Hope safe any longer. I must take responsibility.' He takes a deep breath. 'For a long while I thought I'd never come back here. But Hope changed that. Now it's time for me tae right an old wrong.'

The scruffy black dog presses his head against Sandy's leg, and Sandy crouches and scratches Oliver under the chin.

'Now it's my turn tae ask,' the mage says. 'Are *you* sure about this? It's a big favour I'm asking of yeh.'

'Of course I'm sure,' says Oliver. 'Do you think I would ever let you ride into battle without me and steal all the glory for yourself? Come on, let's get on with it. Work your magic, old boy.'

Sandy smiles. 'Man's best friend indeed.'

He stands, reaches into his tweed coat and brings out a long, thin spell wand with a teardrop-shaped grey blob of dried magic on one end. Then he lights a match and holds the flame to the end of the wand.

The grey flame catches the dried magic and fizzes to life in a brilliant ball of light, white and dazzling as the sun, a shower of sparks spitting all about. Sandy flicks the wand at Oliver, and there follows a blinding flash, and a bang.

Sandy's eyebrows shoot up at the sight before him.

Oliver still stands with him beneath the chestnut trees. But now he is the size of a shire horse, bigger in fact. Bigger than any Ripper Dog.

'What do you think?' he asks.

Sandy grins. 'Aye. You'll do, boy. You'll do.'

In the secret walled garden in the Emperor's castle, the Necromancer sits before her magical fire, basking in the orange flames and the power of the only true colour in the Dominion.

No. She frowns. Not any more.

There is one other place where colour exists, and that is in the body of a child. A child! For a long time, the Necromancer thought the Rainbow Child was nothing more than a fairy tale. But the rumours grew, and the Rainbow League spread and became bold. And then, more recently, as the Necromancer's own power continued to blossom, she had been able to feel a disturbance out there somewhere. A hole in her spell. The Rainbow Child. But not for much longer. Her Ripper Dogs will search every inch of the Dominion and sniff the child out and put out her colour like a candle.

'Is something troubling you, Aunt?'

She blinks. She had completely forgotten that the young

Emperor is sitting nearby, the orange-red flames of the fire peeling back the seconds of the day from his body, keeping him young.

The Necromancer sniffs at the air. 'Something's up, nephew. Something's fishy.'

The Emperor looks sideways at her. He sniffs the air uncertainly. 'It is?'

'I don't like it,' she says, standing. 'Not one bit.'

She raises a hand, and from the fire steps a flaming figure. The Emperor scrambles up and steps back. He has seen this a hundred times, but it never ceases to trouble him.

The flames engulfing the figure die away, and there stands a Black Coat, faceless, silent inside its hood.

'I have a bad feeling,' the Necromancer tells the Black Coat. 'Something in the air stinks. Take a patrol out to the wall. Be on the lookout for anything unusual.'

Silently, the Black Coat bows and walks slowly away, out of the garden.

'What's happening?' the Emperor asks. 'I am the Emperor, and I demand to know.'

'Oh, do shut up, nephew,' she tells him, and when he makes no reply, she turns her attention back to the fire.

Darroch and his grandmother watch the Rainbow League march from Gwendle Farm in the pale, cool light of the full moon.

Sandy leads the way, sitting astride Oliver's wide back.

Behind him, most of the others are on foot, though a few have chosen to bring their horses. The night crackles with nervous energy, with fear and excitement and determination.

Darroch stares after them, his fists balled, his jaw clenched tight. He wishes that he was with them. Not because he thinks that he would be especially good in a fight, or because he feels very brave, but because these people are mostly like him, normal folks who are standing up for what they feel is right. How he would love to stand beside them, to know he did his bit.

Gran's hand squeezes his shoulder and then is gone. Darroch does not follow her into the farmhouse. He wants to watch the League until they are out of sight.

'You'll need these.'

He turns, frowns. Gran stands at the farmhouse door. In one hand she holds Darroch's hunting bow, and in the other his quiver of arrows.

'What?' he asks.

Gran comes towards him. By the light of the farmhouse windows, he can see her face is grim with effort, that she is deeply torn about something. Slowly, she offers him the bow and arrows.

'You'll be needing these,' she repeats. 'You can't go into a battle unarmed.'

Darroch stares. 'What are you saying?'

'I'm saying I know you, son. I know how much you ache to be a part of what's happening. You're too much like me.' A shake of the head. 'Too bloomin' much. But I can't wrap you up forever. You're a young man now.' Her eyes sparkle as tears gather. 'I could keep you here. I could forbid you to go. But that would be selfish of me. I'd be doing it for me, not for you.'

He reaches out, takes the bow, and throws the quiver over his shoulder.

'If I were twenty years younger,' Gran says, her voice breaking, 'I'd be right beside you.'

Darroch grabs her into a tight hug, and she hugs him back, tighter than she's ever done before. He tries to hold back his tears as he whispers, 'Thank you.'

Then the hug is over, and Gran is wiping her eyes. She straightens up, takes a deep breath. 'Well,' she manages to say. 'You'd better go if you want to catch them up.'

He nods, turns, and begins to jog.

'You come back, young man. Yeh hear me? Make sure yeh come back!'

Halfway across the farmyard, Darroch stops, turns and says, 'I will. I promise.'

Then he is away, running faster and faster, past the barn and down the dirt road.

Mrs Gwendle watches him go, her eyes fighting the dark as he gets further away. When at last she can see him no more, she goes slowly back into the house, into the kitchen and, not knowing what else to do, she begins to make bread, her tears dropping into the dough mixture as she works.

*

The road follows the ragged line of the white sea cliffs, the sound of the waves crashing far below, the air moist and filled with the tang of salt.

Then, the Rainbow League come around the final bend, and the grey city wall looms large. The gate is shut, but Sandy has been expecting that, and he has prepared a special spell to deal with it. What he is not expecting, not at this stage, is the pack of a dozen or so Ripper Dogs standing between the league and the gate, shadows against the flickering torches of the wall.

Sandy comes to a stop, holds up a hand, and the League halts behind him.

'This is what we have prepared for these last few days,' Sandy calls to his small army. 'Do not be afraid. Colour is on your side, my friends.'

He reaches back, takes a moonlight-tipped arrow from his quiver, draws his bow and aims.

He lets the arrow loose.

Now, when it matters most, it might be the truest shot he has ever taken.

The arrow rips through the night and plunges into the chest of one of the Black Coats. The thing screams and screeches, then explodes in a cloud of ash. The shot has an instant effect on the soldiers of the Rainbow League. They cheer, and roar, just as the now riderless Ripper Dog throws its nightmarish head back and expels a terrible howl.

Sandy raises a hand. 'For Hope!'

'FOR HOPE!' cheer the League.

They charge.

'Come on, boy. That's it!' Sandy pats Oliver on the back as the giant dog sprints on. 'Get to the gate!'

The Ripper Dogs and Black Coats are riding out to meet them. As Sandy rides, arrows fizz past from the archers on their horses just behind him, but the Ripper Dogs are ready this time, and they jump and weave and dodge.

Nearer and nearer they come, until the two sides plunge together like crashing waves.

The Ripper Dogs grunt and growl, they rip and tear at anything in front of them. Among the screams and shouts, Sandy lets loose another arrow, knocking a Black Coat from its Ripper, turning the rider to dust.

Something slams into Oliver's side. He yelps, and spins, but manages to stay on his feet, and somehow Sandy stays on his back. They spin around, just as the riderless Ripper Dog lunges towards them.

'Down!' Sandy screams.

Oliver drops to his belly, and in one fluid motion, Sandy reaches for his belt and brings out a moonlight-tipped blade, thrusting it up into the guts of the Ripper Dog as it passes overhead, splitting it open.

The Ripper lands heavily and is still. Its demonic flesh peels back and bubbles as the magic does its work.

All around, more arrows rain, hitting Black Coats.

Sandy counts ten Ripper Dogs, then eight, then four.

He aims, looses another arrow, takes out another Ripper. Then he says to Oliver, 'The gate! Let's go!'

Oliver whips around, breaks into a sprint, and they ride towards the large iron gate. As they near, Sandy reaches into his coat once more, this time pulling out a glass bottle filled with a little concoction that Effie helped him cook up before he left for the City.

'Almost there,' he breathes. 'Almost.'

He winds back his arm, aims, throws . . .

Among the chaos of the fight, Darroch Gwendle throws himself to the ground as a Ripper Dog lunges through the air above him. He lands, rolls and springs back up, spinning around in time to see an arrow from somewhere plunging into the Ripper's side, felling the monster.

Darroch's ears ring with the shouts and yell of the battle. Everywhere he looks he sees the bodies of the fallen. Dozens of them. His head pounds, and part of him wishes that he had not joined the fight. Too late now.

From the bubbling body of the Ripper Dog comes its rider. The Black Coat fixes its faceless glare on Darroch. He stares, frozen, into the blackness of the hood as the Black Coat comes nearer, nearer, moving slowly, deliberately, the way a corpse might move if it could . . .

The tip of a moon blade pierces through the Black Coat's front with a sickening crunch. The Black Coat screams, turns to dust, leaving Darroch staring at the person wielding the blade, a woman he recognises instantly. It is Beth, the woman he and Grandma nursed back to health. The woman who brought him the magical paint.

'Thank you,' he says.

She smiles at him.

A thunderous boom rents the air, and a blast of intense heat makes Darroch flinch away.

'The gate!' says Beth. 'It's open!'

Sandy had expected to be met with a fresh wave of Ripper Dogs upon penetrating the gate. Instead, he is met only with empty streets. He has not been in the City for many years, and yet, in the moonlight, it looks exactly as he recalls. The stone streets on the outskirts are narrow, lined with tall buildings, and dotted with alleyways and hidden corners and steeply climbing stairways that lead to courts and other thoroughfares.

It takes him a minute or two to gain his bearings. The castle sits on the south eastern corner of the City, high on a cliff. He can tell from the quiet that the last of the Black Coats and Ripper Dogs from outside the wall have been taken care of, and soon enough the League are following him through the gate.

'No soldiers on the wall?' asks a man on a huge grey-and-white horse, looking up towards the ramparts.

'There were, once,' Sandy says. 'But not any more. Who's going to be daft enough to attack a city guarded by the dead, eh?'

The man on the horse laughs, and they continue on through the streets. Pale grey faces stare down from the windows of the colourless buildings as they pass by.

'Jings, these poor folks,' Sandy says. 'Living here all this time in a city haunted by monsters. It was a great place once, you know.'

'It's too quiet,' Oliver whispers. 'Do you think they're waiting for us?'

'Oh, I have nae doubt of that, old pal,' Sandy says, patting the great dog's back. 'But the only way this ends is if I get into that castle, or I put an end tae the Necromancer. Either way, they aren't coming tae me.'

On they march, through the deserted streets, until at last they come out into the main street and approach the square, and the castle, an awesome collection of towers and turrets that looms over them from a clifftop behind a high, high wall.

Sandy raises a hand again, bringing his small army to a halt. He peers out towards the wall.

'Is that . . .' begins Oliver. But he does not finish the question, because he knows the answer.

There is a lone figure in front of the wall, clear as day in the rampart torchlight. She sits on the back of a pure white bear.

'The Necromancer,' Sandy says.

Someone behind him loses their nerve and fires an arrow, and it rips across the square and bounces off the wall. Sandy swivels around and says, 'Hold!' through gritted teeth. Then he turns back towards the Necromancer, who has not moved, not an inch.

'What should we do?' Oliver asks.

'Let's get a wee bit closer,' Sandy whispers. They edge forward ever so slowly, Sandy's fingers twitching near the arrows in his quiver, ready to draw.

'Wait. What's she doing?'

The Necromancer reaches around to her back and draws a long wooden staff. She holds the staff aloft, and the end of it bursts into brilliant white flame. Then she moves, not towards Sandy and the League, but off to the right, the white bear bounding at a terrific pace, until they reach the far side of the square. There, she touches the flaming tip of her staff to the ground, and the bear bounds forward once again, this time in the opposite direction. As they go, the Necromancer drags the flaming staff across the ground, and a high wall of colourless fire leaps from the earth, spanning the entire width of the square between the League and the castle.

'What now?' Oliver says.

A pause. 'I don't know.'

For an agonising moment that seems to stretch out forever, nobody moves. Not Sandy. Not the League. Not the Necromancer. The roar of the magical flames seems to tear through the fabric of the world.

Then suddenly from the wall of fire, flaming shapes explode out into the dark. Dozens of them. Hundreds. As the flaming things charge at the League, the fire drips away from them, leaving the huge black bodies and glowing white eyes of Ripper Dogs. And upon their backs, as always, are a multitude of faceless, hooded Black Coats. Spirits wrenched from the beyond.

Sandy turns to his League, his face filled with wild rage. 'Fire!' he screams. 'Fire at will!'

Several people who had been standing beside Darroch only moments ago have gone, turned tail and run away from the oncoming wall of Ripper Dogs and Black Coats.

Darroch, though, does not run. He is frightened, more frightened than he has ever been, but he will not die running away. He takes an arrow from his quiver, aims, draws, trying to think back to the countless times he has hunted the wolves that kill Grandma's sheep. He lets the arrow loose.

Thwack!

It hits a Ripper on the hind leg, making it fall.

Then he is on the move. He cannot stay still, not for one moment. All around him are the whizzing sounds of arrows, the snarls and growls of the Rippers, screams and yells and roars, and the clang of moon blades against the dark metal blades of the Black Coats. He shoots another arrow, turning a Black Coat to dust, then he spins away from a charging Ripper, aims, sends a moon-tipped arrow into its backside.

'Good shot!' yells a man beside him, picking an arrow off the floor. But no sooner has the stranger spoken those words than a Ripper Dog is upon him, gnawing, tearing.

Darroch takes his moon blade from his belt, lunges, drives the point into the Ripper's side. The demon falls, but the stranger is already dead.

*

Sandy has lost count of the number of Ripper Dogs and Black Coats he has sent back to the void with an arrow or a blade. But more keep coming. He is exhausted, and a look around tells him that his companions are running out of steam too.

The Necromancer is even more powerful than he feared. How can any army overcome an endless onslaught of monsters that never tire, or feel pain, or fear?

The sheer number of Ripper Dogs and Black Coats is overwhelming. The Rainbow League are going to lose.

Unless.

'We need to get to the Necromancer,' he tells Oliver.

His beloved dog nods once, growls, and then carries Sandy off on a sprint.

The Necromancer has not moved from her spot front and centre of the wall of fire. She has watched the battle calmly, not flinching as arrows zip past her. Oliver scrambles towards her, butting a Ripper Dog out of the way, hurdling another, sending yet another tumbling with a passing swipe of his giant paw.

Nearly there.

Nearly there.

Sandy kicks away a lunging Black Coat.

They are almost upon her.

The Necromancer turns her head and looks at them.

She smiles.

A flaming shape bursts from the wall of fire, crashes into Oliver, sending him tumbling, spinning, skidding, and throwing Sandy twenty paces across the square, where he lands with a sickening thump. He blinks, tries to force air into his lungs, and when the ringing in his ears subsides, he can hear the calls of the surviving members of the League.

'Retreat,' they are calling.

'Retreat.'

Darroch Gwendle is still alive. He does not have much of a recollection of how he has survived this far, only that if he is to live very much longer, he is going to have to get out of the City.

He looks around for a way out, an alley perhaps, or a riderless horse he might mount, when his eye catches something, and he gasps and dashes forward to a mountain of shivering black-grey fur on the ground. It could be mistaken for a Ripper Dog, but Darroch knows better.

'Oliver?' he says, crouching behind the dark mass of Oliver's huge body. 'Oliver, wake up!'

The dog stirs, whimpers and opens his eyes. 'Sandy,' he says, struggling up.

'You're hurt,' Darroch tells him.

'I'm fine.'

'We need to leave,' says Darroch. 'It's over.'

'I'm not leaving without Sandy.'

Darroch's eyes are suddenly wide, and he draws an arrow and, quicker than a blink, sends it zipping into a Ripper that had been charging Oliver from behind.

Oliver stares down at Darroch. 'Thank you. Climb on my back. I'll get you out of here, but we must find Sandy.'

The wind has been knocked from Sandy, and his bad leg feels ready to explode. He blinks, tries to shake away the cobwebs. He attempts to sit up, but a crushing force upon his chest pushes him back down, and he finds himself pinned to the ground under the enormous paw of a snow-white bear. The massive creature stares down at him with eyes like giant black marbles, and its wet black nose shines in the dazzling, colourless light of the fire.

Another grey face comes into view, staring down at him from high upon the bear's back. A face he once knew very well, though there is no recognition in her eyes when she looks at him. And why would there be? Sandy is older, and wears his drifter mage persona like a costume, hiding under his hat and moustache. She has, somehow, not aged at all.

'Crush him,' she says in a disinterested tone.

The bear raises its paw off Sandy's chest, prepares to stamp down on him.

'Wait! I have a message for the Emperor.'

The Necromancer taps the white bear on the back of the head, and its paw stays hovering over Sandy's body. 'What message?'

Sandy tries to catch his breath, stares up into the Necromancer's eyes, and says, 'Tell him that his brother has come home.'

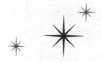

Chapter Thirty-One

In Which Hope Hears the Truth at Last

'Brothers?' Hope's jaw hangs open. Her fishing rod twitches, indicating that she has a bite on the end of the line, but she has forgotten about fishing now. She has forgotten about everything other than the words Effie has just spoken. 'Sandy and the Emperor are *brothers*?'

'Twins,' says Effie.

Hope opens and closes her mouth but makes no sound.

'The Emperor arrived first,' Effie says. 'Course, his name wasn't "the Emperor" then, but I suppose that's neither here nor there. And then came Sandy. His name wasn't Sandy either. It was Alexander. But he's Sandy tae us so we'll stick with that.

'Now, when the Emperor was born, it came as a great shock tae the old King and Queen that their bouncing wee babby arrived in the world in black and white. Not a smidgen of colour about him! Then along came Sandy, filled with colour and life. Well, yeh can guess, Hope, who was the favourite right from the beginning.'

'The King and Queen liked Sandy better because the Emperor was different?' Hope says. 'That's horrible.'

'Oh, they loved the colourless prince in their own way. But nobody in the royal family – the most powerful mages in the land, mind – could work out why he was born with such an affliction. And they could not fix him, no matter what they tried.

'The boys grew and it became very obvious tae the King and Queen that the colourless prince was never going tae get his colour. They decided that the people of the Dominion would never accept a King who was so different, that they would say he was cursed, and the Dominion would shatter. And so, they decided that Sandy should be heir tae the throne.

'Sandy was supposed to be King?' says Hope. Her brain feels like it is melting. 'Sandy? *Our* Sandy? So, what happened?'

'If yeh give me the chance I will tell ych,' says Effie shortly. 'So, as yeh might imagine, the young colourless prince was not very happy when, in his teenage years, his parents finally broke the news that he would not be King. The brothers had been quite close until that point. Sandy had spent time with the young King when so many others had avoided him. But a rift between them opened up, and while Sandy began tae learn about the royal duties that would one day befall him, the colourless prince spent his days hiding away from the world that had rejected him.

'It was then that he grew close tae another member of the family. His aunt. There were all sorts of rumours that she was meddling in necromancy, the dark art of communicating with spirits from the other side. And Sandy thinks it was during this time that she poisoned his brother's mind.'

Effie sits back in her seat on the boat, stretches her neck. The black water of the lake is calm as glass, and the full moon is right overhead. 'Now we come tae the bones of the matter. As the twins approached their twentieth year, their lives could not have been more different. Sandy was popular and clever and talented with magic, while the young Emperor had wasted away tae a skinny shell, spending all of his time locked away in his tower, listening tae the poisonous words of his aunt.

'Sandy had a real talent for inventing spells. Several of his creations made it into famous spell books. But he was headed for disaster. One night, a new spell went wrong. Sandy still does not know how, but his failed magic opened some dark rip in the world, and out came a monster. A dog the size of a horse, with glowing eyes.'

'A Ripper Dog!' Hope breathes.

'The first Ripper Dog,' Effie says. 'He managed tae fend it off with some moonlight, but others in the castle were not so lucky. The Ripper Dog set upon his parents and killed the King and Queen as they slept.

'Sandy was devastated, and more frightened than I can ever imagine. The aunt was first on the bloody scene. She told Sandy that he would have tae leave and never come back, or else the people would hang him for his crime.'

'But it was an accident!' says Hope.

'Aye. It was. But put yehrself in Sandy's shoes, if yeh possibly can. He had nae choice, lassie. He ran, and he ran, and he kept running, and his heart was so broken that he stopped caring about anything at all, even as his brother became the Emperor and his aunt became the Necromancer. Even as they stole the colour from the world and used the power of it tae keep themselves young, and tae summon an army of those same demon dogs Sandy first discovered.

'Sandy changed how he looked, and how he sounded. He learned how tae talk like Rab and me.' She chuckles. 'It took him a fair while, mind. His accent was awful at first!'

'That's why he sounds different when he shouts out in his sleep!' Hope exclaims. 'That's his old voice? His royal voice!'

Effie gives one nod of confirmation. 'Sandy wandered the Dominion, lost and broken, until he found us. Rab and me, we took him in. We helped him best we could, tried tae bring back the light inside him. It took a long, long while, and it never came fully back. Not until he found yeh, Hope. Yeh were the thing that really saved him. Yeh gave him something tae live for. Something tae protect. Something worth fighting for.'

Hope sits back in the boat, breathes the sweet summer night air and listens to the gentle lap of the calm water against the little rowing boat. Her world has changed.

Everything she thought she knew about the man who raised her has been wrong. Heartbreak has been gnawing silently away at him all these years, and yet he has been there for her whenever she has needed him. Everything she is, she is because of Sandy, and she wants desperately to tell him that, to tell him how grateful she.

'I don't want him to die,' she says.

Effie blinks her sad eyes, and shuffles across the boat to sit beside Hope, placing her arm around her.

'I don't either.'

CHAPTER THIRTY-TWO
IN WHICH THERE ARE TWO IMPORTANT MESSAGES

Mrs Gwendle paces the farmyard, back and forth, back and forth, muttering.

'Please let him be all right. Please let my Darroch come back, oh I don't know what I'll do if something happens to him. Why did I let him go?' She wrings her hands. 'But I had to.'

Occasional, far off Ripper Dog howls have reached the farm from the City on the sea winds. Now other sounds draw her out of the yard, make her move more quickly than she has in years. She grabs a lantern and cuts across the yard.

Shouts.

Yells.

The zip of arrows.

Ripper Dog growls.

She runs down the sweep of the dirt track towards the edge of her farm, where the first scatterings of the retreating

Rainbow League are throwing themselves over the border, collapsing on the grass, gasping and heaving.

More follow, sprinting up the hill with huge shadows giving chase. Some of them make it. Others are caught. Others still turn and fire arrows at the chasing Rippers, sacrificing their lives so that their comrades can get to the safety of the farm.

'Darroch?' Mrs Gwendle calls. 'Darroch, where are you?' She stumbles around, turning her lantern to the bone-weary, haunted faces of the prone soldiers, but none of them is her grandson.

A mass of dark shapes with glowing eyes is gathering along the farm's borders, Ripper Dogs sniffing for a way in, a weakness.

A thunderous bark rings out over the hillside, and another dark shape bombs towards the farm. The dog leaps high into the air, over the lunging, snapping jaws of the waiting Rippers. As the dog sails overhead, it shrinks, throwing its rider off.

The rider lands hard, rolls, then gets to his hands and knees.

'Darroch?' says Mrs Gwendle. She takes a step forward, and another, and then she breaks into a run. She reaches him just as he is back on his feet. His face is dirty and cut and grazed, his right eye swollen.

She grabs him, pulls him into a crushing embrace. 'My Darroch,' she says, taking his face in her old hands. 'My boy.' Her eyes spill over. 'Are you hurt?'

He shakes his head. 'Not badly. Listen, Gran, they've got Sandy!'

'What?'

'It's true.' Oliver has shrunk back to his normal size. He sits at Darroch's feet. 'The Necromancer got him. Her white bear picked him up in its jaws and carried him away.'

'What are we to do?' Darroch points out to the farm's edge, where hundreds of Ripper Dogs' eyes glow brightly along the dark border, and others are still arriving in the night. 'We're trapped like rats!'

Later, the surviving members of Sandy's army try to regroup in their campsite near the back of the farm. Those who feel like it, eat hearty bowls of Mrs Gwendle's stew, while a handful of mages treat the wounded with potions.

At the farmhouse table, Darroch and Mrs Gwendle drink hot tea, while Oliver licks a wound to one of his paws on the floor.

'We have to help Sandy!' Darroch says, banging his fist on the table.

'I hate to say it,' says Mrs Gwendle, 'but we have to consider the possibility that he's already dead.'

'No,' says Oliver from the floor. 'The Necromancer won't kill him. After tonight, she knows he's high up in the Rainbow League. She'll do everything she can to get information about Hope out of him.'

'Do you think he'll crack?' says Mrs Gwendle.

'Not ever. But it would be wise, I think, to send a

message to Hope's guardian. Hope must be kept safe above all else.'

Mrs Gwendle nods. 'Aye. And we also need to get messages out to any League members who might still be on their way to answer Sandy's call, tell them to turn back. We can't have them walking into a massacre.'

'Agreed,' says Oliver.

'What about all the folk stuck here?' says Darroch.

Mrs Gwendle considers this. 'The Necromancer can have her Ripper Dogs and Black Coats surround us all she wants, but they are not coming onto our land. I'm certain of that. As far as survival goes, well, we live on a farm. We have enough food to stay alive for weeks. Probably lunar cycles, if it comes to it. Long enough at least for the rest of the League to find a way to rescue us.'

'And if they can't?' Darroch asks.

Oliver and Mrs Gwendle look at each other. They do not answer.

The following morning, Hope walks into the kitchen of Effie's cottage, still half asleep and feeling like the weight of the world is on her back. The night brought little sleep, and she spent most of it worrying about Sandy and Oliver, wishing she was with them. Her colour has come back overnight, but she is in no rush to take her potion. She is safe in this place to be herself.

There is no smell of frying bacon this morning, which is odd. Nor is there any sign of Effie's cheerful morning whistling. Instead, the old mage is sitting at the table when Hope comes in, staring down at a small slip of paper that sits beside her forgotten mug of tea.

'What is it?' Hope gasps. She stands very still, not wanting to take another step, as if staying frozen in place might also freeze time and save her from whatever Effie is about to tell her.

'A raven brought this message half an hour ago,' Effie says. 'It's about Sandy.'

'Is he dead?' Hope's voice is flat and emotionless. She feels like she is being crushed in a vice.

'No. But they've captured him.'

The wrench loosens just a little. 'He's alive? What about Oliver?'

'Aye, he's alive too. It was the wee dog's words transcribed in this message. The Necromancer has Sandy.'

Hope inhales sharply. 'Then we have to help him! Why are you just sitting there? We should leave right now!'

Effie stays seated. 'Hope, listen tae me . . .'

'No. I won't. There's nothing to discuss.'

'Hope! Use yehr brain! Sandy risked his life tae keep yeh safe, tae try and end this. Do yeh think he'd want yeh tae walk right through the Necromancer's front door? If he fails, yeh are the only hope we have left! What sort of way is that tae pay him back?'

'And what about leaving him to die? What sort of way is that to pay him back, Effie?'

The old mage looks broken. 'Believe me, lassie, I want

313

nothing more than tae ride south and storm that castle myself. But I swore tae Sandy I'd protect yeh, whatever it takes. Oliver's message reminds me of that. And that's why we have tae leave. We're moving north, tae the tundra.'

Hope can't believe what she's hearing. 'The tundra? I'm not going there!'

Effie stands up, slams her hand down on the kitchen table, and a ripple of crackling energy breaks across the house. 'Yeh will go where I tell yeh tae go, lassie, and that is the end of it – even if I have tae put a sleeping spell on yeh tae get yeh there! Now, go and pack yehr things, and not another word!'

Hope wheels away, stumbles down the hall and into her tiny bedroom. She flings herself on her bed, her colour lighting up the flowery bedsheets, orange and green, and she cries until she has no more tears.

She wishes she could do something to help, wishes that she had never been born in colour. Maybe the world would have been a better place if she had never been born at all. Maybe, without her to remind them of colour, people would have eventually forgotten, and grown happy in this grey-and-black world. She wishes she could sprout wings and fly away, fly through the stars and leave everything behind.

Fly through the stars . . .

She gasps. A memory comes to her.

She scrambles off her bed, half falling to the floor, finds a deerskin bag full of her possessions from Sandy's caravan

314

and roots around inside. Her breath catches as she spots the object she is looking for.

She brings out the shining object, the one that Sandy gave her almost two years ago.

The mirror is part of a set, of course.

There are two.

So full of excitement she almost forgets to breathe, Hope places the mirror on top of the dresser, then with a trembling hand, she clicks the lid smoothly open.

'Please work,' she says, edging closer.

Something happens to her reflection. The light shifts, ripples, and her face changes. Becomes another face.

A patchwork face with a deep scar and mismatched eyes.

'Hope? Is that you?' Odd says.

'Odd! Oh, Odd it's so good to see you!' She wipes her eyes.

'It's good to see you too, Hope.'

'Odd, I need help,' says Hope, getting right to the point.

He looks concerned. 'Are you in trouble?'

'Yes. We all are. I don't have time to explain right now. I just need to know, is the wyvern still with you?'

Odd smiles. 'Elmo? Yes. I can't get rid of him now, actually. Seems he's grown quite attached to me.'

'That's brilliant!' Hope can barely contain her joy. 'Will you come and get me, Odd? I need to get to the City. I need to get there as quick as I can, and a wyvern's wings are the quickest.'

'Of course we'll help,' says Odd. 'We owe you forever after what you did for us. Where are you?'

'In a cottage on the shore of Urchart Loch.'

'We're on the north east coast,' says Odd. 'Near Rock, remember? It'll take us a few hours to get to you, even as quick as Elmo can fly, but we'll find you. Just sit tight.'

Four hours later, Effie is packing her caravan for the trip north when a huge shadow falls over her. She looks to the cloudless grey sky, lets out a whimper of disbelief, then stumbles back as a huge, winged monster circles down, down, down, and lands on the pebbly shore of the loch close to the cottage.

Panting, she rushes into the caravan, grabs her bow and quiver, and comes out ready to shoot. 'Don't come any closer!' she yells at the strange-looking rider of this huge dragon. No. Not a dragon. Only two legs. A wyvern.

'We're here to save Hope!' the weird boy shouts. He looks like he's made of a patchwork of mismatched body parts. 'We know you're keeping her here!'

'What?' says Effie. 'What nonsense is this?'

'You're keeping her prisoner!' yells the patchwork boy.

'I'm warning yeh.' Effie pulls the string of her bow tight. 'No closer or I'll let yeh have it!'

Hope comes dashing out of the cottage, her heart leaping with joy. She sprints out of the gate and makes a dash towards the shore.

'Hope!' she hears Effie cry. 'No!'

But she is already away, already on the stony beach, running up the wyvern's great wing, onto his back, into the familiar safety of the nook between his shoulders.

'Hope!'

She hugs Odd tight, her bright colour flooding his mismatched parts, pinks and browns and freckled whites. Then turns back towards Effie. 'It's all right, Effie. These are my friends. They've come to take me to Sandy. I'm sorry!'

Effie lets her bow drop. She rushes forward. 'Yeh can't go.'

'But I *am* going. Sandy saved me when I was a baby. I'm only alive because of him. How could I abandon him now, when he needs me?'

Effie comes closer, her old eyes gazing upon Elmo with wonder. 'There's no changing yehr mind?' she asks. Her face is pale grey.

'No,' says Hope.

Effie's shoulders slump a little. 'Then I suppose, if yeh're going, I'm coming too.'

Hope looks at Odd, then at Effie. 'What?'

'I made a promise, Hope, tae protect yeh. Tae lay down my life for yeh if necessary. So, if yeh are intent on going through with this madness, then I will be by yehr side every step.'

Hope stares down at the old mage and feels more gratitude and love for her than she could ever properly express. 'What d'you think, Elmo?' She rubs the wyvern's back, turning the scales she touches from charcoal to pearlescent blackish red.

Elmo answers in a two-tone, rumbling trumpet call.

'I think that means yes,' Odd says.

Effie steps awkwardly onto the wyvern's giant, leathery wing, and he tilts it up, causing her to roll haphazardly down to the safe spot between his shoulders with the others.

Hope smiles, hugs Effie and says, 'Hold on tight.'

With another roaring call, Elmo spreads his wings, takes one step, two, three, and pushes off.

Effie screeches as they climb, each wingbeat carrying them higher, and Hope and Odd both laugh and hang on as the moon wyvern soars so high that it seems they can see forever. Then, with the wind on their faces, they fly towards the City.

Chapter Thirty-Three
In Which a Great Truth
is Revealed

Sandy's eyes crack open. He flinches as sharp, hot pain pulses in his head, and deep in the bones of his spine. He is shivering, despite the oppressive heat. The room is in pitch darkness. He strains his eyes, fighting to pick out any detail, but the blackness is thick.

He struggles for a while against the leather straps that keep him bound to the table, one across his chest, one across his hips, one at the knees, and one on each of his wrists and ankles. It is pointless.

He knows exactly which part of the castle he is in. The old dungeon. It had frightened him as a boy.

The sound of snapping fingers breaks the hush, and Sandy's eyes become pained, narrow slits as a flame leaps to life in an open palm. The colourless flame illuminates the windowless, grey stone cell. The flame also lights up the face of the person who holds it.

'I didn't hear you come in,' Sandy says in a voice as dry and rough as an old twig.

The Necromancer smiles. It is a cold smile. 'Have you come to your senses yet, nephew?'

Sandy sniffs. 'Aye. I think I have.'

The Necromancer comes closer.

'I want tae tell yeh,' Sandy says, gasping. 'I want tae tell yeh . . .'

'Yes?' she says, mad hunger dancing on her face. 'Tell me what?'

'I want tae tell yeh . . . Nothing.'

The Necromancer recoils. Her thin mouth twists into a sneer. 'You think this is a game?'

'I'll tell yeh what I think,' says Sandy. 'I think you know, deep in that black heart, that I am never going tae tell you what yeh want to know.'

She twitches her fingers and the flame in her hand grows a little taller. 'Why do you speak that way, nephew? Like a commoner?'

Sandy chuckles. 'Because I am one. And there's nothing wrong with that. Now, are we going tae get this over with, dear Aunt?'

The cell door opens, and the sight of the person who enters the room steals away Sandy's breath. His eyes scan the colourless face, the grey eyes, the dark hair.

'Crivens!' he breathes. 'Twenty years, and you havnae changed a bit, brother.'

The Emperor comes closer, though he seems hesitant,

as if he thinks Sandy might break free from the table. He swallows. He is still as scrawny and timid as ever. Sandy can tell right away who is really in charge in this room. It is not his brother.

'It's really you,' says the Emperor, coming closer still. He reaches out as if he is going to touch Sandy's face, then seems to change his mind and touches his own. 'We always looked alike, didn't we? Not identical, of course. You were always more handsome. But now, after all this time, you are growing old, while I am still youthful. In some ways you look like a different person, but not your eyes.'

'Your brother was about to tell me where the Rainbow Child is hiding,' says the Necromancer.

The Emperor looks stunned. 'He was?'

'No, brother,' says Sandy. 'I was not.'

'Enough of this,' the Necromancer snaps. Fingers of flame leap from her hand and wrap around Sandy's body. He stiffens, and twitches, and his eyes roll back in his head.

'Where is she?' the Necromancer demands.

The Emperor watches for a few minutes, a horrified look upon his face, before he can stand no more and turns away.

The flames intensify, twisting, twining around the table, around Sandy's arms and legs and torso. They lash at his face.

He screams and keeps screaming.

But he does not break.

*

Oliver the dog wanders around the outskirts of the Rainbow League camp in the field at the back of Gwendle Farm, sniffing at the ground, leaving his scent here and there. As he walks, he attracts calls of greeting from some of the camp, and he barks back at them.

His usual route takes him up a winding track, past the meadow where the sheep graze, lazy and carefree.

By the farmhouse he goes, through the yard and down the dirt track to the place where the farm ends and the rest of the Dominion begins. Ripper Dogs still line the border in their hundreds, their Black Coat riders sitting astride them, faceless and still.

Oliver growls at them, runs back and forth once or twice, yapping and barking, then he cocks his leg, turns around and begins to walk back towards the farmhouse, his head held high.

Something catches his eye then, draws his gaze to the afternoon sky. At first, he does not quite know what he is looking at. But as the object comes closer, a spark of recognition ignites in his head. He sits, watches as the winged creature glides down towards the farm in easy circles.

The flying thing comes closer still and Oliver's tail starts wagging, brushing across the ground. When at last he spots a flash of brilliant colour riding upon the wyvern's back, he barks, and jumps and laughs. Then he sprints off towards the farmhouse.

*

When Elmo touches down upon the field behind the farmhouse, a small welcome party has already gathered to meet them.

Hope leaps down from the wyvern's wing, and his scales lose the colour from her touch at once. Oliver races to meet Hope, jumps up, licks her face as she crouches to hug him.

'I'm so glad to see you,' she says. 'Don't ever leave me again.'

'I'm sorry,' the little dog says. 'I won't.'

Hope's eye catches the two humans who make up the welcome party with Oliver, a stout woman perhaps in her seventies, and a wide-eyed young man. Both look astonished.

'You're real!' the young man says, gawping at Hope, and at the circle of colour on the ground around her.

'Don't point, Darroch,' says the old woman.

'But, Gran, it's her! It's the Rainbow Child!'

'I know perfectly well who she is! You're making a fool of us, boy!'

'Please,' says Hope gently. 'Just call me Hope.'

'I'm Darroch Gwendle,' says the boy. 'And this is my gran.'

'Welcome to our farm,' says Mrs Gwendle. Then she glances up at the wyvern and says, 'and welcome back to you, Effie.'

'You two have met?' Hope asks.

'A few times over the years,' says Effie from the wyvern's back. 'Mrs Gwendle has long been a friend tae the League. Her farm has helped us launch a number of operations against the Emperor and his Necromancer.'

'But are you all OK?' Hope asks. 'There are so many Ripper Dogs and Black Coats surrounding the place! How have you managed to keep them back?'

Mrs Gwendle shoots a look out towards the edge of the farm. 'Our land is safe. My ancestors are buried here. Some of them had powerful magic their blood, and that magic gives us protection. We have looked after the earth, and now the earth looks after us.'

'Well, it looks like we need all the help we can get,' Hope says. 'Can anybody tell me where they're keeping Sandy?'

'He'll be in the dungeon,' Darroch says. 'Beneath the keep. But it'll be crawling with Black Coats and Ripper Dogs.' He tells Hope about the battle, how the Necromancer seemed able to make an endless number of soldiers appear from the magic flames.

Hope looks to her companions. 'I'll go myself,' she says. 'I can't ask you to take such a big risk.'

Effie laughs, and Odd raises a patchwork eyebrow. 'Yeh don't have a choice, lassie,' says Effie. 'We're coming.'

'You'll need someone to show you where to go.' Darroch looks expectantly around at them.

'He's right,' says Mrs Gwendle. 'You'll need to be in and out quick by the sounds of it.'

Darroch embraces his grandmother, then Hope shows him how to climb onto Elmo's back. It is quite cramped up there now, with four of them sitting between the wyvern's colossal shoulders, and Hope's colour spreads to them all, chasing away the grey from Darroch's face, painting it instead with the golden tan of an outdoor life.

'Darroch . . .' Mrs Gwendle steps forward slowly, her hand covering her mouth as she stares at her grandson. She has never seen him in colour before. 'Your eyes. They're just like your mum's.' Her own eyes brim and sparkle when he smiles at her and places his hand on his chest, over his heart.

Then, suddenly, Elmo takes to the sky with a powerful leap, scattering leaves and dust and hay. As they climb, Darroch leans close to Hope and says over the rush of the wind, 'I can show you where the dungeon is, but I don't know how we'll get Sandy out. They say nobody's ever escaped from the keep.'

Hope turns to look at him, her brown hair blowing wildly about, and her brown skin almost aglow in the sun. 'Nobody's had a wyvern before,' she says.

Sandy jolts back into consciousness and feels the cold, soothing touch of a wet cloth dabbing at his forehead and face. The lamp in the wall sconce is lit, casting the Emperor's gaunt face in stark white light and black shadow as he gazes down at his brother.

'What are yeh doing?' Sandy asks.

The Emperor puts a finger to his lips. 'Sssh. She doesn't know I'm down here.'

Every part of Sandy's body pulses with the after pain of the Necromancer's magic fire. Yet his skin shows no burn marks.

325

'Why have yeh come?'

The Emperor continues to dab the cool wet cloth on Sandy's forehead. 'I don't quite know,' he says. 'I suppose because when I saw you, I started to remember things I hadn't thought about in a long time. Memories . . . and feelings.'

'Aye?'

'Listen to you. "Aye"! Mother and Father would have had a fit if they'd heard you speaking like that.' A brief smile crosses his lips, then fades. 'You were the only one who ever treated me like a proper person, you know.'

'That isn't true.'

'No? Then you remember differently than I. Mother and Father were ashamed of me. Why else would they hide me away from our people? As for the servants, well, they had no choice but to pretend that they liked me, but I knew the truth. I knew what they whispered about me. That I was cursed. That I was a freak. But you . . . with you I could always tell the kindness was real.'

'I'm sorry,' Sandy manages to say, his voice weak. 'I'm so sorry for how things turned out.' He flinches at the pain, then says, 'Surely yeh know that what yeh are doing is wrong, brother? The world without colour is a sad place. I know you suffered. I can't imagine how lonely you must have felt. A wee boy made tae feel like a monster. It wasn't right. But punishing the world doesn't make it better, does it? Doesn't change it.'

The Emperor's hands tremble.

Sandy presses on. 'Oh, how I wish I could go back twenty years and stop myself lighting the spell that killed our parents. But I didnae know, brother! If I had known . . .'

A great rumble shakes the room, like the very ground beneath them has shifted.

'What was that?' The Emperor drops the cloth, springs up. He goes to the door, listens. 'Something is going on out there!'

'Take that, ya stinking fur pile! And that! And have some of this!'

The wyvern swoops down over the keep, his great wings roaring through the air. Upon his back, Hope, Effie and Darroch send moonlight-tipped arrows zipping this way and that. Their aim is impressive; arrows find Ripper Dogs and Black Coats, clearing the courtyard enough for Elmo to land. As soon as the wyvern touches down, he whips his massive tail around, sending the remaining Rippers and Black Coats scattering.

'There!' Darroch points to the keep tower. 'That's where we need to be.'

Odd pats Elmo on the back. 'Can you get us in there, boy?'

The wyvern throws out a wing, battering another approaching Ripper Dog into the air, and then charges forward and whips his tail again, clubbing it against the keep wall with a thunderous bang. Cracks appear in the stone, and the collision throws off dust and fragments of rubble.

Elmo winds up and lets his tail loose again, and again, and a final time, making the wall explode inward, leaving a ragged hole.

'Come on, Odd!' Hope leaps down, makes a dash for the entrance and down a winding staircase. She looses another arrow and takes out a Black Coat rushing up to meet them, and then they come to a heavy wooden door at the foot of the stairs.

Hope reaches into her coat, bringing out a tiny spell bottle. She shakes it madly, rushes to the door and places the bottle on the floor. As the liquid inside starts to glow, Hope grabs Odd's hand and dashes back up the stairs.

'Effie says we've to stand as far back as we can. Cover your eyes!'

The spell bottle lets out a high-pitched scream.

Then, with a blinding flash, it explodes.

Hope is still choking on the cloud of dust when she steps into the dungeon cell. She races to Sandy's side at once, grabs his hand, yells, 'Odd! In here!'

The patchwork boy comes through the door, rushes to the table and tosses Hope a wand. She lights the end, holds it to Sandy's restraints, and they disintegrate. Then the two of them help Sandy up, taking most of his weight, and they are out of the door, back up the stairs to the upper level. There they climb through to the courtyard, where Elmo is swatting away Ripper Dogs for fun with his tail. From the wyvern's back, Effie and Darroch shoot moon-tipped arrows, until it seems that the last of this band of Rippers and Black Coats are done.

What happens next happens very quickly.

A flash, and a plume of smoke across the courtyard, and from the smoke comes the Necromancer, her grey face a livid mask of fury. Then, as she scans the area, that fury turns to triumph as she spots a flash of colour over by the keep. Can it be? The Rainbow Child has come to her!

Across the way, Effie catches sight of the Necromancer, cries out and reaches for an arrow. She draws, aims, shoots. The arrow flashes across the courtyard, straight and true.

But it does not reach its target.

The Necromancer's hand blurs upward and grabs the arrow out of the air. She squeezes the arrow, and the arrowhead turns black and smouldering. Then she spins to face Hope, rears back and launches the arrow with a spark of flame.

The arrow streaks across the courtyard like a dark comet. By the time Hope hears the shouts from her friends, it is almost upon her. There is no time to react, to dodge or duck or drop to the ground.

Everyone is frozen.

Everyone except Sandy. Hope's protector, her guardian, her friend, finds the strength to help her one last time. With a roar, he pushes away from Odd and throws himself between Hope and the arrow.

The arrow buries itself deep in his chest.

'No!'

Hope crouches over him, holding his hand as blood pours from the wound onto the cobbles. At her touch, Hope's colour floods into Sandy, lights him up and paints him.

'Brother!' The Emperor has made his way up from the dungeon. He shambles across the courtyard, reaches Hope and Sandy, and stares down at the expanding puddle of black blood. And then Hope's colour reaches the pool of blood too, turning it blazing red.

The Emperor's hand goes to his chest. He inhales sharply, his gaze captured completely by the sight of his brother's blood.

'Brother,' Sandy whispers. He reaches out and grabs the Emperor's hand.

And that is when something amazing happens.

The Emperor, born in black and white, who has never seen himself in colour, stares disbelievingly at his hand as Hope's colour flows through Sandy and into him. His mouth opens and his eyes fill with childlike wonder at the sight of his pale, pinkish fingers.

'No!' screams the Necromancer, watching in horror from across the courtyard. 'That is not possible. Nobody can break my curse!'

The Emperor's smile fades as he replays her words in his head. 'What do you mean "your curse"?'

She begins to walk slowly towards him, very slowly, her lip curled up. 'I mean, dear nephew, that you are the way you are because I made it so, you fool. I cursed you. Did you never wonder how a child could naturally be born without colour?'

He lets go of Sandy's hand, and the colour fades from him again, turning him grey and pale. Then he stands up and strides towards her. 'Why? Why would you do that?'

'Because I was supposed to be Queen! Me!' the Necromancer screams. 'I was supposed to be the one to marry your father. It was me he loved first. But your mother, my stupid sister with her fluttering eyes and simpering ways, came along, didn't she, and stole him from me. So on their wedding day, I put a curse upon their firstborn child.' She smiles. 'Poor little you.'

'Quick,' whispers Hope, to Odd. 'Help me with Sandy while they're distracted!' Odd lifts Sandy, and together they carefully get him up onto Elmo's back.

Across the courtyard, the Emperor has almost made it to his aunt. His hands are by his sides and he walks like he is in a dream. 'All my life, I've believed that I don't belong. When I was a child, I cried every night and wished to be like everyone else. I have been alone every minute of every hour I have been alive, in a world of grey and sorrow. And that is all because of *you*?'

They stand face to face.

'Oh, silence, nephew, you fool! I can't listen to your whinging any more! You sound just like your mother. She used to moan and fret too. And yet she had no reason to. She was the one your father chose. My only regret is that I didn't kill them both earlier.'

On Elmo's back, Sandy stirs, some magical sense bringing him around a little. He turns his head to listen.

'I thought,' says the Emperor, 'that Sandy caused our parents to die? When one of his spells went wrong?'

The Necromancer laughs. 'Do you know how much strength it takes to summon a Ripper Dog? How much magic one needs to tear a spirit from the next world and turn it into a Black Coat? Your brother could never have done those things! You have to mean it, to really *mean* to open a tear and let something through from the dark places beyond. I stowed that spell in your brother's room all those years ago. I switched it for one of his own. All he had to do was light the fuse.'

The Emperor tilts his head, realisation dawning in his boyish grey features. 'You planned all of this, right from the moment I was born, didn't you? You made me this way, made me suffer when I was a child, used me to help you light your fire. You made me think what we've done is right, that it was my idea.'

She smiles. 'You're weak-minded, nephew. It wasn't difficult. And, yes, there was a time when I needed your power as well as my own to keep the fire lit, to keep colour locked away. But now I am strong enough to fan the flames without you. In short, I do not need you any more.'

Her hand moves in a blur, bringing a hidden blade up into his gut. He falls to the cobbles, tears in his eyes, reaching up towards her. Then his hand falls limp, and he suffers no more.

The Necromancer steps over her nephew's body, strides towards the wyvern as it beats its wings. She begins to run, to sprint, and she makes a grabbing leap just as it takes off, her fingers narrowly missing Elmo's tail.

From the wyvern's back, Hope hears the Necromancer scream and curse at them as they fly away.

Hope paces around the grey farmhouse kitchen, shaking her head, going over and over what happened at the castle in her mind, unable to shake off the sight of the pool of Sandy's blood, angry and crimson on the ground.

'He'll be fine,' she keeps repeating to herself. 'He'll be fine.'

Effie and Mrs Gwendle are treating Sandy upstairs. Odd and Darroch sit at the round table in silence, their heads bowed.

After what seems like days, the door opens, and Effie beckons Hope out into the hallway.

'How is he? Can I see him?'

Effie sniffs. 'He's asking for yeh.'

Hope smiles, but her smile fades when she sees the look on Effie's face. 'What is it?'

'We've done all we can,' Effie says. 'But that arrow . . . the tip of it was pure evil . . .'

Hope shrinks away from her. 'What are you saying? He is going to get better, isn't he?'

Effie takes a wavering breath. 'No, lassie. He is not.'

*

Hope pushes the door open and enters the bedroom, feeling like she is walking in a trance. Sandy is lying on the bed, eyes closed, looking peaceful. Oliver is curled up beside him, but when Hope approaches the bed, he gets up.

'I'll leave you two.'

'No,' says Hope. 'You don't have to.'

'I know,' says the little dog, licking her hand. He jumps down from the bed and leaves, his head bowed. Hope edges closer to the side of the bed, until she is near enough to take Sandy's calloused hand in her own, and her colour flows through him.

His apple green eyes open a little at her touch, and a gentle smile creeps into the corners of his mouth. 'Hope,' he whispers. 'My Hope.'

Sandy seems to suddenly look through her. 'My brother,' he says, his eyes spilling over. 'The Necromancer killed him.'

'I know,' Hope whispers, squeezing his hand. 'I saw. I'm here, Sandy. I'm here for you.'

He smiles. 'All this time I thought it was my fault,' he says, breathlessly. 'I thought I killed my own mammy and daddy. But I didnae, Hope. You heard her, didn't you?' His eyes plead with her. 'You heard her say that it was her, the Necromancer, who did it?' He coughs and chokes, and his head falls back to the sweat-soaked pillow.

'I did,' says Hope through her tears. 'I heard. I'm so sorry, Sandy. She stole your life from you.'

He shakes his head, blinks slowly. 'No, Hope. She did not know it,' he says, 'but she gave me more than she took away.' A barking cough escapes him, and a smear of blood appears at the corner of his lips, turned bright red by Hope's colour. When he speaks again, his voice is almost gone. 'I've something tae tell yeh, Hope,' he says. 'Something I've never told yeh before.'

She leans closer.

'You are the best thing I ever had in my life. I am so proud of the young woman yeh've become. I'm just sorry I won't be there for yeh any more.'

She squeezes his hand tightly, forcing back the burning sobs in her throat.

He squeezes back. 'I love yeh, Hope. I have loved yeh from the first moment I picked yeh up and held yeh in my arms. And I will love yeh wherever I go next.'

'I love you too, Sandy,' she says, kissing his hand. 'You are the best father I could ever have wished for.'

His eyes sparkle. Then he takes a quick breath as some realisation seems to dawn on him. 'Death!'

'It's OK, Sandy. I'm with you.'

'Death, Hope,' he says. 'Death and her friend. That's the way tae do it . . .'

Hope frowns. 'You need to rest.'

'No! You need to listen, lassie.' Another wrenching cough. 'We know what she's doing. We know she's stealing souls from the other side. And we know, lassie, that Death has a friend who'd very much like to meet her because of that.'

Hope begins to understand. Her eyes meet Sandy's.

'When I'm gone,' he says, 'let's take the Necromancer for a wee walk, shall we? Across the desert . . .'

He looks up at her one last time, his eyes drinking in every detail, and then he sees no more.

She runs out of the farmhouse, across the field behind the house, until she comes into the shade beneath a huge chestnut tree. There she sits against the trunk and howls. She kicks the ground and bangs her fists on the tree trunk until they bleed. She opens her mouth and screams at the world, and after that she gets up and sprints back the way she came, past the farmyard and away down the track to the border where the farm ends.

Here she stands and stares at the hundreds of Ripper Dogs stationed on the border. She screams at them, curses and shakes her fists, and after that she drops to her knees, exhausted, trembling.

Sandy's voice echoes in her head.

'I love yeh, Hope.'

The thought of those words seems to scatter the dark storm clouds in her soul just enough to let some brightness in. She feels a warm glow starting in her chest, radiating outward, reaching every part of her. Hope's colour burns brighter and brighter, more vivid and dazzling with each passing moment, intensified by every memory of Sandy and their life together. The power of it thunders through her like a mighty river, building in her until she can hold back no more.

She raises a foot and slams it back down hard. When her foot impacts the grass, there is a *BOOM*. A streak of burning colour shoots across the ground. When it reaches the closest Ripper Dogs, they are swallowed in a blaze of colour and light, and they turn to dust, their shadows burned forever on the earth.

The power of colour continues to grow in Hope, burning with a ferocity she could never have imagined, a hundred times the strength it was even in the Night Caves.

The commotion brings her friends from the farmhouse, Odd and Effie and the rest, and from the field beyond come the Rainbow League. They gather around her in awe.

'The Rainbow Child!' they cheer.

'She's come to save us!'

Hope looks around at them. She is still Hope, of course, but it seems for a time that she is sharing her body with another living thing, a force that has been held down for a very long time, that has been lying dormant and is now awake and angry and ready to fight back.

Sandy's last words burn suddenly bright in her head. Words about the Necromancer.

'Death has a friend who'd very much like to meet her.'

And she understands.

Turning, she walks towards her companions, the ground alive with breathtaking colour for twenty paces all around. Every blade of grass, every mote of dust, every fibre in her dress, seems to sing with life and power. Her colour has reached her friends long before she gets there herself, and when she stands before Effie, the old mage stands straighter as the colour floods through her, making her cheeks rosy, her eyes sparkle.

'The day Sandy and I walked with Rab,' Hope begins, 'it began by burning a candle. Could you make me another one now?'

Effie looks taken aback, and then realisation dawns on her face, and she smiles sadly. 'Aye, lassie. It will be my honour.'

Hope returns the smile, leans in, and whispers a plan in her ear.

Chapter Thirty-Four

In Which Hope Meets
the Necromancer

Before they can march upon the City, Hope must first make the way safe for her friends. They have gathered behind her at the edge of the farm, watching with curious awe as she walks to the border. The sphere of colour around her ripples in the air, turns the sky blue when you look through it, the distant trees green. As Hope leaves the safety of the farm and her feet touch down upon the Necromancer's territory, every Ripper Dog caught within that circle of colour screams and burns and scatters to the wind.

Hope looks at the long, long line of Ripper Dogs and Black Coats to the left. She points, and a jet of colour leaps from her hand and stretches in a flash all along the line, leaving only shadow scars on the earth. She turns to the right and does the same.

All is quiet for a moment. Waves crash against the rocks and the birds sing in the trees. Then a great roar erupts from the Rainbow League.

Hope walks on.

She follows the path along the cliff tops, temporarily painting everything her sphere of power passes over, daisies and buttercups, bees and birds and beetles. When she reaches the City walls, her colour blasts away any Ripper Dogs or Black Coats that come near. When she leads her people through the streets, others join them, leaving their little houses and crammed buildings, bewitched by the colour of Hope, long-dormant memories and dreams and imagination awakening in their souls.

The castle. By the time they reach it, there are thousands in the crowd, following Hope's colour. They gasp and cheer when an awesome moon wyvern swoops down from the sky, turning from black to shining red when Hope climbs aboard his back. He takes off, carrying her over the castle wall.

From the air, it is easy to spot the secret walled garden where the Necromancer has built her magical fire.

Hope stares down at the orange flames, the only colour in the City now that she is in the air.

'Here goes, Elmo,' she says. 'Take us down.'

The Necromancer is sitting in front of the high orange fire when the moon wyvern lands. Hope climbs down, sends Elmo away, the beat of his wings blowing her hair as she turns and walks towards the centre of the garden. Her colour spreads out, painting the ever-blossoming trees glorious pink. When she stands opposite the Necromancer, the fire separating them, the Necromancer gets up and brushes herself off.

'Quite an entrance.'

Hope does not answer. The heat of the fire is intense. In those flames, she can sense all the stolen colour from the world, feel it thrashing around like some trapped animal. The power of the fire pulls at Hope's colour, tries to wrench it from her, but it is anchored deep inside her, and she resists. The glow of her skin brightens.

'You feel it?' the Necromancer says. 'All that magic? All that strength? It flows through me. You cannot beat me, child. Just as your poor, dear Sandy could not beat me.'

Anger rises in Hope's throat, runs away with her tongue. 'You stole him away from me. He was a good man, and you took him. But you're wrong about him. He did have the beating of you.'

'Oh?' says the Necromancer. 'Then why am I still breathing when he is not?'

'There's things you don't understand,' Hope tells her. 'Things you will never understand. Because you're the weak one.'

A flash of anger in the Necromancer's face. 'I'm tired of you now, girl.' She snaps her fingers, and a huge tongue of flame leaps from the main fire, engulfs Hope. She staggers back, cocooned in searing orange flame, but she doesn't burn. The power of her colour forms a tight sphere around her. She wills the colour to push back against the fire. Angry flames lick and crack against the barrier around her as it expands, forcing the fire back. On the other side of the fire, the Necromancer's face is contorted

341

with effort, her hands twisting in the air, trying to direct the flames.

Hope takes a step forward, thinks of Sandy, of her friends on the outside of the castle walls. Her colour explodes outward, sending the flames leaping back, containing them.

The Necromancer yells in fury, 'You'll never beat me, girl. You'll never win! To do that, you'll have to kill me. And you don't have it in you to take a life!'

'You're right,' Hope agrees. 'I don't. Sandy knew that too. That's why he figured out another way.' From her coat she pulls a black candle, made for her by Effie. She holds it up. 'I want you to remember,' she says, reaching the candle out towards the fire, 'that your own fire lit this spell. The spell that will end it all. Let's take a wee walk together, eh?'

For the first time, the Necromancer looks frightened. She rushes forward, but Hope has already touched the wick of the spell candle to the fire. The wick flickers alight, the flame first small and blue, and then leaping up, spitting, becoming yellow. A thick fog of smoke chokes the garden, swallows everything, and suddenly they are no longer standing in the Necromancer's secret garden. The fire is gone, and all is silent.

They have gone somewhere else.

'What is this?' the Necromancer says, looking blindly around the fog of smoke. 'Where are we?'

A figure in black comes through the smoke, a woman with dark hair and eyes like amber marbles.

Death nods to Hope. 'Hello, again. Back so soon?'

'Aye,' says Hope.

'And who is it this time?' Death asks, taking her black book in her hands, leafing through the pages.

'Sandy Burns. Well, that's the name I knew him by anyway.'

Death frowns, runs her finger down the open page. 'Burns. Burns . . . here he is.' She frowns. 'And there's another name here too. How interesting . . .'

She closes the book with a snap, and there stands Sandy, looking tall and tanned and happy. He smiles at Hope, a wide, toothy grin beneath his moustache.

'Yeh did it, lassie. Yeh understood what I meant!'

'Aye,' says Hope. 'I did.'

'What is this?' asks the Necromancer. 'Where are we? How can *you* be here?' She takes a step forward, pokes Sandy's arm, checking that this is real. 'Return me to my garden at once!'

Death raises an eyebrow, looks at Hope and flicks her head in the Necromancer's direction. 'Who rattled *her* cage?'

Hope smiles. 'Don't pay her any attention.'

'Shall we walk?' Death asks.

Sandy nods. 'Aye.'

The smoke clears, and the vast white expanse of the Desert of Bones opens up before them. They walk beneath a blood red sky and a burning yellow moon. The smell here is hot and dry, and the air – if it *is* air – is heavy and presses against Hope's skin.

The Necromancer is trailing behind them, staring about.

It seems she is powerless in this place. 'Take me back,' she demands. 'Put me back where I belong.'

They ignore her.

'Look after Oliver, will yeh, lassie?' Sandy says. 'The horse and caravan are yours now. Take care of them.'

'I will.'

They reach the edge of the great black river, where the rowing boat sits at the wooden jetty. The bear-like Ferryman sits in the boat, and a second figure waits upon the jetty, staring out over the water, into the thick mist that shrouds whatever waits beyond.

The figure turns around. It is the Emperor, full of colour.

'What's he doing here?' says the Necromancer. 'What's happening?'

'What's happening,' says Hope, finally acknowledging her, 'is that you are about to repay your debt.'

'Debt?' she spits. 'I owe no one a debt!'

'No?' says Sandy. 'You have been stealing spirits from the other side for many years. Wrenching them away from their rightful place across the river. Forcing them back to the world of the living, where they have no choice but to ride on the backs of your demon dogs. By my count, yeh owe a very great debt indeed.'

The Ferryman lifts a huge oar, points it at the Necromancer. 'It's *your* fault. The beyond is in a state of imbalance because of you. I ferry spirits across, and there they are supposed to stay. But they have been disappearing

344

for a long time, upsetting the river. You are the one responsible for that?'

'She is,' says the Emperor. He stands on the jetty, his hands clasped behind his back, smiling at Sandy. 'I've been waiting. We entered this life together, brother. Let's enter the next life together too. But not, I think, before we see dear Auntie off.'

Death appears at the Necromancer's side. 'Come on, dear,' she says cheerfully, taking the Necromancer's hand, leading her to the jetty. 'Time to climb aboard.'

'I don't want to,' says the Necromancer, her voice full of panic. 'I don't want to go on the boat.' She tries to resist, but it is no good. Death steers her effortlessly on board. The rowing boat rocks as she sits on the bow seat.

The Ferryman stares at her from across the boat, his black eyes shining like beetles. He takes up his oars, begins to row the boat out over the river. The Necromancer turns around, confusion and fear in her pale face. 'Back,' she says. 'Take me back.'

But the Ferryman keeps rowing, out over the black flowing water, until he stops and keeps the boat in place just before the wall of mist begins.

'They're not going over to the other side?' Hope asks.

Death smiles down at her. 'Oh no. Not that one. *That* one has a debt to pay. She belongs where all the hateful, unloving things go in the end.'

Out on the boat, the Necromancer sees movement in the water, pale shapes in the murky darkness. A hand breaks the surface, rotten flesh peeling from the bones. The arm reaches up out of the water, over the side of the boat, grabbing hungrily. The Necromancer screams and shifts to the other side of the boat, but another rotting hand comes from the depths there, and another, and more and more, all stretching out of the water, grabbing and clutching over the sides of the boat.

'No!' she screams, kicking them off. 'No!'

But the hands are relentless. Their cold, deathly grip closes up on her clothes, her arms, her legs. The dead hands pull at her, drag her to the edge of the boat. She flails and scratches and bites, but the dead hands feel no pain. They drag her over, into the water with a splash.

She goes under for a moment, then her head breaks the surface, her eyes wild with terror.

'Help me! Someone help me!'

No one moves.

The hands cover her face, her head, smothering her. She manages one last cry before they pull her under, and she plunges into the depths of the river to join them forever.

The Ferryman takes his boat back to the jetty.

'She's gone?' Hope says, staring out at the bubbling place on the water where the Necromancer went under. 'She's really gone?' She continues to stare, half expecting the Necromancer to come up out of the water like a terrible monster.

'Oh, she's not coming back from there,' Death says. She puts her hands in her pockets. 'Can we get a move on, please? I have a card game to get back to. I really think I'm going to win this time.'

Sandy steps forward. 'I'm ready.'

'Wait,' Hope says. 'Just . . . just wait. Just a bit longer.' A terrible panic rises in her. 'Can't he come back?' she pleads with Death. 'Can't you make an exception just this once?'

Death looks puzzled. 'That's . . . not how it works.'

'It's all right, lassie,' Sandy says. 'It's my time tae cross the water.' He glances out towards the mist. 'I'd like tae find out what's waiting for me there.'

Hope follows his gaze, out into the mist, and she wonders if, somewhere across the river, her parents are staring back from the other side. She runs forward, wraps her arms around Sandy and squeezes tight. Great sobs escape her chest. She does not want to let go, not ever. This wonderful, loopy, brave, magical man has been the best father anyone could ever hope for. Life without him is unthinkable.

'I love you,' she says.

'I love you too, lassie. You're going to be brilliant. You're going tae do wonderful things. Just don't forget me, eh?'

'Never.'

Gently, he breaks away from her and joins the Emperor on the jetty. They embrace and walk towards the boat. The small vessel rocks a little as they climb in and sit side by side.

A nod from the Ferryman, and he takes up the oars and, with a few powerful strokes, rows them out over the dark water.

As they go, Sandy turns for a moment and smiles back at Hope, who waves, tears spilling down her cheeks. She watches until the boat reaches the mist, and the mist swirls around them and swallows them up.

Sandy Burns is gone.

Death's cold hand rests on Hope's shoulder. Everything spins, and she is falling.

She opens her eyes, and there she stands, back in the secret walled garden in the castle grounds. The Necromancer is gone, and the flames of the great fire are acting strangely, spitting and leaping and dancing. She begins to see brilliant streaks of colour in the flames, greens and blues and purples. The flames grow brighter, brighter still, and then they fall back. They shrink and shrink, smaller and smaller, until at last there remains only a single, marble-sized point of blinding incandescence, floating where the heart of the fire used to be.

All is still.

The ball of light trembles. A sound comes from it, like the whistle of a boiling steam kettle. The sound grows in intensity, until Hope must cover her ears, and even then she can hear it, like it is inside her head.

Then . . .

BOOM!

Colour.

All the colour of the world explodes out in a shockwave of dazzling hues. It roars over the castle walls like a supersonic tidal wave, paints the houses and streets, paints the crowds who have gathered.

Darroch and his grandmother stumble back as the force of the colour hits them, a warm blast of radiance, and when it has passed over them, they look at each other, at their own hands and clothes, and at the people standing nearby. They look at the sky and the buildings, and they see colour everywhere, in the red rooftops and the flowerboxes and the wonderstruck eyes of the children. In the purple-gold wash of the evening sky.

Darroch holds his gran, sees that she is crying with happiness.

All around, as the people begin to get over their shock, as they dare to believe that their eyes are telling them the truth, cheers ring out, laughter and songs and shouts of thanks. A great celebration has begun.

The wave of colour reaches every part of the Dominion in minutes. Summer meadows burst to life with dazzling hues. The great forest turns from a grey mass of twisted shadows to a paradise of greenery. Grey cornfields are painted gold. Cold lagoons transform to shimmering, crystal blue-green. And the animals ... Birds fly among the treetops, their feathers blossoming with brilliant shades. Beetles shine gold and silver-red. Yellow-and-black bees land on flowers of every description.

As the colour moves through the land, it turns every Ripper Dog to dust, frees the trapped souls inside the dark hoods of the Black Coats, letting them return to the other side of the river beyond.

The landscape, so long devoid of these wonders, breathes once more.

The Dominion is free.

The world is how it should be.

Chapter Thirty-Five
In Which We Come to the End, and also the Beginning

Hope sits by Sandy's grave, Oliver at her feet. The grass beneath her feet is green, and the flowers she has just laid upon the grave are deep blue. The smell of summer heat hangs in the air.

The spot is peaceful, high on a grassy meadow overlooking the Gwendle Farm, with views of the sea cliffs and the highest spires of the City. All of the spectacular view, every bit of it, is in glorious colour, so much colour that it makes Hope's eyes hurt in a wonderful way.

'I'm going to miss him,' says the little dog.

'I am too,' says Hope. 'But it will get easier. I just wish he'd had the chance to see it for himself.'

'Oh, he knows,' Oliver says. 'Wherever he is, he knows.' He preens one of his ears, then shakes off an itch. 'Do you think Odd is going to be all right?'

'I don't know. He's awful sad.'

'Yes. Why d'you think the wyvern left?' Oliver asks.

Hope shrugs. The day after the world got its colour back, Elmo flew off in the night. He has been gone for a week, and it does not seem like he will return. 'If I was to guess, I'd say all that new colour called to him. Maybe it sparked something in him. Perhaps he remembered something from long ago, something colour brought back to him. Maybe he's gone home.'

They walk down the hill, through golden pools of sunlight and buzzing yellow bees and butterflies with wings of orange-blue, to the farmhouse. The front door, which had been black in the colourless world, is now navy blue. In the warm, wooden kitchen, Darroch, Mrs Gwendle, Effie and Odd sit around the table.

'Ah, Hope,' says Effie. 'We've been waiting.'

'Waiting? For what?'

'Wait there,' Darroch says, getting up, disappearing into another room. When he comes back, he is holding a square object wrapped in brown paper and tied up with string. 'For you,' he says, handing it to Hope.

'What is it?' she asks, taking it from him.

'Well, open it and find out, lassie!' says Effie.

Hope unties the string, rips the paper off. She stares down at the object in her hands, and a lump rises in her throat. It is an oil painting of Sandy. In it he stands holding his bow, smiling beneath his black moustache. The likeness is brilliant.

She does not know what to say.

'I like to paint,' Darroch says. 'I understand if you don't like it.'

'It's perfect,' says Hope. Effie hands her a handkerchief, and she wipes her eyes. 'Thank yeh.'

Darroch beams, then looks around the kitchen and laughs in wonder. 'I still can't believe it's real! When I wake up in the morning, I keep my eyes shut for a while, frightened to open them in case it was all a dream. Then, after a while, I work up the courage to look, and there it is, colour, still here. Still beautiful.'

'And here it'll stay, laddie,' says Effie. 'Forever more.'

'Only thing is,' says Darroch, 'I've been painting this mural on my room's wall for years. Adding to it and painting over it and trying to get it right. I finally thought I'd finished, but now I can see the colours, I realise I've got everything wrong!'

This makes everyone laugh.

'So,' says Oliver with a wag of his tail. 'What next? There is always a next, after all.'

Effie speaks first. 'Well, Mrs Gwendle has asked me tae stay on here for a while, and I have agreed. I've already sent a message tae a friend in the village, asking her tae look in on the cottage and look after my horse. There's going tae be a lot tae sort out in the City, and I have a feeling that they are going tae come and ask Mrs Gwendle for help in making some big decisions. Her family has always been respected, after all. So, I'll be here tae help Darroch run the farm.'

'We've asked Odd to stay too,' Darroch says. 'He's strong, and we could use him during harvest.'

Odd smiles a patchwork smile, but part of him seems to be somewhere far away.

'Oh,' says Hope. 'Well then, I suppose you have a decision to make, Odd. Oliver and me, we were going to ask you if you want to travel with us.'

Odd's mismatched eyes flick towards her, surprise etched on his face. 'You were?'

'Aye. The caravan is going to be awful empty without Sandy, and there's only so much of Oliver's chat I'll be able to take before I lose my marbles. What do you say?'

Odd's strange eyes light up. 'I'd like that.' He looks around sheepishly at the others. 'I'm sorry to turn down your offer.'

'That's all right, laddie,' says Effie. 'Yeh must follow yehr heart. I think there is room for us all tae do that in this new world.'

Mrs Gwendle fills mugs with steaming, tan-coloured tea and passes them around.

They raise a toast to colour, and life, and the power of friendship. Then they sit until the sun goes down in the ruby sky, and tell stories of Sandy, their laughter ringing through the house.

Two days later, Hope takes the reins of Sandy's caravan – Hope's caravan now – and Gloria the shire horse pulls them out of the farmyard and down the track. As they move away from the house, Effie, Darroch and Mrs Gwendle wave from the doorstep, Effie blowing her nose loudly and dabbing her eyes.

They reach the end of the track, and Hope stops the caravan where the track meets the road.

'Which way?' she asks Odd, who sits beside her on the driver's bench, Oliver sprawled across his lap. Odd turns his head to the east, towards the City and the lands beyond, and then the west, to the greenery of the forest and the rest of the world. He jerks a dark brown thumb towards the forest.

'I have a good feeling about that way.'

Hope smiles. In truth, she has a good feeling about either way. There is optimism in the air, and a smile on the lips of everyone they meet. And despite the fresh start that colour has brought with it to the Dominion, the work of a drifter mage is never done. Sandy once told her that. Wherever they go, they will find people to help, and trouble to remedy, and she cannot think of anyone else in the world that she would rather have with her on her travels than Odd.

'Let's go get into some trouble,' she says.

Odd laughs, and Oliver barks as Hope snaps the reins and the fine shire horse pulls them into the great emerald forest.

And high above, the sky is blue.

ACKNOWLEDGEMENTS

The idea for this book has been bubbling in my head for quite some time, and I'm hugely grateful to the entire Andersen team for helping me finally bring it to life. Thank you, Charlie, for the belief you've shown in Hope from the beginning. Working with you is a joy. I also owe a great debt to Eloise and Chloe for their editorial input. They make me look far better than I am. To Paul and Rob, I'd like to say how much I appreciate all that you do to guide me around the country to school visits and festivals and all the rest. I'd be quite literally lost without you!

My agents are simply the best. Thank you, Steph and Izzy, for your advice and guidance, and for helping me make a living doing what I love. I appreciate it every day.

To the readers who continue to seek out my books, I wish I could explain how much it means to me that you enjoy the stories that spill from my head. And to the librarians and teachers who encourage young readers to pick up my books – indeed, any books – I can only say a million thanks, which seems nowhere near enough.

As ever, I could not have written this novel without the support of my family. Mum and Dad, you continue to be my ideal readers. Thanks for always telling me that anything is possible.

Selina and Mollie, thanks for putting up with a dad who constantly daydreams, plots, plans and edits, and for sharing me with the characters in my imagination. I love you.

And Aileen, my love, you are a hero and an inspiration to our daughters, and to me. You and the girls bring colour into my life every day. Thank you forever x

EVERNIGHT

ROSS MACKENZIE

THE EVERNIGHT
HAS BEEN UNLEASHED ...

As far back as she can remember, orphan Larabelle Fox has scraped together a living treasure-hunting in the sewers. In a city where emotionless White Witches march through the streets and fear of Hag magic is rife, Lara keeps her head down. But when she stumbles upon a mysterious little box in the sewers, Lara finds herself catapulted into a world of wild magic – facing adventure, mortal danger and a man who casts no shadow.

'Epic good-versus-evil fantasy'
Guardian

'Beautifully cinematic, *Evernight* is a spellbinding tale'
The Scotsman

9781783448319

FEAST
OF THE
EVERNIGHT

ROSS MACKENZIE

The Evernight has been defeated and the sun has returned,
thanks to Larabelle Fox and her friends Joe and Double
Eight. It should be a time of celebration. But a new threat
is emerging from the mists of the Veil, the dangerous
forest that surrounds the Silver Kingdom's southern lands.
Mysterious killings are taking place, and Double Eight is the
suspect. Lara and Joe journey to
Lake End to discover what's really
happening, all the while trying
to stay one step ahead of the
secret police . . .

9781839130472

The Secret of Splint Hall

KATIE COTTON

1945. War has ended, but for sisters Isobel and Flora, the struggles continue. They've lost their father and had their home destroyed in a bombing raid, and now they must go to live with their aunt and her awful husband Mr Godfrey in their ancestral home, Splint Hall. From the moment of their arrival it seems that this is a place shrouded in mysteries and secrets. As the girls begin to unearth an ancient myth and family secret, the adventure of a lifetime begins.

9781839131967